W9-AAJ-257

Dear Reader,

While researching *Digging Up Clues*, I came across a fascinating story about the discovery of a shipwreck and the recovery of a massive treasure. History records that in April 1717, a pirate ship, the *Whydah*, capsized off of Cape Cod during a fierce storm. The ship had been laden with tons of gold, silver, and jewelry. Only two shipmates survived to tell the tale, and although there were initial attempts to salvage the wealth, the wreck went undiscovered until 1984. Barry Clifford, a professional treasure hunter, discovered the wreck in fourteen feet of water under five feet of sand, all within sight of the shore. Can you imagine his excitement? Clifford had not only made a significant archaeological find but also discovered a massive treasure worth millions that, despite its close proximity to civilization, had remained lost for over 260 years.

The story of the lost *Whydah* made me think about treasures we have around us that we don't notice or appreciate fully. I'm not referring to silver and gold but "treasures" that God has blessed us with. Perhaps it's the budding of the first spring daffodil by our front step, a loyal pet that is always happy to greet us, the smile of a child, or a tender note from a close friend. These small things enrich our lives.

In *Digging Up Clues*, Mary sets out to solve a mystery about a lost treasure and makes some surprising discoveries along the way. I hope you enjoy her adventure as much as I did.

Best wishes,
Kelly Ann Riley

Secrets of Mary's Bookshop

A New Chapter
Rewriting History
Reading the Clues
The Writing on the Wall
By Word of Mouth
A Book by Its Cover
Poetry in Motion
Missing Pages
Between the Lines
By the Book
Disappearing Acts
A Classic Case
Cover Story
A Thousand Words
The Lost Noel
Work in Progress
Words of Wisdom
Lost for Words
Cooking the Books
Snowbound

SECRETS *of* MARY'S
BOOKSHOP

Digging Up Clues

Kelly Ann Riley

Guideposts

New York

Acknowledgments

Every attempt has been made to credit the sources of copyrighted material used in this book. If any such acknowledgment has been inadvertently omitted or miscredited, receipt of such information would be appreciated.

"From the Guideposts Archives" originally appeared in *Daily Guideposts*, 1979. Copyright © 1978 by Guideposts. All rights reserved.

Cover and interior design by Müllerhaus
Cover illustration by Ross Jones, represented by Deborah Wolfe, Ltd.
Typeset by Aptara, Inc.

Printed and bound in the United States of America
10 9 8 7 6 5 4 3 2 1

Digging Up Clues

ONE

M ary Fisher carried a stack of nautically themed novels to the front of her mystery bookshop, where her sister, Betty Emerson, was decorating the front window. Like the other business owners on Main Street, Mary had started preparing for the Cape Cod Shipwreck Festival scheduled for the coming weekend.

"I think that if anyone in Ivy Bay could solve the mystery of the *Lady Beth* treasure, it would be you," Betty said as she carefully set her late husband's model schooner in the display.

"You think?" Mary asked with a laugh. She handed her sister one book at a time as Betty placed them around the model sailing ship.

"Well, you're so great at digging up clues." Betty looked over her shoulder with a twinkle in her blue eyes.

Mary smiled at the pun. "Well, I'm flattered, but even if the legend is true that there's a chest of gold coins buried around here, it has managed to stay well hidden for over 190 years."

"That just makes the challenge more fun."

"That's true," Mary said. Lately, it seemed as if everyone in the small coastal town of Ivy Bay had caught treasure fever after a series of strong storms hit the Eastern Seaboard a couple of weeks ago. The violent surf had churned up the sandbars, revealing more scattered artifacts from the 1824 shipwreck of the *Lady Beth*. Several bottles, belt buckles, keys, nails, and an old tin mug had washed up onshore, but the discovery of two gold coins had resurrected the legend of a lost chest of gold and sent townsfolk into a furor of treasure hunting.

"Hey, Jessie, wait up!" someone yelled outside on the sidewalk.

Mary glanced out the window at Main Street as a group of excited teenagers passed by, carrying buckets, shovels, and a metal detector. Rumor had it that since the gold wasn't found during the excavation of the site in 1986, the gold may have been smuggled ashore before the storm and buried somewhere in Ivy Bay.

Mary turned her attention back to the shop and handed Betty another novel. So far, she had resisted getting involved in the treasure hunting and the mystery of the missing coins. She told herself she needed to concentrate on running her business, but there were moments, such as now, when she wished she were out at Little Neck Beach with the beachcombers.

Betty stiffly stepped back from the window and cocked her head. "What do you think? Should we keep the boat in the center, or perhaps move it to the side?"

"You're the one with the flair for decorating. Whatever you think is best, Bets." Mary smiled at her older sister, appreciating times like these when Betty had a chance to help at the shop. Betty's struggle with rheumatoid arthritis was one of the reasons Mary moved to Ivy Bay, but the most precious perk of living together was the opportunity to renew their relationship after so many years apart.

Betty pursed her lips and looked in the box of sea-related items she'd brought from home. Mary's gray cat, Gus, sniffed the cardboard edges and then hopped in.

"Gus! You can't play in there," Mary affectionately scolded her blue-eyed cat. Gus had shown up outside Mary's Boston home about the time her husband, John, had to be hospitalized during the last few weeks of his life. Gus had remained her faithful companion ever since.

Mary lifted the cat out of the box and set him on the counter. He gave himself a shake, as if brushing off an insult, then jumped to the floor. He trotted over to where Mary's employee Rebecca Mason and Rebecca's daughter Ashley sat on the floor, organizing a shelf of children's books. The cute seven-year-old with blonde pigtails scooped up Gus and hugged him tightly.

Betty held up a small toy seagull. "I need some string to hang this little guy."

"There's some in the closet."

"I'll get it." Betty headed to the back room as the front door chimed.

Penny Fuller strolled into the shop. Navy shorts and a white tank top covered her trim, youthful figure. Flip-flops slapped on the wood floor, and she carried a large canvas beach bag. Mary had only met the young, aspiring reporter the previous week but enjoyed the enthusiasm with which Penny tackled her unpaid internship at the local newspaper. She'd earn the few remaining college credits needed from the University of Maine so she could graduate at the end of the summer. Penny smiled when she spied Mary. "Hey, Mary, good morning. How are you?"

Mary smiled back. "Hi, Penny. Good to see you. All is well here. Is there something I can help you with?"

"Yes, I'm here to grab a new book. But first, you'll never believe… I was in Bailey's Ice Cream Shop, and I overheard someone say that Tom Gordon found a fork on the beach about an hour ago. They think it might be from the *Lady Beth* shipwreck."

"A fork?" Ashley looked up from the stack of books in front of her. "That's not a treasure."

Penny turned her smile toward Ashley. "Trust me. It's an awesome find."

Ashley gave her a funny if-you-say-so look and turned back to shelving the stack of books with her mother.

"They're still finding things on the beach, huh?" Rebecca's brown eyes sparked with curiosity. "I would've thought after a couple of weeks, the sand would've been picked clean."

"It seems a bit unusual, but the tides can do strange things sometimes." Penny set her bag down by the counter. "Shipwrecks are an interest of mine. Comes from having a seafaring family."

Mary smiled at Penny. "I read the article by you and Johanna in the Sunday paper yesterday. It was excellent. Really captured the mystery surrounding the *Lady Beth* and the supposedly lost treasure."

"Thank you. I wish I could take more credit. Johanna wrote most of it," Penny said, referring to Johanna Montgomery, the head reporter at the *Ivy Bay Bugle*. "She's been teaching me a lot. It's a great experience, even though I don't plan on being a small-town reporter like she is."

"What do you want to do?" Rebecca had finished one of the shelves. She stood and rubbed her lower back with one hand.

"Travel writing. I want to see the world."

"That sounds exciting," Rebecca said, sounding a little wistful as she picked up another stack of children's books from a table and carried them over to Ashley to be shelved on the bottom row. Rebecca was also an aspiring writer, and Mary tried to encourage her whenever she could.

Betty came out of the back room with a ball of string, and Mary said, "Betty, have you met Penny Fuller? Penny is here for a couple of months doing an internship at the *Bugle*."

"Why, no, I haven't yet." Betty smiled warmly. "It's very nice to meet you, Penny." Betty studied the girl curiously for a brief moment. "You look familiar, Penny. Do you have family in the area?"

Penny looked surprised at the question. "Oh no, I don't," she replied. "My folks are in Maine. I've never been to Ivy Bay, although my parents brought our family to the Cape on vacation a couple of times," Penny said. "I'm actually friends with Johanna Montgomery's niece Sunny. We went to the same college, and she put in a good word with Johanna and the *Bugle*."

Penny's eyes narrowed slightly. "Pardon me for asking this, but are you the Betty whose brother-in-law was the one who discovered the *Lady Beth* shipwreck? Johanna had mentioned a Betty Emerson who was related to Richard Blakely."

"Oh yes. That's me. My husband's sister was married to Richard. The discovery of the *Lady Beth* was one of the great highlights of Richard's life."

"How exciting for him," Penny said. "Imagine finding treasure right out here in the bay. It's too bad they didn't find the chest of gold, assuming the rumors are true."

"I heard Richard say once that he felt like the ship itself was the treasure."

"I like that. Would you mind if I quoted you?" Penny whipped out a small notebook from her beach bag. "I've been trying to gather material for a more personal piece."

Betty nodded. "If you wish, but, really, my sister-in-law would be the one to talk to."

"Johanna assigned me to interview her, but so far, Mrs. Blakely hasn't returned my call."

"Eleanor spends most of her time these days down at the historical society," Betty said. "You probably already know she's the chairwoman of the festival committee."

"She's really busy right now, but you might mention to her how the interview might help promote the festival," Mary added as she went around to the back side of the counter to get Betty the scissors for her string.

"I'll remember that." Penny jotted down a note.

"Have you talked with Horace Crenshaw yet?" Betty asked. "He was Richard's diving partner."

"Uh, I don't think so..." Penny paused, looking at her notes. She pointed to a line on the page. "Here it is. I've left a message, but he hasn't returned my call. According to my notes, he travels most of the time."

"He has until recently," Betty said.

"I think I saw him this morning, heading into the historical society office," Mary said. She didn't know Horace well. She'd been living in Boston when the *Lady Beth* was discovered and he came into the Blakelys' lives. She did know, through Eleanor, that he'd kept a summer place in Ivy Bay for years and recently decided to make it his home base between travels.

"He's also helping with the festival, so you probably can catch up with him there," Betty said.

"Thanks for the tips." Penny made another note and then put her notebook in her beach bag. She pulled out a Lilian Jackson Braun novel. "I'm almost done with *The Cat Who Saw Red*, and I'm ready for the next one in the series. I'm going to try to read as many as possible while I'm here." She headed for the shelves that contained Jackson Braun's mysteries.

Ashley looked over from where she was sitting cross-legged on the floor by Gus. "I like your ankle bracelet. I want one like that."

Penny glanced down at her red-and-black ankle bracelet and flashed a smile. "This bracelet is special. A relative of mine made it, but you can get coral bracelets down at the marina." She held out her fingers to Gus who sniffed them. "Hello, pretty kitty."

"He's *handsome*," Ashley said, and stroked Gus's back. "He's a boy."

"Oh, sorry, *Mister* Kitty. You're very handsome, and I bet you are as smart as Koko and Yum Yum," Penny said, referring to the two Siamese cats in Jackson Braun's series.

Gus arched his back and let Penny pet him before she turned her attention to the bookshelves.

Mary helped Betty hang the little seagull in the window until Penny approached the counter. She'd selected the next two in the series, *The Cat Who Played Brahms* and *The Cat Who Played Post Office*, and brought them to the counter. "I just love these stories. I'll be sad when I reach the last book in the series."

"I know how you feel." Mary rang up the purchase. "But I've found that if I wait for a while before rereading them, I forget who the bad guys are."

"Something to look forward to, then." Penny laughed. "I hope to own the whole series someday, but I'd better be careful right now. I've already filled up a box with books and another with shells and driftwood. Not everything is going to fit in my little car by the time I head home."

"You could mail some of them ahead," Rebecca suggested.

"Good idea. But right now, I'm just going to enjoy this gorgeous day and see if I can get enough material to write another article this evening. Maybe I'll find a fork on the beach." She shot a grin in Ashley's direction and went out the door.

"It *is* gorgeous out," Betty said, casting a wistful look out the window as Penny strolled past. "Great evening for a walk on the beach, don't you think?"

Mary grinned at her sister. "You want to see what the treasure hunters are up to, don't you?"

"Well, you have to admit it is pretty exciting." Betty laughed.

"Mary, I don't mind locking up if you want to head on home," Rebecca offered. "And I was wondering if I could take a couple of hours off tomorrow afternoon. It's my turn to read lines with the kids for the play they're putting on for the festival."

"That's fine by me, on both accounts. Thanks, Rebecca." Mary smiled. Rebecca had been a wonderful employee since she opened the shop, and Ashley was a ray of sunshine. Life wouldn't be so enjoyable in Ivy Bay without them.

Mary helped Betty box up the items they didn't use for the window display and then enticed Gus into his cat carrier. Ashley walked Mary and Gus to the door, telling Gus she'd see him tomorrow.

Mary and Betty stopped under the elm tree in front of the wooden storefront and studied Betty's display in the large, paned window. Betty had left the ship model in the center and added a small wooden chest in the corner with two books tucked inside, a strand of faux pearls draped over the lid. Shells and starfish were scattered about the other books on display.

"I think it turned out fantastic," Mary said. "Thanks, Bets."

"You know how much I love doing it." Betty's smile lit up her blue eyes.

"Do you want me to carry the box?"

"It's okay. It's not heavy." Betty hefted the container with the leftover sea decorations higher in her arms.

They turned right and headed down the wide boulevard, leaving behind the enticing, homey aroma emanating from Sweet Susan's Bakery next door. Across the street, customers lined up to get into Bailey's Ice Cream Shop. They passed Jimmy's Hardware as they neared the end of Main Street and crossed over a cranberry bog on a small stone footbridge.

On Shore Drive, climbing roses edged the view of the blue bay between the cottages. The white picket fence cordoned off Betty's—and now Mary's—home from the neighbors. Betty led the way up the slate path to the two-story Federal-style house, painted in a light green. Mary unlocked the door and held back the screen door so Betty could enter.

Gus meowed as Mary set down his carrier and let him out. He circled her legs before scampering for his food bowl. They followed him to the kitchen. Betty set her box on the table and rubbed her left shoulder. Mary hoped she hadn't overdone it today, but she held back her concern. Betty hated to have anyone fuss over her.

"How about a supper picnic on the beach?" Betty asked. "I can make some sandwiches if you get the chairs out of the garage."

"That sounds great. I'll go change," Mary said, eager to get to the beach. She trotted up the stairs to the second floor, which had been her domain since she moved in. In addition to Mary's room, there were three other bedrooms. After her husband passed away, Betty had moved downstairs to his old office so she wouldn't have to climb the stairs.

The air was warmer near the top of the house, and Mary flipped on the overhead fan as she entered her bright and cheerful room. She pushed open a window, letting in the sea-tinged air. John had loved the smell of the ocean, and wistful longing filled her as she wished he were here to walk hand in hand along the beach as the sun set. For a moment, her good mood slipped. How she missed her knight in shining armor.

"Lord, thank You for the blessings You've given me," she said, determined not to let sad memories spoil the evening.

She quickly traded her slacks and blouse for capri pants, a light T-shirt, and beige sandals. As she headed to the stairs,

Gus was just coming up. He paused, tail swishing, as she passed him on the way down.

"If you want your supper, you'd better come now," Mary said, teasing him.

A picnic basket waited on the kitchen table. Betty's bedroom door was shut, and Mary assumed her sister was changing clothes. Mary hurried to the pantry, and by the time she'd spooned turkey pâté into Gus's bowl, Betty had emerged from her room wearing a sunny-yellow capris outfit. Her sister managed to look elegant even when going to the beach.

As Betty finished putting a few more things in the basket for their supper together, Mary grabbed their lightweight striped blue-and-white chairs off their garage wall hook. She met Betty in the driveway, and the walk to the beach only took a couple of minutes. It was still early June, but more people than usual roamed the shore.

Betty spread out a blanket she'd brought, and Mary set up their chairs. They ate their sandwiches as they watched the beachcombers. Mary spied Penny walking along the water's edge. She was so intent on her beachcombing she almost bumped into a sandy-haired, muscular man wearing a bright orange bathing suit, who led an eager group along the shore.

Mary recognized the man as Tom Gordon, a thirty-something sportsman who'd recently opened a dive shop at the marina. Mary sometimes saw him hanging around the historical society where he volunteered. He was talking animatedly with his hands and pointing out to the horizon where the *Lady Beth* wreck lay. When he finished talking, the group fanned out over the sand.

The sisters grinned at each other. There was no way they weren't going to join in the fun. Mary kicked off her sandals. The warm sand squished between her toes as she headed for the lapping waves.

"I found something!" a woman from Tom's group yelled. Mary hurried over with the other nearby beachcombers.

Tom examined the encrusted iron stick. "It's an old key. Looks like it could be from the eighteen hundreds." He handed it back to the excited woman.

Penny pulled a camera out of her pocket. "Can I get a photo for the newspaper?"

"Sure!" The woman held up the crusty key, and Penny took a photo. Penny jotted the woman's name in her notebook as the crowd, more energized than before, dispersed.

Mary gazed around the beach thinking about the violent storm that had stirred the bay and unearthed more items from the shipwreck that lay a mile from shore. The water had surged, with a high tide causing flooding worries for the homes lining the shore. Luckily, the rolling line of sand dunes had protected them.

Volunteers had cleaned most of the beach of the storm debris, which had resulted in a couple of lucky people discovering the two nineteenth-century gold coins. Since then, the shore had been scoured every day by eager locals and the tourists arriving for early summer. The festival was bound to draw in even more crowds, which was great for local businesses but perhaps not so good for the torn-up beach.

Mary wandered in the wet sand for a while but didn't have much luck except for picking up a few pretty shells. She eyed the sand dunes. Nobody was searching the storm's waterline. Maybe something had been washed up there on the dunes.

The sand dunes were protected by law, and signs were placed sporadically reminding humans to stay off of them. Mary searched along the edge, careful not to tramp on the fragile areas. Other than some interesting driftwood, she found no evidence of coins or other artifacts. She was about to turn around to head back toward Betty when a barnacle-encrusted board caught her interest. Mary reached up and carefully dragged it down the dune. Could this worn plank be from a ship? Something lay underneath it, and she eagerly flipped it over. A large cluster of dried seaweed was hooked on a rusty nail.

Mary sighed and was about to turn the board back over so the nail wouldn't be dangerous to bare feet when she realized the green strands were wrapped around something that wasn't natural. Blue vinyl flaked off it as she freed a plastic pouch from the seaweed.

Betty strolled up behind her. "What did you find?"

"I'm not sure. It looks like it could be an old coin purse." Mary tugged at the rusty zipper. The little teeth broke off, but she could get two fingers in the opening. Something cold and hard lay at the bottom. Metal? She turned over the bag, shaking it hard several times until a tangled gold chain dropped into her hand. Small stones covered an intricate gold chain and glittered like fire in the sunlight.

Betty leaned closer and gasped. "Are those what I think they are?"

Mary swallowed hard and looked at her sister. "I—I think they're diamonds."

TWO

◆◆◆

Mary's fingers shook as she gently tried to untangle the chain covered in glittering stones. Something round and hard was enmeshed in the center. She finally extracted a man's gold ring with a large blue gemstone. She passed it to Betty. "Hold this, please."

Before she could finish untangling the necklace, Betty gasped. "Mary!"

Her voice sounded so strange that Mary looked at her. "What is it?"

"I know this ring. See this?" She pointed to a bold inscription on the ring. "That's the Blakely family crest."

Mary stared at the ring. Now that Betty mentioned it, it did appear familiar. Could it be—?

"Did you find something?" A little girl dotted from head to toe with wet sand ran up, carrying a pink bucket. "Oh! Pretty! What is it?" She pointed at the sparkling diamonds, hanging from Mary's fingers like Christmas tinsel.

"Mommy! Come look!" the girl shouted. "Come see the pretty necklace."

Commotion filled the air as word spread among the beachcombers, and suddenly a crowd surrounded Mary and

Betty. The word *diamonds* rippled through the spectators. They stayed a respectful distance back from the women, but their excitement seemed to vibrate the air around them.

Penny pushed her way through the throng. "Mary, what did you find?" She caught sight of the necklace and stopped short. "Wow. That's incredible. Do you mind if I take a photo?" She snapped a shot before Mary could reply. "Sorry, this is just so exciting."

"It's okay," Mary said as Penny leaned closer to get a better look at the necklace.

"Okay, people, what's up?" The sea of people parted for Tom Gordon. He towered over Mary. "Hello, Mrs. Fisher. What's all the excitement about?" He caught sight of the diamonds in Mary's hand, and his mouth dropped open. He glanced around them and said loudly, "Okay, everyone stay back," although no one had moved closer.

He ran a hand over his bushy hair and lowered his voice. "Ladies, this looks like a very, *very* significant find. This necklace may even be from the *Lady Beth*. I suggest you get it somewhere secure."

"Good idea," Mary said, feeling a little claustrophobic. She slid the glittering necklace gently back in the bag. But where should they go? The house made the most sense, but did she really want strangers to see where they lived?

She looked over at Betty. "What do you think?"

"We need to talk to Eleanor. I'm pretty sure this is Richard's ring, but she would know for sure. I think she's still at the historical society working on the festival."

"That's as good a place as any," Tom said with another glance around the beach. "I'll walk you there."

"Okay if I come too?" Penny fell into step by Mary. She pulled out her phone. "I'm going to call Johanna. This is going to be a great story. 'Local Shop Owner Finds Treasure.'"

Mary shook her head with a smile. "One necklace doesn't make for a whole treasure."

"True, but maybe there's more where that came from," Penny said as she lifted her phone to her ear.

Penny had a point. Mary didn't know the significance of their find in relation to the *Lady Beth*, but it appeared that the Blakely family was involved.

Mary glanced behind them at the group of beachcombers following them and then grinned at Betty. She couldn't help think they looked like a small parade marching up Main Street.

Betty still had a slightly dazed expression as they reached the stately brick building that housed the historical society. They climbed the steps, and Tom held the door open. They passed through the small front room that had once served as a doctor's waiting room. Through the second door, Eleanor could be seen sitting in her chair in front of a computer. She looked up, and catching sight of Mary and Betty, she waved at them to come back into the office.

Mary squeezed in the crowded room with Betty and Tom. Two other women sat at desks set around the perimeter of the rectangular-shaped room: Virginia Livingston, a descendant of one of the founding families of Ivy Bay and her young second cousin, Charlotte Rose. Mary had recently had a chance to get acquainted with Charlotte at church. Charlotte was working temporarily in Ivy Bay while she finished her master's thesis in colonial history.

Charlotte jumped to her feet, almost knocking over the metal chair. "Oh, hello, Tom." Her hand went to her dark hair that was smoothed back in a sleek, long ponytail.

Virginia's eyes widened as she noticed the people trying to squeeze through the front door. "They all can't come in here." She made a shooing motion with her hands.

Tom turned in the doorway. "The rest of you need to stay out there."

"Wait, Tom. I—" Penny said, but Tom firmly shut the door and leaned against it.

Eleanor's chair rolled back from the computer, and she looked at Betty. An exasperated expression lined her face. "What's going on?"

"We're sorry to bother you. I know you're busy." Betty held out the ring in the palm of her hand. "But we found this on the beach."

"Oh my." Eleanor took the ring and turned it over. She sank back in her chair and sat so still that Betty finally touched her on the arm. "Are you okay?"

Eleanor nodded, and her eyes glistened. "This is Richard's. He thought he'd lost it forever. I can't believe you found it after all these years."

"What's this about Richard?" A tall man walked out of the storage closet, and Mary recognized Horace Crenshaw, a retired professor, shipwreck excavator, and Richard's old diving partner.

Although a little crusty around the edges, like a seasoned sailor, his body remained very fit and deeply tan. He wore his usual outfit of flip-flops, raggedy shorts, and a faded T-shirt. A shark's-tooth necklace hung around his neck.

Betty had introduced Horace to Mary as an old friend of the family a couple of months ago, and Horace always had a smile for Mary when they crossed paths in town, which had become more frequent lately since Eleanor had recruited Horace to set up an exhibit of shipwreck artifacts for the festival.

"They found Richard's ring, Horace. Can you believe that?" Eleanor said. "Do you remember when Richard lost it on one of the dives?"

"Of course I remember," Horace said. "He was always forgetting to take the ring off until we were underwater, and he'd put it in one of his dive pouches to keep it safe. Figured he'd lose it someday."

"Wait until you see what else they found, Horace. You're not going to believe it. Show them, Mrs. Fisher," Tom said.

Mary opened the bag and shook out the necklace onto the desk.

Charlotte gasped. "Wow! You found that on the beach? I have got to get down there more often."

Virginia adjusted her silver glasses as she peered at the stones. "It's in rather poor condition and needs a good cleaning. What do you think, Horace?"

Horace appeared not to hear Virginia's question as he reached for the necklace and gently spread out the sparkling stones on Eleanor's desk. "So the missing necklace has finally surfaced."

Missing necklace? Mary looked at her sister, and Betty shrugged her shoulders.

"Richard was so upset he lost it," Eleanor murmured. "It's a miracle."

"Yes, it is. He'd be so pleased." Horace's voice caught, but Mary wasn't sure if it was from finding the necklace or that he must really miss his old friend. Maybe both.

Tom let out a snort. "You're saying Mr. Blakely *lost* the necklace? That was pretty"—he glanced at Eleanor—"careless."

Eleanor sucked in a breath, but Horace put a hand on her shoulder. "It was an accident."

"What happened?" Charlotte asked.

"Do you mind if I tell them?" Horace asked Eleanor.

She looked down at the ring she'd slipped on her thumb and said, "Richard wouldn't mind now that the necklace has been recovered."

"Well, we were wrapping up the last of the recovery effort on the *Lady Beth* when a storm blew up suddenly," Horace said in his deep voice. "We didn't have the weather equipment we have now. Anyway, the water turned rough, shifting the sand on the bottom of the shallow bay, which actually turned to our advantage. We found the necklace about twenty feet from the wreck, and Richard put it in his diving pouch. The weather got worse, and the waves knocked us around a bit as we tried to get back on the boat. It's then we discovered the pouch had broken loose from his wet suit."

Horace picked up the pouch and showed them one end of the tattered material. "See? This is where the hook had been."

"How unfortunate," Virginia said.

Tom frowned and shook his head. "I would've been so upset."

"You're telling me," Horace said, sounding disgusted. "The next day, we went back and searched, but the sand must've swallowed it up again."

"Richard always felt terrible about losing such a valuable artifact. I kept telling him it wasn't his fault," Eleanor said. "If it hadn't been for Horace and Richard discovering the wreck in the first place, no one would've profited from it."

"So it is definitely from the *Lady Beth*," Tom said with awe in his voice.

"The diamonds are patterned in a similar intricate design as the other pieces we recovered from the *Lady Beth* shipwreck. The jewelry is exhibited over at the Gosnold Museum, if you want to see it."

"I've been there, but I'd like to go again," Charlotte said, stealing another glance at Tom. "Can you imagine owning such beautiful things?"

"You're going to have to marry well or change professions if you want jewelry like that." Virginia laughed. "A professor's salary won't be buying diamonds like that."

Charlotte sighed. "All I get to look forward to for the next few years is more school and then to make enough to pay off my humongous student loans and still being able to eat."

Tom looked over at Horace. "Any idea what it's worth?" he asked in an oddly flat tone. Mary glanced at him. His face seemed pinched, as if he was upset. He caught Mary's eye and looked away.

Horace rubbed his hands together. "If it's like the other pieces discovered, it's going to be worth quite a lot. I'd say about one hundred thousand dollars, maybe more, but it has to be evaluated by an expert."

"I figured it might be." Tom ran his hand over his head and then looked at his sports watch. "Well, I gotta get going.

Eleanor, I'll finish up that ad I talked to you about and bring it by later this afternoon."

"Bye, Tom," Charlotte called as he let himself out the back door to the alley.

"The first thing we should do is to get the necklace authenticated," Horace said. "I can call the museum and see if Dr. Carlson is available for an appraisal. He was involved with the restoration of the *Lady Beth* artifacts." He looked at Mary and Betty. "If that's okay with you, ladies."

Mary blinked and glanced at Betty. It hadn't occurred to her that they could lay claim to the necklace, and from Betty's startled expression, she knew her sister hadn't either. After all, Richard and Horace had discovered it decades ago.

"Mary *is* the one who found it on the dunes," Betty said.

Mary cleared her throat. "Well, I—"

"I'm sure Betty and Mary will agree that we need to get someone in here who can determine the value of the piece before we make any further decisions."

Mary bristled at Eleanor's proprietary tone but willed herself patience. "I agree. Dr. Carlson should examine it."

Betty nodded. "But where should we keep it until then? I'd worry if it was in our house."

"We have a safe here in the storage closet." Eleanor stood and slipped Richard's ring off her thumb.

"Wouldn't it be cool if we could display it at the festival?" Charlotte said. "We could charge admission."

"Or ask for donations for a worthy cause in lieu of charging admission," Virginia said.

"There's time to decide that later." Horace reached for the necklace.

"Would you mind if I took a photo?" Mary asked, thinking she wanted to do a little research on her own.

Horace looked hesitant but didn't object. He stepped back and let Mary take several close-ups of the necklace with her cell phone before he slid it back in the pouch and handed it to Eleanor.

"I probably should put Richard's ring in the safe too until I go home. I couldn't bear to lose it again." Eleanor walked into the closet and returned a few moments later. "There, safe and sound."

She stood for a moment, looking around the room as if settling on what to do next. "Now we need to get back to work. We only have four more days to pull this festival off successfully." She returned to her desk and scooted her chair closer to the computer screen.

"If anyone can pull off an entire festival in less than two weeks, you can, Eleanor," Horace said, heading for the door. "I'll get a call in to Dr. Carlson. His number is somewhere in my desk at home. After that's settled, I'll check with the rental company and see if they located that larger tent we need for the shipwreck display."

"Thank you, Horace," Eleanor said as he exited the office. A few people still lingered in the outer office, including Penny.

Horace paused. "Listen up. I'm sure you're all curious about the diamond necklace that was found today. We will be getting an expert in to examine it. Until then, we all just need to be patient. I'm sure you have lots going on in your own lives to keep you plenty busy." He closed the door behind him.

Virginia turned to Charlotte. "We need to finish the booth assignments. Where did you leave off on the list?"

As everyone settled back down to work, Betty looked at Mary and said, "I think I've had enough excitement for one day. I'm ready to head home. Eleanor, do you need help with anything before we leave?"

Eleanor glanced up at them. "Thank you, but right now, I'm buried in numbers. I still have to revise the budget. Costs are higher than we anticipated."

"We'll let you get to it, then." Mary and Betty slipped out the back door into the alley to avoid any lingering treasure hunters in the front office.

"Want to stop off at Bailey's and pick up a pint to take home for a celebration?" Mary asked as they made their way back to Main Street.

"You don't have to ask twice." Betty grinned. "Ice cream sounds perfect. It's a great antidote to a crazy day."

Mary laughed. She glanced across the street to her quaint shop housed in a building over two hundred years old. The wooden sign advertising Mary's Mystery Bookshop swung in the evening breeze. Rebecca had remembered to turn on the small lamp in the window, which cast a cozy glow over the new nautical display. On the door, the Open/Shut sign that Betty had found at a flea market currently indicated the store was closed. Mary smiled to herself. Sometimes she couldn't believe that her dream of owning a bookstore had come true. God had truly blessed her after an extremely difficult time in her life.

They followed a young couple into Bailey's and were greeted by the sweet scent of waffle cones and the sound of happy voices. They joined a short line that snaked to the old-fashioned counter.

Mary loved that the Baileys' shop was decorated like a vintage ice-cream parlor with bubblegum-pink-and-white-striped wallpaper. Most of the pink padded stools that lined the counter at the front of the store were occupied. Customers also sat at the small round wrought-iron white tables that were scattered throughout the shop.

As they waited in line, Betty nudged Mary and pointed to one of the ice-cream tubs. "Your flavor of the month is almost gone, as usual."

Mary looked over in the glassed ice-cream freezer. After her husband had given her an electric ice-cream maker many years ago, one of Mary's favorite hobbies was experimenting with ice-cream recipes. After Mary had moved to Ivy Bay, she'd found a fellow ice-cream artist in Tess Bailey. Tess had invited Mary to create special flavors for the family-run store.

This month's concoction was called Fig and Mint Delight. Mary had been feeling especially adventurous. She'd discovered fresh figs at Meeting House Grocers and combined them with fresh mint leaves from Betty's garden. The result had been a light, fresh ice cream that reminded Mary of late spring and the anticipation of summer.

As they took a step toward the counter, Mary overheard a woman's voice say, "Ralph, did you hear? Someone found the *Lady Beth* treasure!"

THREE

—◆◆◆—

Mary looked over at the middle-aged woman sharing a table with two gray-haired men who looked as if they could be brothers. They were all spooning up colorful banana splits, each topped with a mound of luscious whipped cream and a bright red cherry.

"It was a diamond necklace, Mildred," the more portly of the two men said with a chuckle.

Mildred huffed. "Well, still. I do hope they plan on donating it to the town."

"Oh, right, Mildred, like I'd believe *you'd* just donate a diamond necklace."

"I'd like to think I would." Mildred sniffed. "After all, it's a part of history. *Our* history. Wouldn't you feel obligated to share it?"

"Nope. I say finders keepers, losers weepers."

"Ralph! That is so childish." Mildred huffed. "That's the problem with this world. Everyone is so selfish."

"Why is that selfish?" Ralph asked. "If I won a million bucks at the lottery, would you expect me to share it with everyone in town?"

"That's different."

"How?"

The other man at the table looked up, his spoon paused over his strawberry ice cream. "I think this is just a sign there are more artifacts out there in the bay. I'm thinking of getting into scuba gear and taking a look myself."

"I'm betting there is," Ralph replied. "Look at what they found on the *Whydah*. An estimated four hundred million dollars in gold coins and other treasure."

Mary nudged Betty, and her sister raised her eyebrows. They turned slightly away from the table. Mary couldn't help eavesdropping. She could still see the trio out of the corner of her eye.

"But the *Whydah* was a pirate ship," Mildred said. "It's not the same as the *Lady Beth*, is it, Tim?"

"The *Lady Beth* was carrying gold too," Ralph pointed out before Tim could reply. "I read about it in *National Geographic*. Some famous explorer was on board. I can't remember his name. They were hunting riches as they were buying and selling all over the Atlantic basin. Remember, they found gold coins on *Lady Beth* too?"

"Not that many," Tim said.

"So?" Ralph said. "The chest of gold coins is still out there in the bay somewhere or buried somewhere onshore."

"Or someone found it and kept it for themselves," Tim said. "Like those guys who discovered the *Lady Beth* wreck. Who knows how much they squirreled away before reporting the find to the town?" Tim's spoon scraped the bottom of the dish. "They could've taken that chest of gold for themselves."

Betty stiffened beside Mary. "Of all the nerve," she whispered.

Ralph nodded. "Unless it wasn't on the ship. Some of the crew could've managed to get ashore in a lifeboat."

"But there were no survivors," Tim countered.

"That we know of." Ralph reached for his glass of water.

"I heard that someone was even selling maps of possible locations," Mildred said.

"You can't believe those scammers." Ralph shook his head at Mildred. "Someone is trying to make a quick buck on suckers."

"I know that. But the necklace was found on the beach by that old lady," Mildred said. "Maybe there is more out there on the beach."

Betty nudged Mary and grinned. "*Old* lady?" she whispered.

"I'd be careful about repeating that. You're older than me," Mary teased back. Betty was sixty-four, two years older than Mary. They moved two more steps up in the line to the counter.

"Hello there, Betty and Mary. Just the two people I was hoping to see," Tess said. She was a pleasantly plump woman who wore her usual uniform of a white bib apron with the words *Bailey's Ice Cream Shop* embroidered in bright pink across the front.

"I heard that there was some excitement on the beach. Someone said you found a bag full of diamonds. Another person said it was gold."

Mary blinked. "Actually, we found an old diver's pouch with a diamond necklace and a ring in it."

Tess's eyes grew round. "So it is true. I just thought maybe people were speculating again."

"The pouch belonged to my brother-in-law, Richard Blakely," Betty explained. "Horace Crenshaw thinks the necklace is from the *Lady Beth*."

"So a portion of the gossip is true. How marvelous," Tess said. "And this will be really good publicity for the shipwreck festival. Hopefully, people will visit the shops downtown here. We're getting some specials ready, just in case."

"We're going to have a sale and a little contest," Mary said.

Someone impatiently cleared their throat behind them, prompting Tess to ask, "What flavor will it be?"

Mary and Betty couldn't decide between two of the flavors, so they ended up getting both: Island Pineapple Coconut and Jamocha Almond Mud. By the time Tess got their ice-cream containers bagged and Betty had insisted on paying for the treat, the threesome at the nearby table had left.

They stepped outside and crossed the street. Betty stopped short on the sidewalk and felt her pockets. "I left my coin purse on the counter." She handed the bag to Mary. "Be right back."

Mary lingered under the striped awning of Jimmy's Hardware. The window display featured buckets, shovels, rakes, sand sifters, and metal detectors. The proprietor, Jimmy Shepard, was in the process of turning off lights, and Mary gave him a friendly wave through the window.

The shop door opened, and Tom Gordon stepped out carrying a heavy-looking plastic bag in each hand. He turned abruptly and almost bumped into her.

"Excuse me." He stepped back, dropping one of his bags, and it hit the ground with the clanking noise of metal hitting metal. "Oh, it's you, Mrs. Fisher. Everything get squared away in the office?" He reached down to retrieve his bag.

"Yes, they are back to work on the festival. You left the office so suddenly I didn't get to tell you how much I appreciated your help this afternoon on the beach. I was so flummoxed by finding the necklace that I didn't know what to do."

"No problem. I…" He gave a little shrug. "Never mind. Have a good evening." He turned to leave.

"Everything okay, Tom?"

He hesitated and slowly turned around. "I guess it's obvious that I'm feeling a bit sorry for myself." He glanced back at Mary. "I just can't believe I didn't find that necklace myself, you know? I've been combing that beach every day since the storms. I don't know why it didn't occur to me to search the dunes. I'm supposed to be a dive expert."

"I just got lucky," Mary said.

"Well, I wish I had some of that luck. Things haven't been going well at the dive shop. We're in the red. I just hope I don't have to close it down."

"I'm sorry, Tom." Mary knew starting a business could be tough these days, especially one that was seasonal. "Maybe the festival will bring in more customers."

"Yeah, maybe." He straightened his shoulders, and the bags rattled again. "I'm sorry. Please forget I said anything. I don't mean to rain on your parade. Congratulations on your find."

"Thanks, Tom." Mary felt sorry for his struggles. He seemed like a nice young man. Ambitious. Friendly. She hoped he managed to keep his business running. He walked down the sidewalk toward the shore as Betty came up behind her.

"Sorry it took me so long. I ran into Frances, and we got to talking about the next book club meeting. We decided to postpone the next meeting until after the festival since Eleanor is so busy."

"That sounds like a good idea," Mary concurred.

They crossed the footbridge and walked up the street to the house and decided to eat their ice cream on the deck.

Betty sat in one of the deck chairs, her face turned toward the bay. The wind stirred her hair. She looked relaxed and younger than her years. Contented. Mary felt a wave of affection for her precious sister.

Mary sat in the chair beside her, and Betty turned toward her. "Have you ever wondered what it would be like to be on a ship like the *Lady Beth*?" Betty asked. "Sailing for months on the seas. No modern equipment but relying on the stars and your instinct."

"People had to be so brave," Mary said, her sister's question conjuring up images in her mind.

"I don't know if you remember, but Edward and I went on a cruise once."

"I remember your fabulous photos and then trying to talk John into going on one. He said we'd go someday." Mary's chest tightened for a moment. There were so many things she and John had wanted to do together.

"Maybe you and I can go on a cruise someday," Betty said. "It'd be fun."

"I'd like that." Mary reached into the paper bag and pulled out the pints of ice cream and plastic spoons. She held them both up, and Betty reached for the Almond Jamocha Mud.

They settled back, comfortable enough with each other in conversation or not. Mary started in on the pint of Island Pineapple Coconut, eating out of the carton, and then switched halfway with Betty for the Almond Jamocha Mud. Both were delicious.

"I hope Eleanor wasn't out of line," Betty said after a little while. "You did find the necklace. You should be the one to say what you think should be done with it."

"But it was Richard's discovery to begin with." Mary set her empty ice-cream container on the table. "Anyone could've found it on the beach."

"Not just anyone," Betty said with a smile. "I'm curious to see what the expert says. Imagine it surviving in the ocean all those years and being in such good condition."

"The bag must've protected it." Mary pulled her cell phone from her pocket and opened the photo album. She enlarged the photo she'd taken of the necklace on the screen. "I did notice that some of the diamonds are missing."

Betty leaned over. "Where?"

"There, along the edges. Just a few here and there. I didn't see any loose diamonds in the pouch."

"Oh yes. I didn't even notice before. Well, I guess it should be expected, considering it was on the bay floor for so long."

"Most likely," Mary said.

"The necklace is so pretty. I can't wait to see it when it's all cleaned up." Betty took a final lick of her spoon. "I think I ate too much, but it was totally worth it."

The breeze had a little bit of a nip to it. Mary rubbed the goose bumps on her arms. The ice cream no doubt was making her feel chilled. She stood and stretched.

Betty yawned as she picked up their ice-cream containers. "I'm so tired. What an exciting day it was."

"I'm wiped out too. I'll go get our things from the beach and see you inside." Mary walked back to the shore and retrieved their blanket, basket, and chairs that she'd almost forgotten about in all the excitement. She had just returned to the kitchen when the doorbell pealed.

"I'll get it," Betty called as Gus took off toward the front door. Betty hurried after him. "It's Eleanor."

Mary rounded the corner and saw Eleanor standing on the porch, red-faced, with slightly smeared lipstick and disheveled hair, which was shocking for someone who always appeared polished and refined.

Eleanor's suitcase hit the floor with a thud. "I've been robbed."

FOUR

◆◆◆

O h, Eleanor, you poor dear, come in." Betty grabbed
Eleanor's arm and ushered her quickly into the house.
"Here, sit on the couch."

Mary picked up the suitcase and set it inside, and then
helped Betty fuss over Eleanor by putting her feet up, offering
water, herbal tea, and a cool cloth.

Gus jumped on the couch and arched his back against
Eleanor's arm repeatedly until she said faintly, "Shoo, cat. Go
away."

Mary picked up Gus and gave him a hug before putting
him on the floor. "Stay down."

"Drink some more tea and try to relax," Betty said.

"I'll try. It's just very difficult." Eleanor's hand shook as
she lifted her cup for a sip. When Eleanor said, "This is a little
weak, Betty. The tea should have brewed longer," Mary knew
Eleanor was feeling better.

"I'll remember next time." Betty took Eleanor's hand.
"Do you need to see your doctor? The robber didn't hurt you,
did he?"

"No, no." Eleanor sighed deeply. "He just ran out the
back door."

"So he didn't actually confront you?" Mary asked.

Eleanor shook her head.

"Praise the Lord for that," Betty said, and Mary agreed. The Lord had indeed been watching out for Eleanor.

Mary sat in a chair near to the couch and leaned forward. "Can you tell us what happened?"

"I—I'll try." Eleanor took the cool cloth off her forehead and propped herself up straighter on the cushion. "I arrived home, and everything seemed as usual. I was walking down the hall to the kitchen, and I heard a noise. At first, I thought it might be my housekeeper. She sometimes works late if she doesn't get all the cleaning done. So I called out hello, and suddenly a man ran out of Richard's office and there was this awful crash. He knocked over that vase I keep on the table in the hallway."

Betty's hand covered her heart. "Eleanor, I'm so sorry. I know that vase meant a lot to you."

Eleanor nodded. "I know. It is irreplaceable. Richard gave it to me on our twentieth wedding anniversary. He would bring me home flowers every week to put in it." She sniffed and dabbed at her eyes with the washcloth.

"We can be thankful that you weren't hurt." Mary wasn't unsympathetic to Eleanor's angst over the vase, but she was anxious to hear the rest of the story. "Is that when you called the police?"

Eleanor shot her an irritated look. "Of course. I called the police right away. I asked specifically for Chief McArthur, and they sent this *boy* deputy. The chief was too busy to come.

"He was down at the marina. But that's not the point. He could have assigned that case to someone else. Richard and I have been very supportive of his department over the years."

Betty patted Eleanor's hand. "I'm sure he would've come if he could have. What did the deputy say?"

"Not much. He had me look around to see if anything was stolen. As far as I know, nothing was taken, but I was so shaken up I could've missed something. He took a report and said they'd get right on it. He said there are a lot of strangers about town right now due to renewed interest over the shipwreck."

"He's right about that," Mary said, thinking about the crowd on the beach. "Did you get a look at the burglar's face?"

Eleanor shook her head. "It all happened too fast. I was so upset about everything that happened I just packed a bag and came over here."

"You did the right thing. You'll stay right here as long as you need to. And tomorrow, we'll go over to your house and take a look around." Betty gave Mary a beseeching look.

Mary hesitated before she replied. Eleanor had never been overly friendly to Mary, and she was pretty sure that Eleanor didn't want her help. Mary didn't like Eleanor's stuffy attitude, and Eleanor seemed to feel that Mary had intruded upon Eleanor and Betty's relationship, but they tolerated each other politely for Betty's sake. Still…Mary couldn't let her sister down.

Besides, she was curious about the intruder and what he may have been looking for. "We'll go over first thing in the morning and see if we can put things right."

Betty rose from the couch. "Let's get you settled, then." She hooked an arm under Eleanor's and walked upstairs. Mary grabbed Eleanor's suitcase and followed them to one of the guest bedrooms next to Mary's. The room's sage-green walls and the vintage nine-patch quilt on the bed created a restful atmosphere.

Eleanor's eyes narrowed as she looked around the room. "It smells a little musty in here."

Mary took a deep sniff and only picked up a lingering smell of citrus disinfectant from the last cleaning of the bathroom.

"That may be because it's been closed up." Betty crossed the room to open a window. "It was cleaned recently, and the linens are fresh, but I can change them if you wish."

Eleanor sighed. "No, I'll be fine. It's only for one night."

"There are towels in the cupboard and a robe in the closet," Betty added.

"Well, I'm heading to bed. Sleep well. I'm next door if you need me, Eleanor. Good night." Mary set the suitcase down and backed out of the room, scooping up Gus in the hall where he'd been lingering, waiting for a chance to dart into the guest room.

Mary closed her door, relieved to be away from that underlying tension between her and Eleanor. She could sympathize with the older woman. Mary's shop had been broken into before, and she remembered that feeling of violation. She certainly wouldn't want it to be her home. Betty had installed a burglar alarm, and she was pretty sure Eleanor had one too. So how did the thief get in? She'd have to ask Eleanor in the morning when they went over to the house.

Mary took a shower to wash the beach scent off and then picked out one of her favorite sets of light cotton pajamas, a Christmas gift from her husband. He had said the pretty blue flowers on it reminded him of the color of her blue eyes.

She picked up the most recent Sue Grafton novel and tried to immerse herself in the adventures of Kinsey Millhone, PI, but she couldn't focus on the page.

Her mind whirled, replaying the day's events. After overhearing the conversation in the ice-cream shop, Mary was pretty certain the news of the necklace and Richard's ring had spread throughout Ivy Bay. One of the men had even suggested that Richard and Horace had squirreled away some of the treasure for themselves. Could that type of speculation, spurred on by the discovery of the necklace or maybe even the *Ivy Bay Bugle*'s Sunday article on the shipwreck, have prompted someone to break into Eleanor's house to look?

And if that were the case, were they in any danger here?

She retrieved her laptop from on top of her dresser and did a search for more information on the *Lady Beth*. She found it interesting that, even in other articles, there was still speculation that the ship's chest of gold had been taken ashore before the storm. Since there were no survivors, it was pure guesswork to where it could've been hidden.

Another theory, a more likely scenario, suggested the storm may have scattered the contents of the ship even farther than thought, and any gold was now buried under the ocean floor. Over the years, a few gold coins had been discovered onshore and on the sandy bottom.

It was an intriguing mystery, and Mary could understand why it has captured people's interest. Was there still more treasure out there in the bay? Or perhaps it was hidden right under their noses somewhere in Ivy Bay.

In one article about the artifacts found on the *Lady Beth* was a photograph of Horace Crenshaw and Richard Blakely, the discoverers of the wreck. Richard wore a polo shirt and neat khakis. Horace was clad about the same way he'd dressed today, including his shark's-tooth necklace. The partners had their arms wrapped around each other and held dueling pistols. The article noted that the dueling pistols had been stored in an almost-watertight case, so the guns had been spared a lot of the usual concretion. Many of the other *Lady Beth* artifacts had to be carefully restored and were sold to the museum. Richard Blakely and Horace Crenshaw had donated a percentage of the find, valued at around $250,000, to the town of Ivy Bay.

Mary leaned back against the headboard, deep in thought. The discovery of new worlds, and in the case of the *Lady Beth*, exploring and trading for riches from all over the Atlantic basin and the Caribbean, had to be a thrill that was difficult to find today. Would she have been brave enough to venture out like that?

She thought about one of her favorite Bible verses, Hebrews 11:1: *Now faith is confidence in what we hope for and assurance about what we do not see.* Early explorers surely must've had strong faith.

Gus jumped up beside her and ran across the computer keys. "Hey! Are you trying to tell me something?" Mary exclaimed.

The cat stretched out on the bed and rolled to his back with his legs sticking up in the air. Mary laughed and rubbed his tummy. "Okay, it's time for bed."

She closed the computer and set it on the nightstand. She was too tired to read the novel now. But before she turned off the light, she padded downstairs to make sure Betty had turned on the alarm system.

FIVE

◆◆◆

Mary had just poured herself a mug of freshly brewed coffee when a shriek shattered the quiet of the morning. She dropped her mug and charged down the hall and up the stairs. The guest-room door was open, and Eleanor, still in her bathrobe, stood in the middle of the room.

Mary gasped. "Eleanor! What's wrong?"

"There!" Eleanor pointed to her open suitcase on the floor.

"Your suitcase?" Mary asked, puzzled until a gray furry head popped out from beneath the clothing. Gus stared at her for a second and flipped over digging his way under a sweater.

"Gus!" Mary clapped her hands. "Get out of there."

The cat looked at Mary with wide eyes and darted under the bed.

"I'm sorry, Eleanor—"

The cat tore out from the bed, skidding in a half circle and dove in the suitcase again with a flip.

"Gus, no!" Mary said, trying hard not to laugh. She scooped up the wiggling cat and tucked him firmly under her chin. "He's just very curious and likes to play with new things."

"Maybe he doesn't get enough exercise," Eleanor said stiffly, picking up navy-blue slacks and shaking them. "My cats always stayed outdoors so they wouldn't scratch the furniture or get hair *everywhere*."

Mary bit her lip. "Well, Gus likes being in here with me. I tend to worry when I don't know where he is at. He means a lot to me." Maybe she was a little overprotective with her pet at times, but Gus had become such a cherished companion. He had made the nights less lonely after John had passed away. Since then, she'd made sure he was well taken care of. She stepped across the hall into the bathroom, grabbed a lint roller, and took it to Eleanor. "This should get the hair off. I'll try to keep him out of your room."

Mary carried Gus downstairs. Eleanor would be going home today, and Mary planned to just make sure Gus stayed out of Eleanor's way until then. She walked into the kitchen and set him down.

Betty was wiping up the coffee Mary had spilled on the counter. "What was that all about?"

"Oh, Gus was playing in Eleanor's suitcase. She was a bit upset." Mary tried to keep a straight face, but her lips twitched.

"Mary!" Betty scolded and then wagged a finger at the cat. "Shame on you, Gus. We have to treat our houseguests with respect, especially my sister-in-law."

Gus stared at her intently for a moment and then nonchalantly lifted a paw to lick.

A little giggle escaped Betty. "I bet he had loads of fun, though."

Mary grinned. "Unfortunately, yes. I just hope he didn't do any more damage than just leave hair behind."

"We'll hear about it if he did." Betty set two skillets on the stove. "Poor Eleanor. I had trouble sleeping last night thinking about someone breaking into her home. We're lucky here because we at least have each other, but Eleanor is all alone over there most of the time."

"I'm glad we have each other too. Eleanor has a burglar alarm, doesn't she?" Mary asked, getting out a bottle of orange juice and a milk carton from the refrigerator and setting them on the table.

Betty broke eggs into the bowl and whisked them. "Yes, but it didn't stop her home from being broken into. Maybe it wasn't working."

Or maybe it hadn't been turned on, Mary thought. She'd have to see if the system was checked by the police when they went over to Eleanor's later.

"Would you mind making some toast?" Betty asked as she put turkey bacon into one of the skillets.

"Sure." Mary popped two slices of whole wheat bread into the toaster.

By the time Betty had finished cooking the scrambled eggs, Eleanor strolled into the kitchen. She looked like her old self, with perfect hair and flawless makeup. Her shoulders were straight under her elegant suit jacket as she sat primly at the table and looked around with a confident gleam in her eyes.

"Smells wonderful in here," she said. "I've always enjoyed a good breakfast. Sometimes, Richard only wanted coffee in the morning or just a bite of toast. I think he would've been healthier if he'd listened to me and eaten better. As you know, breakfast is the most important meal of the day."

Betty set a platter of cantaloupe on the table and took a seat. "Mary, would you say the blessing?"

Eleanor set her fork down. "I'm used to eating breakfast alone these days."

Mary provided a prayer, asking that the Lord continue to nourish them and bless them to do His will. And she added a silent prayer for peace. Already she could feel a sense of tension at the table.

"These eggs are great," Mary said, enjoying the smoked salmon and green onions Betty had added to the eggs.

"My previous housekeeper used to make the most delicious scrambled eggs. They were so creamy. The secret is to add a dollop of sour cream," Eleanor said and looked at Betty. "Not that these aren't good too, dear."

Mary stifled a sigh, wondering why Eleanor's tone always sounded slightly condescending around Betty.

Betty appeared not to notice and picked up the platter of bacon. "Would you like some bacon, Eleanor?"

"No, I'd better not," Eleanor said. "I need to watch my calories."

"It's turkey bacon, so it's lower in fat," Betty added.

"If I shouldn't have the real thing, then I don't want this pretend bacon."

"I'll have some, Betty." Mary took several slices. The bacon tasted almost the same to her as regular bacon. Gus liked it too. He appeared at her feet, his nose tilted in the air.

"Behave, young man. I'll give you a piece later," Mary said, rubbing the cat with her foot.

Eleanor poured herself a half glass of orange juice. "Should you be giving people food to the cat? I thought it wasn't healthy."

"Normally, I don't," Mary said. "But he loves bacon, so I sometimes give him a small piece when we have it."

Eleanor turned her attention to Betty. "I was shopping last week and saw the most adorable curtains that would be perfect in that upstairs bathroom. There was also this divine antique rug that would look fabulous in the hallway. That is, of course, if you are thinking of ever updating things around here someday."

"Oh well, I hadn't thought about it," Betty said. "But I suppose it would be fun to at least look. Did you want to go shopping?"

"It will have to wait until next week after the festival. I'm swamped until then. Maybe we could even take a trip up to Boston."

Betty nodded and smiled. Mary felt a rush of warmth toward her sister. She was trying very hard to make her sister-in-law feel welcome. Betty had spent most of her life living up to the standards of the wealthy Emerson family and did a marvelous job. Mary knew from experience she didn't have to worry about Betty being a pushover. Betty wouldn't change anything about the house unless she wanted to, but Mary just wished Eleanor would appear to accept Betty for the delightful, talented woman she was.

Mary picked up the *Bugle* newspaper she'd planned to read before Gus had been discovered in Eleanor's bedroom and read the headline: Hospital Scandal Threatens Employee Pensions.

Mary skimmed the article written by Johanna Montgomery. The details were still emerging, but they suspected fraud, and Mary felt sorry for the people affected.

Mary turned the page and discovered a photo of her and Betty on the beach that Penny must've snapped. Beside it was a close-up picture of the necklace in Mary's hand. The article under the photo had the byline of Penny Fuller and Johanna Montgomery. Mary thought that Penny was probably thrilled her name was listed first.

"There's an article in here on the necklace."

"Oh, please read it out loud," Betty said. "I'm curious to hear what they have to say about yesterday."

"'Lost Treasure Found?' is the title," Mary said. "'With hundreds of treasure seekers descending on Ivy Bay's beach, there have been some great discoveries. Tom Gordon, owner of the Dive Shop, reports that he has been recovering the items found along the shore and by some of the customers who take his specialized diving tours around the site of the *Lady Beth*'s final resting place. These items have included a mug, a silver fork, nails, and buttons. But the most exciting discovery was made onshore by local business owner Mary Fisher.'"

"But of course," Betty interrupted with a tease.

"'A diamond necklace and a gold ring were discovered among the dunes,'" Mary continued. "'Her sister, Betty Emerson, immediately identified the ring as belonging to her brother-in-law, the late Richard Blakely.'"

"Well, that's not exactly true. I suspected it was Richard's, but Eleanor confirmed it," Betty said.

"The article mentions that next," Mary said, and read the next paragraph. "'Eleanor Blakely confirmed that the ring and the diving pouch was her husband's. Richard Blakely had allegedly lost the diver's pouch during the excavation of the shipwreck.'"

"Allegedly." Eleanor rolled her eyes. "Well, of course Richard lost it, or otherwise how would it have washed up onshore? Are they trying to imply something?"

"I think it's just police jargon," Mary said, trying to diffuse Eleanor's defensiveness, and continued reading. "'Horace Crenshaw, Richard's partner in the discovery and excavation of the *Lady Beth* in 1986, stated that Richard had found the necklace during the excavation of the *Lady Beth,* but due to rough water, the diving pouch in which the necklace had been stored was lost. Horace believes that the diamond necklace is part of a matched set that had been recovered from the shipwreck. The museum has been contacted and will be sending down an expert within a day or two to evaluate the find.'"

"Well, that part's accurate," Eleanor said. "I suppose the museum will offer to buy it. They did with the other jewelry Richard found."

Betty turned to Mary. "That is okay with you, right, Mary? After all, you found the necklace this time around. You could get someone else to evaluate it."

Eleanor blinked, as if surprised. "I just assumed that we were all in agreement about what should be done."

"It's fine, Eleanor. I really don't think of the necklace as mine," Mary said. "If it is sold to a museum, though, it'd be good to see some of the funds go to charity. But we're jumping ahead of ourselves here."

"I suppose there might be some paperwork to sort out when it comes to ownership." Eleanor glanced at Mary again.

"Richard had some agreement with the Gosnold Museum and Ivy Bay about how much was to be donated and what he and Horace could keep. I think they signed some sort of contract. Horace would know for sure."

Betty looked at the paper still in Mary's hand. "Is that all the article said?"

"There are a few more paragraphs." Mary picked up the paper. "'Ned Krantz, an avid Ivy Bay historian, always thought there should've been more artifacts recovered from the site. "I'm afraid they botched the job," he said.'"

"Oh, that Ned. Always jealous of Richard," Eleanor said with a huff. "He was an accountant before he retired. What would he know about excavating? Botched job! He should go down there and dig. Since then, people have been out there with more modern equipment and nothing has shown up." She looked at Mary. "What else does it say?"

"Longtime Ivy Bay citizen Stella McGuire shares another popular opinion," Mary read. "She says, 'I think the treasure is buried here somewhere in Ivy Bay. There were a couple of letters from the sailors on board hinting about gold among the cargo. Not much gold was ever recovered. My great-grandmother said that when she was a young girl, she heard a treasure chest was buried onshore. Personally, I think the ship was looted *before* it was excavated, if you know what I mean.'"

Mary paused, wondering if Stella was insinuating that Richard or Horace had stolen the gold, or just assuming that over the years, people had pilfered the wreck. The assumption seemed to have passed by Eleanor so she continued. "'Most of the artifacts recovered from excavation of the shipwreck can be found at the Gosnold Museum. Patrons may also be able to view artifacts selected by the historical society this weekend during the Cape Cod Shipwreck Festival.'"

"Which reminds me," Eleanor said. "I'd better get down to the historical society right after we go by my house. We only have a short time to get ready." Eleanor set her napkin on the table and hurried toward the stairs. Gus started to follow her, but Mary grabbed him.

"Here you go, Gus," Mary said, putting a piece of turkey bacon in Gus's bowl. The cat eagerly ate it up, and Mary filled his dish with cat food. She returned to the table to help clean up.

Betty waved Mary away when she reached to get Eleanor's plate. "Don't worry about it. I'll clean up." She seemed so insistent that Mary left the plate but grabbed Eleanor's glass when she took her own plate and glass to the sink.

Mary went back upstairs to brush her teeth. She stuck the article in her purse, wondering why the article had quoted Horace Crenshaw and Tom Gordon, but no one had come by to interview Mary or Betty since they had found the necklace. Mary didn't need to see her name in the paper, but the story would've been more thorough if she had been interviewed. But then, with Johanna apparently busy with the hospital scandal, she may not have had much time to spend with Penny on it.

She looked around for Gus and realized he was probably still hanging around his food dish. She grabbed his carrier and headed down the stairs. As she walked into the kitchen, she spied Eleanor holding the back door open and Gus was trotting outside.

"Gus!" Mary rushed to the door, startling Eleanor. The cat paused, flicked his tail, and then headed for the street. Mary raced after him and caught him on the sidewalk.

"Where were you going? We have to go to work soon." Mary held him close so he wouldn't wiggle.

Eleanor still stood by the door. "He wanted to go out. Was he not supposed to?"

Mary bit back her initial sharp reply. She had just mentioned to Eleanor upstairs that she worried about Gus when she didn't know where he was. "Eleanor, please don't let Gus out."

"I'll try to remember," Eleanor said stiffly, and turned to walk back to the kitchen.

"I appreciate it." Mary carried Gus over to his cat carrier.

Lord, grant me patience.

At least she had one thing to be grateful for. Eleanor would be going home today.

SIX

❖◆❖

Eleanor unlocked the door to her large gray Federal-style house in one of the most prominent locations in town.

"Eleanor, was the alarm on yesterday when you got home?" Mary asked as she and Betty waited on the porch until Eleanor tapped the disarm code into the burglar alarm control panel.

"Yes, I always set it when I leave, but it must not have been working yesterday. The company is going to come out today and check it." Eleanor looked around the foyer with a wary expression. "I don't know if I will ever feel safe here again."

"That's totally understandable," Betty said. "I get shivers every time I think about it. But the good thing is that the Lord was looking out for you and you didn't get hurt."

"I am grateful for that," Eleanor said. "Now I just don't want it to ever happen again. Maybe I should get a big guard dog. Maybe a rottweiler."

Mary set Gus's carrier by the door and glanced around at Eleanor's beautiful antiques, many of which were original to the house. Great care went into keeping them polished and preserved. Sterling-silver frames with family photographs were set on the end tables and lined the mantel. The floors were kept shining and the area rugs spotless. Mary had a hard time picturing a large dog running about the elegant rooms getting hair everywhere and possibly knocking things over, especially after Eleanor's reaction to Gus this morning.

Betty must've had her doubts too because she said gently, "That's one option, but a dog would require a lot of care. You're so busy with your volunteer work you're not home much. Maybe you just need an updated burglar system."

"Did the police have any idea how the burglar got in without setting off the alarm?" Mary asked.

"That young policeman looked around and didn't seem to have a clue. Then he decided that maybe the thief came in upstairs since I left the window open in the guest bedroom."

"The upstairs?" Betty asked. "He'd have to be a cat burglar to get in up there."

Eleanor sniffed. "You can see why I wanted Chief McArthur."

"Do you mind if I look around up there?" Mary asked.

"Go ahead," Eleanor said. "I'm going to check my messages."

The stairs were near the doorway. The treads creaked and groaned under her feet. She reached the wide-planked hallway at the top and admired the mahogany side table lining one wall. On the other side, a Federal-style convex mirror hung above an old steamer trunk.

Mary turned right into the first bedroom. An antique sleigh bed filled up the center of the room. A lovely dresser occupied one wall opposite a tall window. An off-white antique-looking floor rug lay in between. The scent of lemon wood polish hung in the air. Everything looked shining clean and untouched. She went to the window and saw what the young policeman had. An ancient oak with long leafy branches grew near the house. One of the branches stretched about four feet from the window. An experienced burglar or even someone athletic could possibly reach the window if they were willing to take such a risk. A fall from this height would break bones.

She shoved the window upward and pushed on the screen. It wasn't locked in place. A tug on the bottom and someone might be able to slip in. She looked around the floor for a clue. There was a tiny smudge on the edge of the off-white rug. Mary rubbed it with her finger. It was possible Eleanor's housekeeper had missed it or maybe the policeman had left the smudge when he had inspected the room. She checked the other bedrooms upstairs and found them as immaculate as the first. None of them had trees close to the windows.

She went back downstairs. In the formal living room, Betty sat on a stiff, low-to-the-ground love seat upholstered in an intricate tapestry design. Mary sat next to Betty. Even with the thin pillow that Eleanor had set on the cushion, Mary found the seat uncomfortable.

Eleanor's agitated voice rose in the distance.

Mary looked at Betty. "What's going on?"

"Eleanor got a crank call by someone accusing her and Richard of hoarding the treasure. She called the police station to report it."

Mary's stomach dropped. "Did they threaten her?"

"Yes, but it wasn't specific in what they would do. I'm worried."

"Betty," Eleanor called.

"Coming, Eleanor." Betty rose hastily, and Mary followed her to the kitchen.

Eleanor sat in a chair, her face pale and grim. "Can you believe the nerve of some people? The police said they'd make a report. That was it. What if that person is serious and comes over here?"

"Oh, Eleanor." Betty placed a hand on her sister-in-law's shoulder.

"Do you mind if I listen to the voice mail?" Mary asked Eleanor.

"No, no, go ahead." She explained how to access the recording.

"Greedy selfish pigs!" a muffled voice growled. "You stole from the people of Ivy Bay? You'd better turn over the treasure before we make you." There was a click. Mary checked the caller ID and dialed back the number. It just rang.

"No one answers," Mary said, not surprised. "The police will want the number." Mary suspected the phone was either a public one or disposable.

Eleanor nodded. "I just hate feeling like a victim. We used to get crank calls after the excavation of the *Lady Beth* too. This probably happened because of those articles in the *Bugle*. People get crazy when they think they are entitled to something."

"We can't keep people from calling, but maybe we can help the police catch your burglar." Betty looked at Mary. "Surely there is something we can do."

Eleanor rubbed her temples with her fingers. "How?"

"Let's go step by step over what happened and see if we can get any ideas," Mary suggested.

Eleanor took a deep breath and stood. "It can't hurt."

"Let's start at the front door," Mary said. "Go through the motions."

They walked back to the front of the house, and Mary opened the door.

"Oh, you want me to start outside?" Eleanor sighed.

When Eleanor was on the threshold, Mary asked, "When you walked up to the house, did you see anything unusual?"

"I was preoccupied," Eleanor said. "I had left Richard's ring back at the historical society. I almost went back but then decided it could wait."

"So then you went in the house," Mary said. "You sure the door was locked?"

Eleanor hesitated. "Yes, I think so. I turned my key in the lock anyway. Besides, the alarm would've gone off if someone went in without disarming it."

"Then you turned off the burglar alarm, right?" Betty asked.

Eleanor nodded. "As I told the police, it's a habit. I arm it when I leave and disarm it when I get home, and of course at night when I'm alone. I've been doing that for years."

"Where did you go next?" Mary asked.

"I set my keys down on the table." Eleanor walked over to a little table where her keys were now resting in a beautiful silver tray. I turned on the light and headed down the hall to the kitchen, and I heard something. Like a squeak."

"Like the stairs?" Mary asked, suddenly wondering if there had been more than one intruder in the house.

"No, it came from the office. Then this person came out of Richard's office, crashed into this side table, and the vase crashed to the floor. I loved that vase." Her voice caught.

Betty patted Eleanor on the shoulder. "What did you do then?"

"I—I froze. I didn't even scream. He was gone before I knew it."

"He went out the kitchen door?" Mary asked, walking the distance to the door. She looked through the window to the backyard. "What was he wearing?"

"All black. Black shoes, pants, sweatshirt and hood that covered his face except for his eyes and nose. I told this all to the officer."

"How tall was he?" Mary continued, although she could sense Eleanor was getting to the end of her patience.

Eleanor stared at her, her eyes narrowing. "I really couldn't say. I was so frightened. But I suppose he was taller than me, probably average height for a man, and lean." She blew out a huff. "How dare someone come in here like that? But, I'm going to make sure it doesn't happen again. I'm going to get all the locks changed and upgrade the security system."

"Those are good steps to take." Mary glanced down the hall to the office. "And maybe we can also help get the crook off the streets and in jail. You mentioned you didn't find anything missing, right?"

"That's what I thought, but we can take another look, though." Eleanor led them to the back of the house and opened a door. "I haven't changed it much in here from the way Richard left it. It makes me feel closer to him when I come in here."

Mary could understand that. She kept some of John's possessions in the closet in her bedroom, just for that reason.

The small, tucked-away room was as immaculate as the rest of the house, but gone were the uncomfortable antiques and lightly colored tapestry fabrics. This room was definitely a man cave.

A large wooden desk occupied the space in front of the windows and tan suede easy chairs cozied up by a set of shelves filled with books. Mary scanned the titles. Some of the books were novels written by Tom Clancy and James Patterson, some were biographies, including several of Abraham Lincoln, and many colorful books on travel and diving rounded out the collection.

A television was attached to a wall in a corner of the room. Underneath was an exercise bike.

Glass shelves climbed to the ceiling on the opposite wall, full of what looked like artifacts from Richard's diving adventures. Mary moved closer to examine them when Eleanor gasped.

"I was wrong last night. Things are *not* right!"

"What do you mean?" Betty hurried over to the desk where Eleanor stood. "Everything looks okay."

Eleanor shook her head. "See that lamp? It's been moved."

Mary looked at the green-shaded reading lamp on one side of the desk.

"It has to sit precisely in that corner or it casts an annoying shadow."

"Maybe the housekeeper moved it when she dusted?" Betty suggested.

"No, she knows better. Besides, I was in here writing bills just two days ago and it was fine. She hasn't been in here to clean since."

"Was that drawer open too?" Mary asked, pointing to a drawer that was cracked open.

"Not that I know of. I don't use it unless I run out of supplies." She opened the desk drawer that contained paper, pens, a calendar, and a box of paper clips. The other drawers appeared untouched.

"Surely if someone was looking for anything valuable like that necklace, he wouldn't think I'd be foolish enough to leave it in a desk drawer, would he? I'd put it in the safe, and that wasn't touched."

"Maybe he was looking for money or credit cards when you interrupted him," Betty suggested.

"Or maybe the thief wasn't very bright," Mary said, although she really wasn't getting that impression in this situation. Normally, a burglar would probably snatch what he could and run. Surely he had enough time to at least get something if he heard Eleanor coming in the door.

Eleanor walked over to the glass shelves. "This is not right either." She flipped a switch, and light washed over the artifacts. "That bell is supposed to be over there, and the key is too close to the edge. Someone was touching them."

Mary hurried over to see what Eleanor was talking about.

"Richard put his finds in chronological order of when he discovered them," Eleanor explained. "He was very methodical."

Betty looked over the display. "I haven't been in here in years, and everything looks the same to me. Is anything missing?"

Eleanor frowned. "I don't think so. None of the main ones, at any rate. But there are so many artifacts it's hard to be sure. Richard kept records, but I stored those files in the attic years ago."

Betty turned from the shelves. "I seem to remember that you had some old photographs of Richard standing right here. Are those still around? Maybe you can compare what's here with the photos."

Eleanor thought for a moment. "I think I put that album in a bedroom armoire. I'll be right back."

After Eleanor left, Betty shivered and crossed her arms over her chest. "I don't like this. I used to think that having a burglar system gave us some measure of protection."

"It does. But it can't protect against every scenario. That's where faith comes in," Mary said gently, thinking about Hebrews 11:1 again.

Betty blew out a little sigh. "You're right."

"Anyway, I think the policeman was right that the burglar could've come in the window upstairs. The screen is loose, and the windows are not wired for the alarm."

"I didn't want to say anything in front of Eleanor, but she can be forgetful sometimes." Betty lowered her voice. "I know of at least two other occasions she forgot to set the alarm."

"If that was the case, someone either got lucky or...they were watching the house," Mary said.

Eleanor swept back into the room and set a large leather-bound album on the desk. She flipped it open.

Betty giggled and pointed at a photo of her and Edward that looked as if it might've been taken in the late eighties. "Look at my 'big' hair." She patted her modern and chic blonde hairdo. "I had to use lots of hair spray to get it like that."

Eleanor turned the page to reveal a photo similar to the one that Mary had seen in one of the articles she'd found online. Richard and Horace stood side by side holding matching antique pistols and grinning at the camera.

"Here is the photo Betty was talking about." Eleanor pointed to one of Richard standing by the shelves. He was placing something on the shelf.

"That's the bowl of a pipe he found when he was diving off North Carolina," Eleanor said. "It's not an antique, probably from the fifties, but he was excited. That was after the *Lady Beth.*"

Mary located the pipe on the shelf. It was in the same spot where Richard had placed it. In the next photo, Richard stood off to the side of the shelves. The flash had caught the edges of the glass and reflected it back, but Mary could still make out the items.

The artifacts ranged from the small silver bell that perhaps was used by a mistress of a household to bullets, a cannon ball, buttons, belt buckles, a long iron key, a battered wooden case with metal edging, and an assortment of bottles in different colors and shapes. Mary compared the items on the shelves to the photo. Richard had added more finds, but the initial artifacts were still in the exact order as in the photo.

Three gold coins in individual small glass cases were front and center. Easy to grab and pocket. Again, she wondered about the motive of the burglar.

Mary paused by the case and lifted the lid. An old pistol was nestled inside. "Is this the same pistol that was in the photo with Horace and Richard?"

Eleanor looked up from the album. "Yes, the men got so excited about finding those silly dueling pistols. Richard took one and Horace the other."

Betty moved closer to look and accidentally bumped the edge of the case. Mary grabbed it as it tipped over, and Betty caught the pistol before it hit the floor.

"That was close. Feel how heavy this is." Betty handed the pistol to Mary. The pistol did feel solid and heavy. She would have had a difficult time shooting it unless she held it with both hands. Mary placed the pistol back in the case and closed the lid. A series of letters stamped on a metal plate on the one corner caught her attention. They looked like initials.

"JPV," she read out loud and looked at Eleanor. "Do you know what these letters mean?"

"Richard thought they were the initials of whoever owned the pistols. He never found out who the owner had been."

Mary stared at the initials for a few moments longer, wondering about the person the initials belonged to. Surely Richard checked against the names of the sailors on the *Lady Beth*.

Mary stepped back. "Okay, so which of these items came from the *Lady Beth*?"

"It would be everything on those two shelves." Eleanor pointed. "The pistol case, the cannon ball, the small bell, buttons, the coins, and the key."

"And only these shelves were disturbed?"

"That's my impression," Eleanor said with her hands on her hips.

"So he was looking for something from the shipwreck," Betty said.

"It appears so." Mary squatted so she could look up under the shelf.

"What are you doing?" Eleanor said.

"Looking for fingerprints," Mary said, but the glass panes were as spotless as the rest of the house.

"You won't find any. The burglar was wearing gloves," Eleanor said. "I'm pretty sure anyway."

Mary straightened and joined Betty and Eleanor at the desk. They were all quiet, as if lost in thought.

Mary looked around the room again. Unless Eleanor discovered something missing later, it appeared she'd been blessed to only suffer the damage to her prized vase and her peace of mind. It could've been worse. So much worse.

Eleanor let out a soft sigh. "I think after I get the security system fixed, I'm going to put Richard's ring with the *Lady Beth* artifacts."

A bell chimed in the hallway. Eleanor headed for the door. "That must be the security company."

Mary gave the *Lady Beth* artifacts one last glance. Again, the thought struck her that if the thief had been hunting for *Lady Beth* treasure, why hadn't he taken anything? And if he was searching for the necklace, why bother moving the other artifacts around? What had he been looking for?

She heard Eleanor talking to someone down the hall, and she went to join them at the front door. A man wearing a uniform with Ivy Bay Security embroidered on the pocket was examining the security panel. Betty indicated she was going to stick around for a while.

Mary picked up Gus's case from the porch. The cat was curled up in a furry ball. Gus lifted his head and gave her a sleepy, questioning meow.

"I'm hoping this will be the end of the trouble too, Gus," she answered softly. "I really do." But she didn't really believe it.

SEVEN

Mary exited Grace Church feeling extremely blessed after her prayer group meeting. The weekly gathering was a safe haven where she and the other women could share problems and ask for divine guidance without judgment.

Although Mary hadn't been able to share the details of why she was concerned, in order to protect Eleanor's privacy, she'd still asked for prayers on how best to proceed with a project she was working on. Just being surrounded by women of faith gave her a shot of strength.

She paused at the corner of Main Street and Meeting House Road, waiting for the light to change, and inhaled the tantalizing aroma of baking bread and other mouthwatering offerings from Sweet Susan's Bakery. Those scents drifted out into the street and into her shop whenever customers entered, especially in the morning when most of the baking was done.

Mary placed a hand on her grumbling stomach. Breakfast seemed ages ago. Maybe she could just pop in there and pick up a treat to stave off hunger until lunch. Of course, she'd share the treat with Rebecca and Ashley to show how much she appreciated them. Rationalization complete, she stepped off the curb and headed for the bakery.

People were sitting on benches outside of Sweet Susan's, sipping coffee and enjoying baked treats. Mary entered the yellow-fronted bakery next door to her bookshop. Susan Crosby, the owner and enthusiastic baker, sold cupcakes, cakes, cookies, pies, and sweet fare. But cupcakes were her specialty.

Susan, wearing a yellow apron, stood behind the counter and helped a customer pick out pastries. The pleasantly plump woman's warm smile made you want to smile right back, and no matter what kind of mood you were in when you stepped inside, you left the shop feeling happier.

There were several people in line in front of her, so Mary sidestepped until she could see in the display case. There were the usual flaky croissants, hearty scones, and glazed cinnamon rolls. Baskets of cupcakes with hand-printed little signs announced the flavors of the day. Today's offers were blueberry, poppy seed, and spring triple berry. A variety of golden loaves of fresh breads lay piled next to one another.

Farther down, a triple-layer coconut cake sparkled behind the glass. Next to it was a German chocolate cake, and beyond the Lemon Supreme, to Mary's delight, was a cake shaped like a schooner, with realistic brown frosting ship planks, pretzel masts, tiny candy cannons, and billowing fondant sails. A miniature captain manned the wheel. *Lady Beth* was inscribed on the bow with black frosting. From the depicted drawings of the *Lady Beth* that Mary had seen, it appeared Susan had done a magnificent job capturing the image of the ancient ship.

Mary was having so much fun examining the ship cake that she didn't realize her turn at the counter had arrived until Susan said with a giggle, "Earth to Mary."

Mary looked up. "Oh, sorry, I think I'm in love with your *Lady Beth* cake."

"Thank you." Susan beamed. "I've been getting lots of compliments on it and subsequent orders. They're also going to be auctioning off two of the cakes at the festival on Saturday."

"I'd love to get one too, but I'd better stick with just the treats I came in for," Mary said.

"Speaking of shipwrecks"—Susan's eyes twinkled—"I read about your find in the newspaper this morning. That must have been quite a surprise."

"Oh, it was," Mary said. "The fact that it belonged to Betty's brother-in-law is icing on the cake."

Susan grinned and shook her head at Mary's attempt at a joke. "Well, it certainly has people talking about diamonds and gold. One of my customers this morning mentioned that people are swarming all over the beach again, hoping they find something valuable too. They had to post an officer to patrol out there."

"I didn't hear about that," Mary said, suddenly worried that she had inadvertently put the dunes at risk with her discovery. "I hope there won't be any problems."

"Me too, although I have to admit I am enjoying the boost in business from the treasure hunters and tourists coming in." She smiled. "So, what can I get for you?"

Mary had been so distracted by the ship cake she hadn't made up her mind about what to take back to the shop. There were just too many choices. Luckily, she was the only one in line at the moment. Mary surveyed the row of glass jars containing scrumptious-looking cookies. Several jars had nautically themed labels on them: Sand Dollars, Starfish Pinwheels, Sea Horse Sugar Cookies, and Shipwreck Chunky Delight.

"What's in the Shipwreck Chunky Delight?" Mary asked.

"Dark and milk chocolate chunks, pecans, dried cherries, and a surprise. Want a sample?"

Mary took the piece that Susan handed her and bit into it. "What is that popping? *Rice Krispies?*"

Susan nodded. "Rice puffs."

"It's different, but so yummy. I'll take three of those."

"You have to try the Sand Dollars too. They melt in your mouth," a voice said behind Mary.

Mary turned to find Penny Fuller standing behind her, dressed in jeans and a bright pink blouse. A camera hung on a strap around her neck.

Penny leaned close and lowered her voice in a teasing whisper, "Actually, they are *all* good. I had to try *every* one."

Mary chuckled. If she had Penny's thin figure, she'd be tempted to get one of every cookie in the place. "I think I'll take three of the Sand Dollars too," she said to Susan.

"You won't be disappointed," Penny said.

Susan smiled at the reporter. "Since Penny arrived in town a couple of weeks ago, she's becoming one of my best customers and promoters down at the newspaper."

"I stop by here every morning and buy treats to take over to the office." Penny winked. "I'm trying to bribe them into giving a good evaluation to my professor. Can't hurt anyway."

"I don't think you need to bribe them, but I'm sure they appreciate the cookies." Mary smiled. "I read your article this morning, and you did a great job."

"Thanks. It wasn't as thorough as I had hoped," Penny said. "I was hoping to get more quotes from you and Mrs. Blakely. I went back by the historical society after I got the first draft done but just missed everyone, and we had to rush to press." She grinned. "Love how that sounds. *Rush to press.*"

Mary laughed. "You seem to be really enjoying your time over there."

"Oh, I am. I'm so grateful to Johanna for agreeing to let me intern here. The last place I was at, all I did was get coffee for everyone and run errands. The closest I ever got to being in print was editing the obituaries."

"Have you been helping Johanna with the hospital scandal?"

Penny nodded. "I did a little research for her, but mainly she wants me to stick to reporting on the festival. One of the reporters is on vacation and another's sick, so they're a little shorthanded. Lucky for me, if you know what I mean."

"Here you are." Susan exchanged the bakery bag of cookies for the bills in Mary's hand. "Enjoy."

"Do you know when that expert from the museum is arriving?" Penny asked as Mary turned to go. "I'm curious about what he has to say, in case we do a follow-up article tomorrow."

"I don't know when Dr. Carlson will get here. Eleanor should be at the historical society office by now. You could ask her."

"Thanks for the tip," Penny said. "I still haven't been able to set up an interview. I'll give it a try again. Have a great day."

"You too." Mary said good-bye to Susan and stepped out into the sunshine.

The traffic had picked up on Main Street, and once again, she saw people heading to the shore with buckets and metal detectors. She again hoped the beach wasn't getting torn up too badly with all the digging. She opened the door to her shop, and Rebecca looked up from behind the counter with a big smile. "Good morning."

"Good morning! Everything going okay?" She looked around the shop. One lone customer browsed the new arrivals.

"Sure is," Rebecca said. "It's been really busy up until a few minutes ago."

Ashley sat on a stool, sorting some promotional author bookmarks on the counter. Beside her, Gus stared accusingly at Mary from his perch on a newly arrived box of books and flicked his tail. He hadn't seemed to appreciate being dropped off in the empty shop while Mary attended her prayer group meeting.

Ashley looked up, and her gaze zeroed in on the bakery bag in Mary's hand. "Oh! Did you bring us something?"

"Ashley, it's not polite to ask." Rebecca grinned. "Although something smells really, really good."

Mary held up the bag. "Cookies, and yes, they're for all of us. These cookies were made to celebrate the shipwreck festival this weekend. I'm afraid I overbought, but they all looked so good."

"You can never have too many cookies," Ashley said in her wise seven-year-old voice.

"I agree," Mary said, "especially if they're from Sweet Susan's."

Mary went to the back room to put on a fresh pot of coffee and grab some napkins. She offered the customer, a young

man, a cookie. He politely declined, and Mary let Rebecca
and Ashley choose the cookies they wanted and then tried
Penny's favorite, the Sand Dollars. Penny was right. They did
melt on the tongue.

She wondered if Penny had found out what time
Dr. Carlson would be in town. Betty had said she'd call when
she heard from Eleanor. Like Penny, Mary was curious to
know what the expert would say about the necklace.

Ashley held up one of the Shipwreck Chunky Delights.
"Oh, this one pops in my teeth."

"Susan put a secret surprise in them."

Ashley grinned, obviously liking the idea. She took
another big bite.

After sampling the cookies, Mary got down to business,
checking in the newly arrived books. This was one of
her favorite jobs. Opening the boxes and seeing all of the
wonderful books inside was like Christmas morning.

Gus still sat on the delivery box, as if it was his throne,
but for once didn't seem to mind when Mary lifted him and
gave him a hug before setting him on the floor. She pulled off
the plastic-covered invoice and then opened the box. Nestled
inside were new mysteries. Mary ran her hands over the covers
before setting them to the side and putting a check mark on
the inventory list.

The morning passed pleasantly with a brisk stream of
people going in and out of the shop. Not all of the visitors
were customers; a few of the locals dropped by to ask Mary
about the necklace.

"I almost forgot," Rebecca said to Mary as she finally
turned back to doing her inventory. "The skit rehearsal for

the festival got postponed until this evening, so I can stick around this afternoon, if you need me."

"If it stays as busy as it was this morning, I'd appreciate the help." Mary went back to her inventory list she'd left on the counter. Maybe she could finish while the store was quiet. It looked as though the book distributor had accidentally sent her an extra book. She made a note to contact them.

Mary checked off the last book. She or Rebecca would place the new books on the shelves this afternoon. She had sorted out the five children's books for Ashley to shelve.

She looked over at Ashley in the rocking chair, reading quietly to Gus. Mary had given one of the newly arrived children's books to Ashley earlier to see what she thought about it.

When Ashley closed the book, Mary asked, "How was it?"

Ashley sighed. "It's good, but the middle is a little slow. I would've put in another troublemaker besides the frog. Maybe a caterpillar or ladybug. It was too easy to figure out who stole the baby rabbit's dandelions." She cocked her head and thought for a moment. "But I think the little kids, like three- or four-year-olds, will like it."

"Good to know. Thank you." Mary would read the book later, but she trusted Ashley's judgment. The little girl seemed wise beyond her years and had great intuition about what made good children's fiction.

Mary slid off the stool and went into the back room. She grabbed a bottle of water and stared at the contents of the minirefrigerator, contemplating what to do for lunch. With Eleanor joining them for breakfast and then rushing off to her house, Mary didn't take the time to make a sandwich. She considered heading down to the Tea Shoppe, but the thought of running into more people who wanted to know about the necklace just made her feel tired. She could just run home for a quick bite and see if Betty was there.

The front door chimed, heralding another visitor. Mary heard Rebecca say, "She's in the back," and seconds later, Betty rushed in.

"Hi. I was just thinking about you and—" Mary cut herself off when she caught sight of Betty's face. "What happened?"

"Eleanor called me. There's been another burglary."

Mary's breath caught. "At Eleanor's?"

Betty shook her head. "The historical society. The *Lady Beth* necklace is gone."

EIGHT

———◆◆◆———

Mary and Betty hurried up the crowded sidewalk and shifted restlessly as they waited for the light to turn green so they could cross Main Street. A police squad car was parked in front of the historical society building, and the sign on the building door had been flipped to Closed.

Not good, Mary thought. "Did Eleanor say how they broke in?"

Betty shook her head. "Eleanor didn't give any details, only that the necklace was gone. She called the police immediately." The traffic light turned, and they crossed the street and hurried up the steps and into the building. Horace Crenshaw and Virginia Livingston were sitting in the outer room. Chief McArthur stood inside the office door, talking to Eleanor.

Virginia glanced up from her conversation on her cell phone and just shook her head as though she couldn't believe what was happening.

Horace gave them a nod. "The chief told us to wait out here."

"I'm just going to see if Eleanor needs me," Betty said, and Mary followed her inside the office. Deputy Bobby Wadell was standing behind the chief, taking notes. Mary wondered if he was the "boy" cop that had taken the report at Eleanor's house.

Chief McArthur glanced over at them with a frown, but Eleanor said, "I want them to stay in here with me."

The chief gave a little shrug. Mary knew if he really wanted them out of the room, he'd say so. Chief Benjamin McArthur had been Ivy Bay's chief of police for over thirty years. At sixty-five, he was three years older than Mary. At six feet, he towered over her by a good eleven inches.

He walked into the narrow storage closet. His uniform stretched over his big build as he turned in the small space in front of the safe. He bent down and looked inside, using his pen to lift some papers. Mary stood on tiptoes, trying to see over him, but couldn't make out if there was anything unusual about the contents.

The chief turned and stepped out of the closet. "Okay, let's run through this from the beginning, Eleanor. The building was locked when you arrived at...?"

"Shortly after ten," Eleanor said. "I was running late because of that break-in at my house last night, and I had to wait for the home security rep to arrive." Her eyes narrowed slightly as she glanced at the young deputy and then back at the chief, but she refrained from repeating her complaint about the chief not personally attending to her crime.

"And you said the doors were locked."

"Yes. I came in the front door, and I unlocked it with my key. Then later, I had to take some trash to the alley, and the back door was locked too."

"And did you check the safe when you first got here?"

Eleanor sighed. "There was no reason to, and I was busy. I didn't look until Jayne and Rich Tucker came in asking to see the necklace, and that was right before I called you."

"Who else was in the office this morning?" Mary asked.

"That young reporter, Penny something, from the newspaper was here, pestering me about when Dr. Carlson was expected. Oh!" Eleanor gasped. "I'd better call him and cancel."

"Penny Fuller is the reporter's name," Mary told the deputy. He shot her a quick smile as he jotted it down.

Eleanor looked at Betty. "Can you tell Horace to call Dr. Carlson if he hasn't already thought of that?"

Betty nodded and slipped out the door.

The chief sighed. "Who else was in here?"

"Horace Crenshaw and Virginia Livingston came in around eleven. Charlotte Rose and Tom Gordon have been in and out too."

"And the safe? Was it open?"

Eleanor nodded. "The door pulled right open. It looked closed, which is why I didn't notice it earlier, but it wasn't latched. That's when I discovered the pouch missing with the necklace and my dear husband's ring."

"Can you give me a description of the jewelry?" the chief asked.

Eleanor grabbed a tissue and delicately dotted it under her eyes. "The ring was gold, with a sapphire gemstone and the Blakely family crest. Very distinct."

"I have some photos of the necklace," Mary said. "I took them on my phone camera yesterday."

Chief McArthur glanced at her, approval in his eyes. "That's helpful. If you could e-mail the photos to the office, Deputy Wadell here will add them to the file."

Deputy Wadell fumbled in his shirt pocket and produced a business card. "That's the e-mail address."

Mary tucked the card away as the chief continued, "Mrs. Blakely, you're sure the safe door was latched and locked last night?"

"Of course. I was a bit frazzled trying to get the budget finalized for the weekend, but I'm positive I locked the safe," Eleanor said. "And I locked the place up before I left."

"The doors show no signs of being tampered with, although I would suspect the back door might be easy to pick since the lock is so old. If the safe was securely locked as you claim, then we have a safecracker running around Ivy Bay, or it was someone who had the combination. So my next question is, who has the combination to the safe?"

"Oh!" Eleanor's face flushed. "You don't think—"

"I'm just gathering information, Eleanor."

"Well, let's see. Charlotte, Virginia, and I do since we are here most of the time and sometimes need to access the cashbox, in case someone wants to purchase a map or postcard."

"Anyone else?"

"Technically, no, but…" Eleanor's face turned an even brighter shade of pink. "Everyone kept forgetting it so we hid the combination here. She took a stapler out of the drawer and turned it over. A tiny slip with numbers written across it was taped to the bottom.

The chief sighed loudly and shook his head. "Why even bother locking the safe?"

"How would anyone know we put the combination there?" Eleanor said, sounding indignant.

"Someone observant," Chief McArthur said. "Perhaps someone on the committee."

"I can't imagine anyone who volunteers here is a thief."

"We have to look at all possibilities." He glanced over at Deputy Wadell. "Let's get a list of everyone who has been in the building since yesterday when the necklace was brought in."

As Mary listened to the conversation, it seemed as if the whole town had been in the building yesterday. She knew that was an exaggeration, but the front room was open to the public, and there had been the beach crowd that had followed Mary and Betty in yesterday. Plus, tourists had been in this morning, asking questions, as well as Jayne and Rich Tucker, and Penny Fuller.

It was going to take time to record everyone's alibis. From the stress lines that had deepened around the chief's eyes, Mary was pretty sure he was thinking the same thing.

"Thank you, Eleanor, for your cooperation." He glanced at Mary. "All right, I'm going to ask you both to wait out front while we investigate the crime scene."

Eleanor grumbled about not being able to work, but followed Mary out into the front room.

"I contacted Dr. Carlson and told him that we needed to reschedule his visit to see the necklace. I didn't give him a reason why."

"Thanks, Horace," Eleanor said.

"You poor dear. You must be exhausted with stress. Have a seat." Virginia Livingston stood and offered Eleanor the chair. She glanced in the office. "Do you think we're about done here? I hate to leave when we have so much work to do today, but I have a luncheon appointment."

"You'll have to ask the chief," Eleanor said, sinking into the chair. "We can't work right now anyway."

Virginia leaned into the office and asked her question.

"I can get your statement later this afternoon," the chief replied.

"Are you planning on going out to lunch, or would you like me to bring you back something?" Virginia asked Eleanor.

"I'm staying," Eleanor said. "As soon as they leave, I'm going to try to finalize contracts with some of the vendors. Since you asked, a fruit cup from the Tea Shoppe would be nice."

"All right. I'll see you in an hour." Virginia waved as she went out the door.

"No one would blame you if you took the afternoon off," Betty said gently to Eleanor. "You've been through two stressful ordeals in less than twenty-four hours. Just tell me what you need to get done, and I'll do it."

Horace looked up from the newspaper he was reading. "Betty's right. The festival is not something to ruin your health over."

"I appreciate your concern. I really do, but I'll be fine. Keeping busy keeps my mind off losing that necklace and Richard's ring."

"Tell me about it!" Horace said, rattling the newspaper pages. "This is the second time that necklace has been lost."

"I'm sorry, Horace," Eleanor said. "The chief seems to think I left the safe open by accident. I was responsible."

"Not your fault. Not mine either, but I feel responsible too," Horace said. "I should've been here to close up yesterday. Make sure everything was secure."

"I thought you had a doctor's appointment?" Eleanor asked.

"It was just a checkup. Nothing serious. Something I could've skipped."

"Mary and I could've stayed and helped you too," Betty said.

"We could've," Mary agreed. "So there's no point in trying to cast blame except on whoever took the necklace."

"You're right." Eleanor rubbed her forehead. "But this has been a nightmare, and it just keeps getting worse. After Betty and Mary left this morning, some people with metal detectors came around and walked right across my lawn."

"People have been snooping around my place too," Horace said. "Treasure crazies thinking they might find a chest of gold buried on my property, as if I was involved somehow. Now if they come onto your land again, then you have every right to call the police and report trespassing. I've been known to shoot off my old shotgun into the air to disperse them, but that's frowned upon these days. I have a rottweiler now that just has to look at someone to get them off my property."

Betty glanced at Mary with a half smile. So that's where the idea of Eleanor getting a big dog might've come from.

Eleanor sighed. "You know, I just don't remember people ever being this fanatic, not even when you and Richard first found the *Lady Beth*. Do they really think that we kept the gold?"

"Seems like it. But seriously, if I had a chest full of gold, would I live like I do?" Horace said with a chuckle. "I'd be out on a yacht in the Caribbean."

"Well, I think you all were wonderful to take the proper steps to preserve the artifacts and share the history with everyone," Betty said.

"Other people in town feel that way too," Mary agreed. "Some people would've tried to keep it all for themselves."

"Well, I must admit it was tempting," Horace said. "Problem is that people who get obsessed with treasure hunting can be easily delusional. A lot of people were seething with jealousy that we found the *Lady Beth*. Richard was an easier target since he was already successful. I was just a lowly professor. He had a nice house, nice clothes, and drove a nice car. It's easy for people to wonder where his money may have come from and question if we took more than we reported."

"That was so ridiculous," Eleanor sputtered. "My Richard was a savvy, self-made man. He worked very hard. That's what attracted me to him in the first place. He used some of the money from the wreck to pay off a loan and invest in the business. We also donated part of it to charity. No one had accused him of stealing the treasure in the past. At least not that I knew of."

"I've known you and Richard a long time." Horace patted Eleanor on the shoulder. "I know how protective he was of you. Richard may not have told you everything, just to keep you safe."

"He did adore you, Eleanor," Betty said.

Eleanor took a deep breath. "Well, it does no good sitting around here wasting time. I need to run to the post office. I have some parking permits and banners that have to be overnighted to some out-of-town festival participants. If I don't get over there now, they won't go out in time." She walked over to the counter and picked up several large envelopes.

"I can do it for you, if you'd like," Betty offered.

"No thanks, dear. I could use some fresh air."

She walked to the door. "Chief McArthur, I need to get my purse to go to the post office."

"Do you mind if I look in your purse before you leave?" the chief asked.

"Yes, but go ahead," Eleanor said. She pressed her lips together in a thin line as the chief quickly went through the bag and then handed it to her.

"Sorry about that, Eleanor," the chief said. "But it's to protect you too."

Eleanor snatched up the bag and marched back toward the door.

Betty hurried over to Eleanor. "Do you want me to go with you? I could use a walk."

Eleanor gave her a quick nod and swept out the door.

Horace watched them go and shook his head with a worried expression. "I hope she'll be okay. Eleanor is used to being treated with deference. Me, on the other hand, I was always getting into scrapes my whole life, being in the work I did. I'm used to being accused of all kinds of things." He grinned and shrugged.

Mary smiled at his jovial attitude. "I read about you and Richard on the Internet. It must've been thrilling to discover the wreck."

"One of the best days of my life. People think that we just went out there and got lucky. But I spent over fifteen years—Richard, probably at least five—researching that wreck. No one was sure where it went down. I had searched on my own. Then when I teamed up with Richard, we did twenty-seven dives before we discovered the site. And that was almost by sheer accident. We'd gotten off course of where we were supposed to be searching that day. I always said that God added a little boost to the current that sent us over the top of the *Lady Beth*."

"What an amazing adventure." Mary tried to imagine it.

"In more ways than one." Horace gave a hearty laugh. "I'll tell you a secret. Not many people know this, but that day, Richard and I were so excited that we ran out of air earlier than normal. All that adrenaline surging through us. So there we were hovered over the ship site, both of us with decades of experience, and suddenly our air alarms were going off."

"Oh my," Mary said. "What did you do?"

"Well, it could be a potentially fatal oversight in some situations, but no harm came of it. The *Lady Beth* is only in fifteen feet of water, and we surfaced and swam back out to our boat. Have you ever been out there to see it?"

"I've been over the site in boats, but never have been down under the water."

"You should go someday," Horace said. "It's an easy dive. You can even snorkel it."

The door burst open, and Tom Gordon entered. He held a sheet of paper in one hand and was heading for the office when he skidded to a stop.

"Whoa. I saw the police car outside, but I didn't think they would be in here. What's going on?"

The chief came to the door before Mary could reply. "Mr. Gordon, you saved us the trouble of having to drop by your shop."

"Well, hey, Chief. What do you need? You thinking of taking me up on trying a scuba lesson?"

"At my age, I'm not looking for any new hobbies that could be dangerous to my health," Chief McArthur said. "Are you aware the diamond necklace that Mrs. Fisher found yesterday was stolen?"

"No way!" He dropped the flyer, and it fluttered to the floor. "But how?"

"It appears that someone removed it from the safe."

"This is just insane." Tom looked at Mary. "Are you okay? This must be terrible for you."

Mary blinked, realizing that Tom expected her to be devastated about the loss. They were all staring at her, waiting for her reaction. "I'm concerned about it, of course, but I never considered the necklace mine. I'm more upset for Eleanor since Richard's ring was taken too."

"Tom, we're checking the volunteers' whereabouts for last night," the chief said.

"That's easy. I was home all evening and got to bed early because I had an early diving class this morning. My shop assistant Bri can verify the class for you."

"Can anyone corroborate that you were at your place?"

Tom hesitated and ran his hand over his head. "'Fraid not. But I didn't take it. You can search my place and shop. Truck too." His face was carefully earnest, but his eyes shifted slightly, and Mary sensed he wasn't telling them the complete truth. A glance at the chief's grim set mouth gave her the impression he wasn't buying the whole story either.

"I don't think it will come to that yet, but I'll keep your offer in mind."

Mary picked up the paper that Tom had dropped. It was a flyer advertising his dive shop. He was giving a special discount for the weekend of the festival. She handed it to Tom.

"I was coming in to make copies, but obviously this is a bad time." Tom sighed. "I'll go over to Meeting House Print. Tell Eleanor I came by."

"Tom, I know it goes without saying," the chief said, "but please do be discreet and not discuss the crime with anyone else while it's still under investigation."

"Sure, of course."

When the door shut behind Tom, the chief turned to Horace.

"Doctor's appointment with Dr. Teagarden yesterday evening. I was his last appointment of the day. Errands all this morning after breakfast at the Black & White Diner. Then I was down at the marina, pharmacy, and the grocers. I'm sure I could find someone who saw me. In fact, I have receipts in the bags in my car."

"Did you get all that?" the chief asked Deputy Wadell.

"Yes, sir."

"What about last night?" the chief asked Horace.

"Same as Tom. Home alone," Horace said. "But I did have a long talk on the phone with a former colleague of mine. We're thinking of organizing a trip to the Great Barrier Reef. I can get you the number later, if you want to check."

"Betty and I were at home last night," Mary volunteered before the chief could ask. "Eleanor came over and spent the night because of the break-in at her house."

The door opened, and Eleanor and Betty came back in. "I'm glad you're back," the chief said. "I would like everyone to keep the details of this investigation quiet for as long as possible. It might buy us a little more time in following up on some leads and finding the necklace before it possibly leaves town, if it hasn't already. There have been several recent burglaries we are following up on, and we may get a lead."

"Good luck with keeping it a secret," Horace said with a snort.

"I know it's almost impossible to keep it a secret in this town, but let's try," the chief said.

"What about Charlotte Rose?" Eleanor asked. "She's supposed to be working here this afternoon, and she's bound to ask about the necklace. We were thinking of putting it on display this weekend. Can we tell her it's been stolen?"

"That's fine. I will be contacting Charlotte Rose as soon as possible to get her statement. Call me if you think of anything else that may help." The chief strode to the door. "Let's go, Deputy Wadell." The young man hurried outside after his boss.

Eleanor took her place behind her desk and stood looking at it, her hands on her hips. "This is a nightmare. I've lost a good chunk of the morning and now part of the afternoon."

"I'll help." Betty straightened a stack of papers overflowing Eleanor's in-box. "I'd rather be here keeping busy than be home alone and thinking about burglars."

"All right. Stay, then," Eleanor said. "I was going to have Charlotte make some calls, but you can do that. Now where is that list?"

As Eleanor got Betty set up with a checklist and phone numbers, Mary looked around the office. The safe door was still open. She knelt in front of it, examining the contents.

Mary counted three small plastic bags, two with Indian arrowheads in them and another with musket balls. There were also three shiny silver dollars in coin-collector frames. Whoever had gotten into the safe was apparently only after the necklace.

She tried to get up too quickly in the tiny space, bumped her shoulder on a low shelf, and sat down with a thud. She glanced toward the door, hoping no one had observed her clumsiness, and spied something partly lodged under the throw rug. She picked up a small red pill. What was it doing there?

NINE

M ary pulled the pill loose from the rug and rolled it around in her hand. Who had dropped it? And when?

Eleanor stood over her. "What are you doing on the floor?"

"I was looking in the safe and tripped." Mary got to her feet. I found this." She held out the red pill. "Looks like prescription medication of some type."

"Huh. Well, it's not mine. I don't normally take medication." Eleanor turned back to the stack of papers she was sorting.

Betty hung up the phone and looked over her shoulder. "Can you tell what it is?"

Mary held it up to the light. "There's a number etched into the side."

"I'm back," Virginia announced, coming in the office door. She handed Eleanor a bag with the Tea Shoppe advertised on it. "Here's your fruit salad."

"Thanks," Eleanor said, setting it on the corner of the desk before going back to her sorting.

"I ran into Chief McArthur out front. He said he was done in here for now and we can get back to work." She set her purse down on the desk next to Betty and looked at the phone number list that Betty had been checking off as she called each number. "Oh, thanks. You saved Charlotte some time."

"Virginia, does this pill happen to belong to you?" Mary asked. "It was on the floor."

"*Hmm*, maybe." Virginia lifted her silver reading glasses that hung from a chain around her neck and examined the pill. "No, I guess not. I thought maybe it was one of my blood pressure pills. They're red too, but no, this one is too big. Where did you find it?"

"It was snagged on the rug."

"Well, it couldn't have been there long. Yesterday afternoon, I dropped the water pitcher I keep on my desk and glass went everywhere. Tom took the rug outside and gave it a good shake over the Dumpster and mopped up the water before anyone slipped."

Horace strolled in the door and looked from Virginia to Mary. "What are we looking at?"

"A pill." Mary held it out. "Do you recognize it?"

He studied the pill briefly and gave a little shrug. "Nope. Never seen it before." He turned abruptly to Eleanor and frowned. "Bad news. We're going to have to get more extension cords if you want a light in the exhibit. The ones that were stored at the school are frayed. I can go over to Jimmy's Hardware and get more."

"I didn't budget for new extension cords." Eleanor grabbed her spreadsheets and moaned. "But go ahead. We have to have lights in there."

Mary looked around for something to put the pill in and spied some plastic bags in the closet. She slipped the pill in one and put it in her purse.

"Eleanor, you know what? We've got this covered," Virginia said, crossing the room and placing her hand on Eleanor's shoulder. "I can do the phone calls, and Horace can go out and get the extension cords and stake out the booth sites. Why don't you go on home and rest? It's going to get really hectic the next couple of days, and we need you in top condition."

"What?" Eleanor looked up from the accounting sheet she was studying. "I don't think—"

"Now, now. We insist for your own good and the good of the festival. Charlotte's on her way in, and she can handle any tourists out front."

Eleanor stared at Virginia for a long moment. "Well, at least let me pay you for the fruit salad."

"Don't worry about it. My treat," Virginia said. "You've been such a sweetie handling all this. Now off you go and recharge those batteries."

"I suppose. But call me if you run into any snags."

"Thanks, Betty. You too, Mary." Virginia waited for Betty to get her purse and walked them to the door as Eleanor showed Horace the file she was working on. "Make sure she gets some rest." She shut the door after them with a firm click.

"Do you get the feeling she was trying to get rid of us?" Betty said.

"Seems like it," Mary said, hoping that concern for Eleanor was the only thing motivating Virginia.

"I'd better walk Eleanor home. Virginia was right about her being frazzled. Did you see her hands were shaking when she left for the post office? I think this whole situation has been exhausting, only she won't admit it."

"No doubt," Mary said, but it was the fatigue edging Betty's voice that concerned Mary. "Would you like me to go with you?"

"Only if you're not too busy."

"I have an ulterior motive. I'd like to get another look at Richard's office. Just let me check and see how things are going in the shop."

Mary hurried across the street to the bookstore. Rebecca assured her that she and Ashley were handling the shop just fine. Gus was stretched out in a patch of sunlight in front of the window, enjoying his afternoon nap.

As she was returning to Betty, she spied Tom heading for the historical society office with a stack of papers in his hand. "Tom, hello."

He stopped at the bottom of the steps by Betty and waited for her. "Hey, Mary. What's up?"

"I have a quick question." She pulled the bag with the pill out of her purse. "I know this is an odd question, but I found this in the office and was wondering if it was yours, or if you know what it is."

Tom glanced at the bag. "Have no clue. Sorry. Is that all?"

"Yes, that's it. Have a good day."

"You too."

Tom trotted up the steps as Eleanor came down. She had a fat file under her arm and her purse slung over her shoulder. "Well, how do you like that? It's starting."

"What's starting?" Betty asked as they proceeded up the sidewalk.

"They are starting to suspect me," Eleanor said. "They think I might have something to do with the stolen necklace."

"Who? Virginia? Horace?" Betty asked, glancing back at the building. "Oh, they wouldn't. How could they?"

"How could they not? I was the one who locked the necklace in the safe. I was the one alone in the building. And I was the one who claimed that the necklace belonged to Richard."

"But that doesn't mean you'd just take it." Exasperation edged Betty's tone.

"There are people already saying the necklace should belong to the town since it's a historic artifact of Ivy Bay. And others are saying that since Mary found it, it's rightfully hers." Eleanor glanced at Mary. "I mean no offense."

"Some people will gossip and speculate, but the truth will come out," Mary said, although she also realized that sometimes the truth didn't matter once people got a notion in their heads.

"In the meantime, my reputation will be ruined. So will Richard's."

"Now, that's nonsense. You need to stop thinking like that," Betty said. "Chief McArthur will get to the bottom of this. You are a well-respected Ivy Bay citizen. So was Richard. Look at all the good you've done. Didn't Richard give up a large portion of the money from the shipwreck? Money he could've kept for himself? Just don't pay any mind to what uninformed people might say."

Eleanor sighed, and they walked in silence. Mary trailed a few steps behind them on the narrow sidewalk. Betty was doing her best to comfort Eleanor, which was more than Eleanor would've done for Betty under the same circumstances. Based on past experience, she could predict Eleanor would distance herself from Betty if there was a scandal, just like Virginia seemed to be doing to Eleanor. Not that Eleanor would purposely be cruel, but status and reputation were extremely important to Eleanor Blakely and the people she associated with.

Mary picked up her pace when she realized she had fallen farther behind. If Betty could overlook her sister-in-law's shortcomings, then Mary should too. The most productive thing she could do in this situation would be to help find that necklace.

Eleanor's house came into view. A breeze gently stirred the air, carrying the scent of Richard's rosebushes. Eleanor checked her mailbox and pulled out several envelopes before they headed up the sidewalk. Eleanor put a foot on the first step and froze.

"What's that noise?" Eleanor asked. "There it is again."

"Sounds like someone's digging around back." Mary pulled out her cell phone. "Go on in the house. I'll take a look."

"You're not going back there by yourself," Betty said.

"There's a panic button on the alarm box that will summon the police." Eleanor unlocked the door. "Just say when and I'll push it."

Mary and Betty tread cautiously to the corner of the house. Two young men were standing among Eleanor's rosebush garden. They held shovels and soil shot into the air.

One of them caught sight of Mary and punched the other on the arm. "Dude!"

"Stop whatever you are doing. This is private property, and you are trespassing," Mary said loudly. "I'm calling the police."

The two guys looked at each other. Then, as if by some inaudible command, the trespassers dropped their shovels and ran past Mary out into the street.

Eleanor came around the corner of the house. "I saw them leave. Oh!" She caught sight of the hole and a toppled rosebush, and let out a cry. "My Snow Queen. How could they?"

"The poor thing." Betty hurried over to the fallen branches and gingerly lifted them upright. "I think if we get it back into the ground right away, it should survive."

"I'm going to report the trespassing." Mary tapped in the number for the station.

"They looked like some of the teenagers that hang around Bailey's," Betty said. "I think they might be friends of Tess's daughters."

Eleanor reached for a shovel and gently pushed dirt over the roots of the rosebush. "I don't understand why they were digging here in the first place."

Mary's phone connected with the station, and a brisk female voice came on the line. "Ivy Bay Police. How may I help you?"

"Is Chief McArthur there? This is Mary Fisher. It concerns a case he is working on today."

"If you can hold, ma'am, I'll see if he's available."

"I can hold," Mary said as a strange brown car slowly rolled past the front yard and stopped, idling. Mary started to walk toward it, and with a screech of the tires, it sped away.

The dispatcher came back on the line. "Chief McArthur is unavailable. Is this an emergency?"

"No, but it is rather urgent." Mary explained the situation, and the dispatcher said she'd have someone right there.

The rosebush was upright again, and Eleanor tossed the shovel down. "I don't think I can stay here tonight."

"Of course not." Betty rubbed her hands together to get rid of the dirt. "I insist you come home with us for the night."

Eleanor sighed. "I don't want to impose again, but..."

"It's not an imposition. Right, Mary?" Betty said.

"Of course not, Eleanor," Mary said, keeping an eye on the street.

"Oh, Betty, your fingers are bleeding," Eleanor said.

Betty held up her hands. "It's just a few pricks from the thorns."

"Come along. You'd better get it cleaned up or you might get an infection." Eleanor led the way to the house and ushered Betty inside.

Mary waited on the porch until a squad car rolled to a stop at the gate. Deputy Wadell emerged from the car.

"Hi, Mary. What is going on?" he asked.

"Trespassers. Two teenage boys," Mary answered, glad that the officer who had responded was someone she knew. "They dug up the rose garden." She showed the deputy to the site where Betty and Eleanor had replanted the rosebush.

He strode around the yard. "Did you know there are other holes?"

Mary's gaze swept across the yard and garden. She groaned. "I think people might be digging for buried treasure."

"Believe it or not, that doesn't surprise me," Officer Wadell said. "People are digging along the shore also. We've had to have a patrol go by the beach every half hour. Some fistfights have broken out with people claiming a spot belongs to them, and it's public land. I'll write this up, and I'll have a squad car come by here every couple of hours."

"Thank you," Mary said, looking out over the rose garden again. The treasure hunters were probably harmless, but still, one never knew if an unscrupulous one might try to get in the house like last night.

But why would they dig here? Surely most people wouldn't think Richard Blakely would hide treasure on his land and have it still be here after all this time? Judging from the amount of digging that had gone on, this wasn't just one or two people. There had to be another motive, and Mary was going to find out why.

Mary set a mug of orange-spice tea in front of Betty along with a plate of light wafer cookies. Her sister's shoulders drooped, and weariness edged her face. She appeared as tired as Mary felt.

Mary patted her sister on the arm before sitting down on the other side of the kitchen table. It had been a long, stressful day, and Betty had made a valiant effort to support and bolster her sister-in-law's spirits.

After Deputy Wadell had left Eleanor's property, Mary went through the house and checked to make sure every door and window was locked. She had Eleanor test the alarm system before leaving, and it seemed to be working fine. Eleanor's security system upgrade wasn't scheduled until later in the week.

Mary didn't get the chance to spend any more time in Richard's office other than passing through it to check the window. Eleanor was, after all, seventy-five years old and had had a very busy day. She seemed exhausted by the time they got back to the house.

Mary smiled at her sister as they sat in silence, just enjoying the quiet and each other's company. Mary looked under the table to make sure Gus was still there and not upstairs meowing or slinking around Eleanor's door. As soon as they'd arrived home this evening, he'd made a beeline for Eleanor and her suitcase again. Mary wasn't sure what was motivating her cat to pay so much attention to someone who didn't particularly like cats, or at least not him. Maybe he sensed she was going through a stressful time and needed comfort. Or maybe he was just being ornery.

Mary felt restless and needed to do something to make sense of what was going on. She grabbed one of the small pads of paper they kept by the phone and placed it on the table in front of her.

"What are you doing?" Betty asked.

"Making a list of suspects."

Betty nodded. "Good idea."

Mary picked up a pen. "It can't hurt, and who knows what we may come up with to help the chief? Let's start with those working in the office. There's Virginia Livingston and Horace Crenshaw."

"Don't forget Charlotte Rose," Betty said.

"Right." Mary put her name down. "And there's Tom Gordon. That's four. Now who else might've had access to the safe?"

"What about visitors? Maybe a tourist? Or a stranger in Ivy Bay," Betty said. "Eleanor said she was in and out of the office. What if she stepped out back into the alley to empty trash or something, and someone stole the necklace while she was gone?"

Mary nodded. "That would assume they knew about the necklace and that Eleanor left the safe door unlocked as the chief suggested. Or the thief knew the combination or where to find it." She tapped the pen on the paper. "*Or*, like the chief said, there is a safecracker in Ivy Bay."

"That's a lot of assumptions," Betty said with a little laugh. "First of all, I still don't think Eleanor would leave the safe unlocked, no matter what the chief thinks. You know Eleanor. I know I said she was forgetful about turning on her alarm system a couple of times, but generally she's a stickler for routine and adamant about doing things the right way."

"She is that," Mary agreed, although she privately thought that sometimes Eleanor's methods and standards weren't always the right ways for everyone. And with getting older, Eleanor could be slipping in her routines.

"Here's another idea," Betty said. "What if Charlotte or Virginia or someone else got the combination from the drawer and opened the safe that morning for some innocent reason and left it unlocked? And now they don't want to admit it since the necklace is gone."

Mary considered the possibility. "Okay. Let's suppose that the safe door was unlocked. Suppose a visitor came in the door, saw the office empty, and searched it quickly and stole the necklace." Mary groaned. "That scenario opens the possible suspects to anyone in town."

However, for the thief to be able to act so quickly, then the person would've had to know the necklace was in the building. Of course, Penny's article in the *Ivy Bay Bugle* might've tipped people off, except she hadn't specifically said where the necklace was being kept.

"I keep wondering if the burglar who broke into Eleanor's house could be the same person who stole the necklace. Maybe he was looking for it there," Mary said. "The thief seemed interested in the *Lady Beth* artifacts and left plenty of other valuables alone."

"That crossed my mind too," Betty said. "What if someone had come looking for the necklace?"

"Eleanor said she hadn't gotten a good look, but she thought the burglar was lean and around average height, which applies to"—Mary looked down at her list—"just about anyone on the list except maybe Horace. He has rather beefy, muscular arms and a solid build."

Mary tapped her pen on the table, thinking. "Let's start at the top and see if we can come up with any other ideas." She looked up to see Betty yawn. "Unless you're too tired."

Betty yawned again. "Sorry, I can't help it, but I don't think I can sleep right now worrying about Eleanor."

"All right. First on the list is Virginia Livingston," Mary said. She already knew that Virginia was a descendant of one of the founding families of Ivy Bay, and that status got her invited, like Eleanor, onto many of the town committees.

Virginia and her family attended Grace Church, so Mary saw her often, even if they didn't speak to each other much. Virginia was also a member of Betty's exclusive book club.

"Virginia had the combination to the safe, but I can't think of a logical reason why she'd take the necklace," Mary said.

"Me either. I've known Virginia most of my adult life," Betty said. "Her family is well-to-do, and she is a pillar of society. I can't imagine she would break the law or risk the family name over a piece of jewelry. She even commented on what bad shape it was in. Besides, have you ever seen her collection?"

"I've noticed some pretty necklaces and rings she's worn to church," Mary said.

"Those are heirloom pieces, and she has more that she only wears on very special occasions. Those, I imagine, have the same value, if not more than the *Lady Beth* necklace."

"Okay. What about Charlotte Rose? Do you know much about her?" Mary asked.

"Other than that she's Virginia's second cousin and staying with them for the summer, not too much. I know she's trying to finish her masters and get into a doctoral program. She's always been pleasant to me when I've been over at the historical society."

"She knew the combination to the safe, but would she risk her future to steal the necklace? She has plans to continue in school, and an arrest could certainly jeopardize that." Unless, of course, Charlotte expected to get away with it. Mary made a note to try to find out more about Charlotte and where she was the night the necklace disappeared.

"I think she has a crush on Tom Gordon," Betty said with a smile.

"I thought I sensed something too," Mary said, remembering how Charlotte gazed at Tom at the office. She went to the next name on the list. "Let's talk about Horace Crenshaw."

"Ah...Horace," Betty said with a small smile. "He's always been a character. I know Richard was really fond of him, which is why Eleanor tolerated him taking up so much of Richard's spare time with their diving."

As they chatted about him, Mary jotted down notes. Horace was at the doctor's the evening of the break-in at Eleanor's house. He was a big guy and didn't fit Eleanor's description of her burglar—although Eleanor only got a quick look. Horace had a key to the historical society, but Eleanor mentioned he didn't have the combination to the safe. But he may have known where the combination numbers were hidden. And if Eleanor had left the safe open accidentally, he would've had access. He was excited about the find, but he was a pro at this type of thing. He had even suggested they give it to the museum.

"What about Tom Gordon?" Mary asked.

"I don't know him well enough to make a judgment." Betty got up to rinse out her cup and put it in the dishwasher.

"Well, I know he could use the money. He did tell me his business was struggling and ready to go bankrupt."

"That's sad," Betty said. "You hate to see people work so hard and then lose it all."

"He was also kind of upset that he didn't find the necklace, but..."

"What is it?"

"Didn't Tom leave the historical society office before the decision was made to put the necklace in the safe?"

"I believe he did." Betty nodded.

"So he wouldn't have known the necklace remained in the office unless someone mentioned it to him. Virginia said he'd been in later in the afternoon. He had taken the rug out and mopped the floor for her after she had dropped a glass pitcher. He did seem kind of glum about not being the one to discover the necklace. What if he thought the necklace was at Eleanor's? He knew that Richard had found it originally and could've assumed Eleanor would lay claim to it."

"But he seems like such a nice guy."

Mary nodded, but sometimes nice guys did dumb things. He fit the general description Eleanor gave of the thief. He hadn't been there when they put the necklace in the safe. Was there something else valuable among Richard's dive artifacts that they just didn't know about?

Despite the recent influx of business, Tom could still be on the verge of bankruptcy and feeling desperate. That could be motive enough. So, then, why hadn't he taken the gold coins that were sitting right on the shelf in plain sight?

"I'm afraid I'm more tired than I thought," Betty broke into Mary's musings. "Hopefully I won't dream about burglars and safecrackers. You should get some rest too. If we spend any more time on this right now, we might start thinking each other is guilty."

Mary smiled at Betty's teasing and leaned back in her chair. "Good night, Bets. I'm just going to finish my tea before I turn in too." When she heard Betty's bedroom door close, Mary added one more suspect to the list.

Eleanor Blakely.

Eleanor was family, and she knew Betty would defend her. Mary didn't really think Eleanor would steal the necklace, but Mary needed to consider all possibilities. The police were. Eleanor had a key to the building and the combination to the safe. She had at least one motive. Eleanor could've taken the necklace out of some misplaced loyalty to Richard. Maybe she felt she had a right to it since Richard had found it. She'd mentioned that Horace and Richard had signed a contract with the town of Ivy Bay to split profits found at the shipwreck. What if Eleanor didn't want to share it? Eleanor was a bit greedy, always wanting the nicest things. She'd inherited money from her family and the sale of Richard's business, but what if her savings were dwindling?

For Eleanor's and Betty's sake, Mary needed to discreetly look further into Eleanor's possible role in the events of the last two days. Even if only to prove Eleanor's innocence.

TEN

⬩◆◆⬩

The next morning, Mary opened the front door to fog soup and could barely see the newspaper lying on the sidewalk. Gus ran out the door, and Mary scooped him up before he blended into the gray world. She tucked him under her arm as she retrieved the paper and returned to the house.

Betty and Eleanor were probably still asleep, judging from the quiet permeating the house. Mary had awoken before the alarm clock and couldn't go back to sleep. She'd lain in bed for about an hour, thinking about the necklace and what could've happened to it, before finally getting up and putting on a pot of coffee.

She carried Gus to the kitchen, set the cat on the floor, and placed the newspaper on the table. The coffee had finished brewing so Mary poured herself a cup. She turned around and discovered Gus perched on top of the newspaper.

"Silly cat, get down. You know better than to get on the table," Mary scolded.

Gus stared at her with his big blue eyes, and only the slight twitch of his ear acknowledged that he'd heard her.

"What is it? Are you waiting for your breakfast? Is that the problem?" Mary set him back on the floor and went to the pantry to get a can of food for him. When she returned, the cat was back on top of the newspaper.

"Gus! Get down," Mary said with an exasperated giggle. She could just imagine what Eleanor would say if she caught Gus on the table, and it wasn't good.

Mary supposed it was her fault since she let Gus have free rein to be on the counters or shelves at work, but at home, the cat usually was good about staying off the kitchen table and counters.

Gus flicked his tail and with exaggerated slowness hopped down and meandered over to his food bowl.

"That's a good boy." Mary rolled the rubber band off the paper and spread it out. The top headline was a continuation of the hospital scandal and took up the entire first page. Johanna had done a thorough job investigating. The web of deception had grown. Now it appeared that there had been insurance fraud as well, and someone at the state level may have helped alter the books.

Mary took a sip of coffee as she turned the page and then nearly choked when she read the headline: *Lady Beth Necklace Stolen from Historical Society.*

What happened to Chief McArthur's order about keeping the news of the theft quiet? Not even twenty-four hours had passed. Oh, the chief was not going to be happy.

The byline was by Penny Fuller. Apparently, Johanna had let Penny take the lead by herself this time.

A historic and valuable artifact has allegedly been stolen from the historical society office on Main Street. The diamond necklace discovered on Little Neck Beach by Mary Fisher, owner of Mary's Mystery Bookshop, was believed to have been recovered from the excavation of the Lady Beth *shipwreck in 1986.*

Mary skimmed over the next couple of paragraphs that recapped information about the wreck that had been reported and paused.

A source familiar with the office in the historical society building, and who wished to remain anonymous, reported that security at the building may have been compromised as the safe combination is shared by several staff members and stored inadequately. Other possibilities, such as the safe being left open accidentally, are being investigated.

Some Ivy Bay citizens were hopeful that the Lady Beth *necklace would've been displayed at the Cape Cod Shipwreck Festival. The weekend event is being organized by Eleanor Blakely, who is currently the chairwoman of the historical society event committee.*

Anyone who has knowledge of the necklace and its whereabouts should contact the Ivy Bay police station. As of the filing of this story, the police have no comment on the investigation.

Mary sucked in her breath at the report that the safe may have been left open. Where had Penny gotten this information? It was possible that she and Johanna hadn't known that the police chief had wanted to keep a low profile about the theft for a few days. She made a mental note to call Johanna.

The door to Betty's bedroom opened. "Good morning!"

Mary's face must've been grim because when Betty got closer to the table, her smile faded, and she exclaimed, "What's wrong now?"

Mary instantly felt regret about ruining Betty's cheerful mood, but Betty would hear about the news article sooner or later. "It's an article about the necklace being stolen."

"I thought we weren't supposed to talk about it yet," Betty said, picking up the newspaper.

"Apparently, someone didn't get the memo," Mary said, trying to lighten her tone. Hopefully, the chief and his staff were able to interview the persons of interest they had wanted to last night. They could have someone in custody right now, for all she knew.

Betty shook her head. "This doesn't look good for the historical society."

"What doesn't?" Eleanor asked, coming around the corner into the kitchen. She looked ready for business, already dressed in a lovely pink linen pantsuit, her purse tucked under her arm.

Her gaze narrowed in on the newspaper Betty had discreetly put her arm over. "Is there something in the paper about the historical society?"

Betty sighed and pushed the newspaper over. "There's an article about the necklace being stolen." She stood. "What would you like for breakfast?"

"I'm going to pull a Richard and just have whole wheat toast and coffee. I have a million things to do today for the festival." Eleanor settled at the table. "Now, let's see what has gotten you all perturbed."

Betty popped the bread in the toaster and poured Eleanor a cup of coffee. Gus started to meander over toward Eleanor, and Mary redirected him gently with her foot.

Eleanor's lips thinned as she read through the article. After a long pause, she set the paper down. "Well, the article does seem to imply that the historical society staff is either incompetent or we have a thief in our midst. And who is this anonymous source she quoted? It better not be anyone on my staff." She sighed. "But, there's not much we can do about it right now except put on a great festival and hope the police do their work and find that necklace soon."

"I think you're right. People are going to have a wonderful time this weekend." Betty cast a relieved look at Mary. Eleanor was sounding her normal determined self again.

The toast popped up, and Betty placed it on a small plate. She carried it over to Eleanor, along with butter and strawberry jam.

Eleanor picked up the knife and reached for the jam. "Oh, did I tell you about this marvelous jam I discovered on my last trip to Boston? Loganberry. It's imported from Sweden, and the flavor just bursts on your tongue." She went on to tell Betty about the other wonderful items she found in the store while Mary fixed herself an English muffin with peanut butter and honey.

Mary wished she could dismiss the article as easily as Eleanor seemed to. Someone had wanted the paper to know about the necklace, but why?

She thought about the list of suspects she and Betty had compiled last night. Who would benefit from having the crime exposed? Surely not the thief. Was there another motive? Was someone trying to misdirect the investigation? Or maybe cast blame?

Someone had been in that office and stole the necklace. She thought about the red pill in her purse and decided she'd visit the pharmacy as soon as possible to see if Jacob Ames could identify it. If the timing was correct about when Tom cleaned the floor, then that pill had to be there sometime after the necklace was placed in that safe, along with whoever owned the medication.

Eleanor's cell phone rang, and she took it out of her purse. She glanced at the screen and then her watch. "It's Virginia. She's got an early start to the day." Eleanor sounded pleased. "It's going to take a mighty group effort to get this festival nailed down by Saturday."

"Hello, Virginia," Eleanor said. "Oh, it's no problem. I was just going to head to the office in about fifteen minutes."

Her pleased expression turned to confusion. "What do you mean?" Eleanor fell silent. "Well, if that's the way they feel.... Of course we have to do whatever is best for the committee. I would've insisted on it myself, but I didn't want to let anyone down. Let me know if there is anything else I can do."

She briskly turned her phone off and dropped it back in her purse. Her fingers shook slightly as she picked up her piece of toast.

"Is anything wrong, Eleanor?" Betty asked.

"No, everything is moving along just fine with the festival." Eleanor set the toast down without biting it. "But you know what? I feel a migraine coming on. I'm going to have to lie down for a while."

Betty got to her feet. "Eleanor, I'm sorry. Is there anything I can do?"

Eleanor moaned and rubbed her forehead with her fingers. "I have pain medication in my purse upstairs."

"I'll get them for you," Mary offered.

"Thank you," Eleanor said faintly. "They're in the outside pocket. Prescription bottle."

"Be right back." Mary hurried up the stairs and into the guest bedroom. Eleanor's purse was on the bed. She unzipped the outer pocket and pulled out several bottles until she found the one with a prescription label on it. She was stuffing the others back in when she noticed one of the unlabeled vials contained small red pills. She lifted the vial to the light. The pills looked like the one she'd found at the historical society. Mary put the vial back in the bag. She went down the stairs intending to ask Eleanor about them, but Eleanor was lying on the couch with a washcloth covering her face.

Betty hovered over her, holding a glass of water. "Mary is back. Can you sit up and take your pill?"

Eleanor pushed the cloth to her forehead and leaned forward. Betty propped up Eleanor's back with her arm as Mary shook one of the pills into Eleanor's hand.

Eleanor swallowed her medication and then lay back down.

"Can we get you anything else?" Betty asked.

"No, dear, I just need to lie very still in a quiet room." She let out a little moan.

Gus circled Mary's feet, and she picked him up. She'd ask Eleanor later about the red pill. It was probably nothing, she tried to assure herself. But why had Eleanor acted as if she'd never seen those kinds of pills before?

Her beloved two-hundred-year-old building seemed eerily dark with the fog pressing against the windows. Mary flipped on the lights to the bookshop and let Gus out of his carrier. He scampered across the hardwood floor and leaped up on the counter, his tail swishing.

She still had time before she had to open the shop to the public, and now might be a good time to drop in at the pharmacy and see if Mr. Ames was available.

"I'll be back soon," she said to the cat and locked the door behind her. Cars were moving slowly along Main Street, their headlights knifing through the mist. She hurried down the street, resisting the temptation to stop and investigate that scrumptious cinnamon scent from Sweet Susan's.

She made a left on Meeting House Road, and as she walked past the county clerk's office, Mary paused and looked in the window to see if her friend Bea was at work yet.

Bea Winslow, a petite woman with short, closely trimmed silver hair, stood behind the cluttered counter. Her reading glasses were perched on the end of her nose as she studied a paper in front of her.

Bea had notarized the documents transferring ownership of Mary's bookshop from its previous owner, and they had struck up a friendship. Mary admired the woman's zest for life. Bea was almost seventy years old, ran 5K races, and had been energetically invaluable in the past, helping Mary look up information when she was investigating.

Bea looked up and caught sight of Mary. Her face creased with a big smile, and she motioned Mary to come in.

Mary opened the door and took a deep breath of the air, musty from centuries-old, yellowed, and crumbling birth, marriage, and death certificates, and real-estate records that were packed in file cabinets and cupboards around the cramped office.

"Good morning, Mary!" Bea said. "I was just reading about the necklace in the paper. You've been living on quite a roller coaster of a ride these last forty-eight hours."

Mary smiled. "Between you and me, I'm ready to get off, but I can't until we figure out what happened to that necklace."

"Do the police have any ideas?"

"Chief McArthur had some possibilities he wanted to check out yesterday, but so far he hasn't let us know if he's gotten anywhere."

"What do *you* think?" Bea asked with a gleam in her eye.

"I'm not sure." Mary hesitated. She wasn't comfortable talking about family members to outsiders, although she knew she could trust Bea completely. "I'm still collecting information. I'm starting to wonder if current events are tied to the past somehow. I wasn't here when Horace Crenshaw and Richard Blakely discovered the *Lady Beth*."

"I remember it pretty well." Bea pushed up her spectacles. "The excavation of the *Lady Beth* benefited the town and Cape Cod immensely. Some treasure hunters may have tried to make off with all the wealth they found, but Mr. Crenshaw and Mr. Blakely made sure that historical artifacts were preserved."

"Someone had mentioned that Mr. Crenshaw and Mr. Blakely signed a contract with the town in order to share in the profits."

"Oh yes. There was an agreement on how much each of the excavators, the town, and the university would share.

They had it notarized here, but even so, I didn't get the impression that it would've been especially legally binding if push came to shove. At least it was a gesture so no one would feel cheated. I thought Mr. Blakely and Mr. Crenshaw were very honorable, and it allowed for a more peaceful recovery of the ship's artifacts."

"I'd heard they were generous," Mary said, thinking of the relatively few items Richard had kept from the *Lady Beth*. She wondered if that contract applied to the necklace now. How much of it would have belonged to Richard's estate, Horace, the town, or the university? That might give motive to Eleanor or Horace or anyone else connected to the contract to take the necklace for themselves rather than share.

"Would you happen to know what would've become of that contract?" Mary asked.

"Well, since the contract involved the town, it should be over at the town hall unless someone thinned out files and archived it. Then it may have ended up over here," Bea said as the door opened behind Mary. "I'll take a look this morning."

"I'd appreciate it," Mary said, stepping back to let an aggravated-looking woman carrying a thick folder step up to the counter. "I can try to stop back by this afternoon."

"That would be fine, but are you busy for lunch?" Bea asked. "I was going to grab a quick bite at the Tea Shoppe. If you don't have any plans, why don't you join me? I'll bring a copy of the contract if I find it."

"No definite plans other than I'd like to get over to the library sometime today. What time are you going to be there?"

The other woman set her folder on the counter and sighed noisily. Bea gave her a tolerant smile. "I'll be right with you, ma'am."

She looked at Mary. "I should be there around twelve thirty."

"Okay, see you then." Mary stepped back outside, thinking it'd be nice to have lunch with Bea.

Mary walked along the sidewalk until she reached the stone steps in front of the cheerful white building that housed Little Neck Pharmacy. Chimes rang out when she pushed open the black door. She could hear Jacob Ames talking to someone in the back of the store where the medication was doled out. She hurried past the rows of over-the-counter medication, a few beauty products, and sunscreen and other beach supplies.

Little Neck Pharmacy had been in the Ames family for as long as anyone could remember. The current owner, Jacob Ames, a man in his late sixties with a comb-over, stood behind the counter speaking to a young mother who was trying to control her two preschoolers.

"You have to finish all the pills," Mr. Ames said gruffly. "Do you understand what I'm saying to you? Even if you are feeling better, you must finish the prescription."

"Yes, uh…" The mother turned to grab one of the towheaded boys as he reached for a box on the shelf. "Alex, stand still." She pulled the child toward her. "Now, what were you saying, Mr. Ames?"

Mr. Ames sighed loudly and then suddenly produced two homemade suckers. The boys' eyes grew round, and they stopped wiggling.

"Can I have one?" Alex asked, and his younger brother added, "Me too!"

"Only if your mother says you can *and* you behave. You have to stand still and be very quiet."

The boys looked at their mother, and she nodded.

"Now, not a word out of either of you," Mr. Ames said as the boys took the suckers. They stood perfectly still as Mr. Ames went on with his medication instructions to their mother.

Mary smiled, her mouth suddenly watering for one of those suckers. The recipe was kept a strict secret and had a long family tradition in the pharmacy. Jacob's father used to give Betty and Mary suckers when they would come in with their grandparents during their summer visits to the shore.

Jacob's father was also rather prickly and was offended if anyone refused one of his homemade suckers. But like his father, Jacob carefully listened to the people who came in asking for advice, and she had seen the precision and care he took with his prescriptions, always double-checking them and making sure his customers knew how to use the medicine and what side effects to look for. So despite his gruff exterior, Mary knew he had a heart of gold.

The mother turned and gave Mary a weary smile. "I know the suckers are bribery, but some days, I'll accept whatever works."

"We all have days like that," Mary said. "And I think your boys are really cute."

"Thanks. This is the kind of day that I forget that," the mother said with a little laugh. She grabbed the white pharmacy bag. "Come on, Alex and Jeb. Let's get going."

The boys followed their mother out, and Mary moved up to the counter.

"Mary Fisher, I do hope you're not sick." Mr. Ames frowned. "Change of seasons always seems to bring out the colds."

"I'm fine. Not a sniffle. Betty is fine too," she said before he asked after her sister. "I was wondering if you could help me identify a pill."

"Dispose of it right away," he scolded. "You should know better than to take any medication without being sure of what it is."

"Oh, I wasn't going to use it," Mary said hastily. "I found it on the floor and am trying to figure out who might've lost it. I thought if anyone in Ivy Bay could identify it, it would be you. After all, you are the expert around here."

Mr. Ames's frown softened at Mary's effort to butter him up. "Well, let me see it. I don't have all the time in the world."

Mary took the plastic bag out of her purse and passed it over the counter. "There's a number on it."

Mr. Ames held the pill up to the light and then mumbled something about irresponsible people leaving medication lying around before walking into the back room where prescription medicine was kept.

The minutes ticked by. Mary scanned the store looking to see if there was anyone she recognized. She saw a couple of customers that came into her shop occasionally. One of them gave her a smile before she turned down an aisle featuring lotions and other skin products.

Mary turned back to the counter and eyed the suckers in the glass jar, wondering if Mr. Ames was going to offer her one. Somehow, she doubted it, and she smiled at the thought.

Jacob came out of the back room and pronounced, "It's just what I thought it was. A common, generic over-the-counter decongestant." He came around the counter and handed her the bag. "Look over there. You can get it in the package, or I can dispense it from the back."

"A decongestant?" Mary asked. "And you say it's common?"

"That's what I said. Lots of people have been buying them. The wind from all those recent storms really stirred up the pollen, making it seem even worse than usual."

"I don't suppose you could tell me if anyone was in here buying some recently."

"You supposed right. I wouldn't if I could, and in this case, I can't anyway," Jacob said. "Customer privacy. Besides, I don't keep records of these kinds of meds dispensed other than quantity sold, at least not for that brand."

"Well, thank you very much for your help," she said. "Have a great day." Mary felt a wave of disappointment at the results as she started toward the door. She was hoping the pill would've been something more particular or prescribed. Even if the pharmacist couldn't tell her who it might belong to, maybe he could've told the police. She'd better inform Chief McArthur about her find anyway.

"Mary!" Mr. Ames's voice pierced through her thoughts.

Now what? She turned, and the pharmacist was holding out a homemade sucker. "You look like you could use one of these."

Mary smiled and nodded. "I sure can." She thanked him again and stuck it in her mouth the second she was outside. The sweet goodness made the dreary day seem brighter.

She walked down Meeting House Road toward the police station. The fog had lifted some, but visibility still remained at only about a block. Two policemen were getting into a squad car in front of the station. She squinted. Was that Chief McArthur? It sure looked like him.

"Chief!" she called and broke into a trot. "Chief McArthur! Wait!"

He paused, one hand on top of the car door. "Mary Fisher, what is that you're waving around?"

Mary came to a halt, breathing hard. "What?" She looked at her hand. "Oh, it's one of Mr. Ames's homemade suckers. I was just at the pharmacy."

"Ah yes, on a morning like this, I could use one of those myself." He smiled. "So what caused you to run a block to catch me? If it's news on the necklace case you're wanting, I'm afraid I have nothing I can share with you right now."

"This does have to do with the case, but it's information for you." Mary used her free hand to fish around in her purse and snagged the plastic bag with the pill inside. "I found this on the historical society office floor after you and Deputy Wadell left yesterday. It was stuck under the edge of that throw rug by the safe."

The chief frowned and took the bag with the pill bouncing around inside. Mary hurried on with her explanation, hoping she wouldn't get lectured for butting into their police investigation.

"The rug was shaken and the floor mopped on Monday afternoon, right before they closed, so chances are that this was dropped sometime after that."

The chief lowered the bag. "I see where you're going with this. So far, the only person that was alone in the building before it was locked up for the night was Eleanor Blakely, unless, of course, someone was lying."

"And everyone in the office denies that the pill was theirs." Including Eleanor. Mary thought of the red pills in Eleanor's purse and prayed they weren't the same as the one she found. "Unfortunately, Mr. Ames says it's a common medication for decongestion. He's been selling lots of it this spring."

"In that case, we may have an even harder time pinpointing who dropped it, and of course, it might not be related to the theft at all," the chief said.

"That could be true," Mary said, although she was so hoping the pill would somehow be a useful clue.

"Don't look so glum." The chief smiled. "There is something I can share with you about the stolen necklace. We put out a bulletin, and hopefully, if someone tries to sell the necklace, it will be reported back to us. The piece is unusual, which will make it easier to identify."

"Unless someone just salvages the diamonds," Mary said.

"If I was a thief, that's probably what I'd do," he said. "Less chance of getting caught. Take the money and run. But then we might be dealing with someone who values the historical aspect of the piece or has an emotional attachment."

Mary nodded, feeling a chill unrelated to the fog. The people who would value the historical aspects of the necklace could be anyone at the historical society, but there were two that would have to be especially motivated by emotion. Horace Crenshaw would be one, considering Richard was his friend and he'd been with Richard when they found it. The other would be Eleanor. After all, it was her late husband who found it. And lost it.

ELEVEN

M ary hurried back to her shop. It was almost ten o'clock and time to open for business. She was surprised to see a glow coming from the windows. She thought she had turned off the lights after she'd dropped Gus off and left for the pharmacy.

Rebecca was vigorously dusting the bookshelves as Mary opened the door. She looked over her shoulder with a big smile. "Good morning, Mary. I hope you don't mind that we came in early for an hour or so. I thought I could catch up with the cleaning and then come back later in the afternoon. It's been so busy in here this week."

"And too yucky to go to the beach. We were going to go look for buried treasure," Ashley added as she pushed the dust mop along the floor. Gus peeked around a corner of one of the shelves, crouched, ready to attack the mop if it came close.

"I'm sorry you couldn't go," Mary said to Ashley. "But the fog will probably lift by this afternoon. Maybe you can go then."

"You don't mind?" Rebecca asked, reaching down to run the duster along the floor in front of the shelf.

"Actually, this works out great if you can stay until about one thirty. I'm having a meeting with Bea over lunch, and then I want to pop by the library." Mary looked around her beloved shop that she normally kept neat and shining. "And you're right. Things could be spruced up some, especially since this weekend will probably be really busy with the festival."

"We're just about done." Rebecca tackled another bookshelf and then let out a shriek as Gus sprang from his hiding place to grab the feather duster. He got his paws into the duster and turned upside down, his hind legs kicking the feathers.

Ashley laughed so hard she dropped her mop handle with a clatter. Gus sprang up in the air and disappeared into the back room.

Mary laughed too as she walked to the door and turned over the sign to Open. Gus still hadn't reappeared, so she went to the back room to check on her pet and make sure he hadn't done any damage in his mad dash. His eyes glowed as he peeked out from under the love seat. Mary fixed herself a cup of coffee and thought longingly of the pastries next door, but resisted since she was having lunch out at the Tea Shoppe. She might treat herself to something yummy there.

She went back out to the front room just as Penny Fuller opened the door. "Good morning. Isn't it a lovely day?"

"It's foggy," Ashley said glumly.

"I know and I love it," Penny said. "It's like the fog we get back in Maine. So dense you can feel it brush up against your skin and mix with air. And it's so mysterious."

"Mysterious?" Ashley paused in her mopping and looked out the window.

"You never know who or what might be lurking just out of sight. Scary, huh?" Penny said in a spooky voice.

Mary glanced at Rebecca, worried that Penny might be frightening Ashley, but the girl just shrugged. After all, she did spend a lot of time in a mystery bookshop. "I'm not scared of the fog."

Penny smiled and set her large canvas bag down by the counter. "Well, that's good. I'm not either anymore. My brother used to tease me about the fog and make up awful stories." Penny turned to Mary. "I finished the third and fourth books of *The Cat Who . . .* series and need more."

"I wish all my customers read as fast as you," Mary said.

"I figure I'd better grab the time to read while I can. In fact, I probably should buy the next five or six. I'm heading out of the country next week, and who knows when I'll get to a bookstore."

"You're leaving so soon? I thought you were going to be here until the end of June."

Penny nodded. "An awesome opportunity came up in the Caribbean. I'll get to sail from island to island. I might have to take turns scrubbing decks, but it will be worth it if I can do some travel writing."

"That sounds fun. Are you still graduating at the end of summer?"

"Oh, sure." Penny gave a dismissive wave. "I'll still get the credit for interning here. My professor has been pleased with how much they've let me do already. Did you see my article this morning? Johanna didn't have much time to work with me on it."

Mary nodded. "Yes, I did. Great job, although—"

She glanced at Rebecca and Ashley and then smiled at Penny. "Would you like a cup of coffee? I just brewed a pot."

"Sure. That sounds good. I was going to grab one on the way to the office." Penny followed Mary to the back room and looked around. "This place is just so cozy. Makes a nice place to escape to if things get crazy."

"Thanks, Penny. Have a seat, if you want," Mary said to Penny who lingered by the doorway.

"Thanks. I have a little time. I'm due at the *Bugle* office in a half hour." She perched on the edge of the couch. Her fingers fidgeted in her lap, as if they didn't know what to do without a pen or notebook. She smoothed her lightweight blue-and-white-striped sweater over her jeans.

"Do you take cream or sugar?" Mary poured coffee into a mug, feeling a little nervous. She didn't like butting into other people's business unless it was absolutely necessary. But since Penny had thrust herself in the middle of the mystery surrounding the necklace, Mary decided she needed to pry a little into how Penny was getting her information.

Please, Lord, guide my words.

She handed Penny the cup and passed the sugar and creamer, both of which Penny dumped in. Mary picked up her mug and grabbed a chair so she could sit by the couch. "So how are you enjoying your stay in Ivy Bay? Is it much different from Maine?"

"In some ways. The shoreline was rockier where we lived and the water much colder. I love being able to get out in the bay and swim." Penny tasted her coffee and added more sugar.

Mary leaned back in her chair. "Are your folks still there?"

Penny nodded. "My mom is a schoolteacher, and my father is a fisherman. My brother runs the fishing operation with my dad now. Haven's Point was a nice place to grow up."

"That's the way I feel about Ivy Bay. I have wonderful memories of staying with my grandparents here. So, why did you decide to be a journalist?"

Penny gave a little shrug. "I've always loved books, and it just seemed a natural direction to go. I suppose that's why you own a bookstore?"

Mary nodded. "Yes, I've had a love affair with books, especially mysteries, for as long as I can remember. Did you have a favorite book when you were a kid?"

"*Treasure Island*, if you can believe that." Penny laughed. "I've always loved the idea of an adventure. I can't tell you how many times I got lost when out exploring as a kid. My mother said it turned her hair gray prematurely."

Mary smiled. "You seem to be applying that love of exploring to your work. You got the scoop about the stolen necklace. Did you know that information you dug up about the necklace being stolen was supposed to be kept confidential for a few days?"

Penny took another sip of coffee. "Well, you know how small towns are. Nothing stays secret for long."

"That's true," Mary said. "I like the small-town feel of Ivy Bay, and you probably experienced that too in Haven's Point. People have a chance to get to know and care about one another easier than in a big city. Of course, it's only an asset as long as the gossip doesn't get out of hand—then it has the potential to hurt someone, or their reputation."

Penny nibbled on her lower lip and then lifted a shoulder in a small shrug. "I agree, but we haven't reported anything that isn't true as far as I know, and if we interfered with the police investigation, that was totally unintentional. No one told us *not* to write about it. After all, the people of Ivy Bay deserve to know what's going on. If what we wrote turns out to be wrong, then we'll print a retraction. No permanent harm done, right?"

Mary didn't answer right away. Of course, the longer the rumors went on, the greater chance Eleanor's and Richard's reputations might be tarnished. Sometimes the public tended to remember the worst about people. Penny was still so young. She probably didn't realize the damage speculation could cause.

She changed tactics slightly. "I'm sure whoever gave you the information about the office safe didn't mean any harm either."

"I'm sure they didn't."

"Chief McArthur may want to know who revealed the information to you," Mary said gently.

"I can't reveal my sources. He'll understand." She drained her coffee cup and stood. "I'd better buy my books and get to work or Johanna will be calling. Before I go, have you learned anything new in the investigation?"

Mary took Penny's mug and set it on the small table.

"Nothing yet that can be backed by facts." Mary winked in the spirit of keeping things light.

Penny smiled. "Touché. I get your point, but, really, why should anyone worry what was printed if they didn't do anything wrong?" Penny headed back into the shop and over to the series section.

Mary followed, disappointed she hadn't learned more, but she also understood Penny's refusal to reveal her anonymous sources. Penny's doggedness would probably serve her well as a reporter. Mary just hoped she retained a sense of balance in the process.

Three more customers had come in, including a handsome, silver-haired muscular fisherman who was browsing the new arrivals. Henry Woodrow was sixty-three years old and one of Mary's favorite childhood friends. They'd grown close when she had spent summers in Cape Cod with her grandparents. They both attended Grace Church of Ivy Bay, and they were both experiencing a major life change. Henry's beloved wife, Misty, had passed away recently, and like Mary's children, his twin girls, Karen and Kimberly, were both married and had lives of their own. Henry tried to visit them as often as possible, as Mary did with her two. Mary was glad they'd been able to reconnect after all these years.

He looked up from the hardcover thriller in his hand, and his smile reached all the way to his sea-green eyes.

Penny sidled up to Mary at the counter and said quietly, "He's really good-looking for an older guy. I've seen him down by the docks and hanging out in here a couple of times." She placed her novels on the counter and pulled a wallet from her bag. "You interested?" She nodded toward Henry.

Mary smiled. "Not in the way that you mean. We're old friends."

"And that doesn't mean you can't date, does it? Or is he married or something?"

Mary slid the books in the bag. "He's a widower."

"Oh." She considered that. "So that means he's available, right?"

Mary's exasperation spilled over. "Penny!" she said with a laugh.

Penny grinned. "I'm just teasing." She passed over her debit card, and Mary ran it through the machine. "Thanks, Mary, and try not to worry. I know what I'm doing." She took her bag of books and went out the door just as the sunshine found a hole in the fog. The misty cover was rising as forecasted.

Ashley had finished mopping and was in the upholstered bathtub in the children's area. A square of sunlight formed on the wooden floor. She looked out the window and grinned.

Henry walked over to the counter with a warm smile for Mary. "Good morning."

Mary returned his smile. "Well, hi! I didn't expect to see you in here so early." The last time she'd talked to Henry, he had said he was booked all week for fishing trips and a couple of bay tours.

He leaned on the counter with his arms. "The fog had me canceling a tour this morning. Hard to entice the tourists to go sightseeing when they can't see anything. Fishing wasn't a good idea either—I didn't want to go too far out until the weather cleared."

Henry spent most days on his boat, the *Misty Horizon*, which he used both for fishing and for doing tours around the bay. With the influx of tourists looking for the treasure and those attending the festival, Henry was booking good numbers for tours and fishing trips. Hence, Mary realized she'd been missing him over the last few days. He was one of her regular customers, and she enjoyed discussing mystery plots with him.

"I thought I'd drop by and see what new books came in," Henry said. "And to see if you're up for that sunset sail. The fog should be all gone by then. We'd talked about it a couple of weeks ago. I figured you'd still be interested, especially after the last few days."

"You figured right. I'd love to get away for a while," Mary said. "I see you've been reading the paper too."

"Along with everyone else in town. It caused quite a stir at the marina. People want to go out to see the wreck site or take a boat up and down the coast to scout the shoreline for sites of buried treasure."

"How is the Dive Shop doing?" Mary asked.

"Seems to be doing pretty well, actually. I heard that Tom is so busy he's been hiring Horace Crenshaw to take some groups out."

"Really? That's great," Mary said. So, maybe Tom's business could be saved, after all.

"There have been some minor artifact finds close to the wreck site as well as along the shore. No one has been anywhere close to as lucky as you."

"That's the way it appears, but there are other possibilities. And that reminds me," Mary said with a pang. "Eleanor stayed with us the last two nights, and she may be there again this evening. It might not be good for me to disappear, in case she needs moral support."

"Well, we certainly can go out on the boat another time, but why not bring her along? And Betty too. We can all have a relaxing evening," Henry suggested.

"I'll ask them. Thanks, Henry," Mary said. He was such a kind and considerate man.

"I'd better get back to the docks. I told my morning customers to check back if the fog lifted."

Mary looked outside at the sun burning off the mist overhead. The day had the promise of being beautiful, but as she watched Henry leave, a dark cloud seemed to settle over her.

———

Mary arrived at the Tea Shoppe promptly at twelve thirty. The quaint shop was located on Main Street, not far from Mary's store, and sold a wide selection of teas, as well as teapots, tea cozies, and other paraphernalia. Mary walked inside and inhaled the fragrant scents emanating from the many jars of spiced teas and the baked goods. The scents rivaled Sweet Susan's, with the Tea Shoppe adding an exotic and adventurous perfume to the air.

Mary resisted the temptation to linger over the newly arrived merchandise, including a cute creamer shaped like a cat, and headed for the far corner to a small café where full afternoon tea was served, along with a selection of quiches and pastries. The refrigerated cooler held several premade deli sandwiches and salads, but Mary studied the daily specials advertised on the teacup-shaped chalkboard hanging above the counter. Today the specials were a California vegetable quiche and a five-bean soup.

The store owner, Sophie Mershon, a tall and lithe thirty-year-old, used to dance with a Boston ballet company before moving to Ivy Bay to open the Tea Shoppe. Even now, her movements were graceful and fluid, whether she was pouring tea for her customers or making food behind the counter.

Her back was to Mary when she approached the counter, but then Sophie spun on the balls of her feet, her long, blonde braid swinging about her waist, and gave Mary a toothy smile. "Hi, Mary! How's it going?"

"It's been busy at the shop, which I love," Mary said, bracing herself, expecting the inevitable questions about the necklace.

But Sophie just said, "I'm glad. I'm enjoying the busyness too. So many interesting people in town. What can I get you today?"

"What's in the California vegetable quiche?"

"Oh, it's great, especially if you like avocado. There's also fresh grape tomatoes, basil, mushrooms, green onion, artichoke hearts, olives, and Swiss and aged cheddar cheese."

"That sounds yum. I'll try that, and I'll have a glass of your Caribbean black iced tea."

Mary turned to scout a place to sit. The mission-style tables with matching chairs scattered over the wide-plank floor were occupied, but a couple was leaving the table closest to the window. Mary waited for them to pick up their empty paper plates and dispose of them and then claimed the table. The lacy curtains cast pretty shadows over the table and planked floor, and Mary was glad to be sitting in the sun after such a dreary morning.

Bea came rushing into the shop and hurried up to the counter. She placed her order and then joined Mary. She slung her black bag over the back of the chair. "Sorry I'm late. Remember that woman who came into the office while you were there this morning?"

"The one with the thick file?"

"Yes, that's the one. She's a new teacher at the high school and is teaching an adult-education class on genealogy. She's doing this huge project, trying to trace family trees of students whose families have been here for a couple of generations. She thought it might be easier to get copies of the records rather than bring the whole class in, but I don't think she anticipated what a big job it was going to be. Even using the computer, it's been slow going trying to make the necessary connections. After a bit, she asked if I could come to the school and talk about records and the history of the town."

"That's right up your alley. They're going to enjoy it," Mary said. When Bea talked with enthusiasm, it was hard not to get caught up in it.

"Anyway, another reason I'm late is that I stopped by the town hall to see if they had a copy of that contract Horace Crenshaw and Richard Blakely had drawn up about the artifacts collected from the *Lady Beth*, and get this—"

Sophie walked up with two plates. "Here you are. You both ordered the quiche special." She set a plate in front of Mary. The golden quiche with bright green avocado chunks on top looked scrumptious. Sophie had placed some fresh strawberries on the side.

"This looks wonderful," Mary said.

"Sure does," Bea agreed.

Sophie smiled. "Enjoy."

Bea salted an avocado chunk and speared it with her fork. "I love avocado and wish we could grow the trees here." She took a bite and sighed deeply.

Mary sampled her quiche. The fresh flavors melded delightfully together. Another winner of a recipe for Sophie. She waited for Bea to get several bites down, and then she couldn't stand it any longer. "What were you saying about the town hall?"

Bea dabbed her lips with her napkin. "The receptionist said the file was there, but the contract was missing."

"The file was empty?" Mary asked. "Do they have any idea where the paperwork is?"

Bea shook her head. "Nope. That's the odd thing. They didn't seem to have a clue. After all, it's been almost thirty years since it was filed away. And I wasn't the first to come looking for it. Someone had been in earlier asking for it."

Mary leaned forward. "Who was it? Did she say?" she asked, wondering if Horace or Eleanor had been in there.

"She didn't really want to say, but eventually I got her to tell me it was that guy that teaches those scuba classes down at the marina. The blond young man who usually looks like he needs a shave."

"Tom Gordon? He owns the Dive Shop."

"Is that his name? I've seen him around town but haven't gotten to meet him. Anyway, the receptionist said he wanted a copy for research on the wreck. She told him she couldn't look for it until later and forgot about it until the next day. Didn't matter much since the contract was missing. I'll still look around my office, just in case, but I have a feeling it's long gone."

TWELVE

G one? How could a contract just disappear?" Mary asked, her appetite suddenly gone.

Bea shrugged. "Who knows? Someone could've misfiled it, or it just never got put back and maybe got tossed by accident. Those things happen, but I'll keep looking. A copy may still be in the clerk's office."

"Thanks, Bea. It's not urgent, but I am curious since it pertains to the *Lady Beth*," Mary said.

The conversation shifted to the upcoming festival. Bea was helping out with a game booth that the church social committee was sponsoring, and she was full of ideas.

Mary came up with a few of her own but was having difficulty concentrating as she pondered why Tom would want a look at the old contract. What kind of research was he doing? If anyone would have an interest in the contract right now, it would be Eleanor, Horace, and those listed as benefiting from the excavation of the *Lady Beth*.

Bea looked at her watch and jumped up. "Got to run. Thanks for having lunch with me. I'll let you know if I find that contract."

"Thank you, Bea." Mary picked up her purse to follow Bea out but noticed a woman standing by the antique china cabinet on the wall opposite the door. She didn't appear to be looking at the array of teapots and matching cups, but kept shooting glances at Sophie, who was chatting away with a young man from behind the counter.

Her dark hair was tied back in a severe knot. A large bag that looked packed to the max hung off her shoulder. She turned her head, and Mary realized it was Charlotte Rose. Charlotte cast another look at Sophie and then set her book bag on one of the nearby chairs. The bag tipped over, and books tumbled out and slid out across the floor.

Mary hurried over to help her pick them up.

"Oh, thanks, Mrs. Fisher," Charlotte said as Mary handed her a large colorful book.

"You're welcome. You have quite a load here." Mary noted that most of the books seemed to have history-themed titles.

"Research. Between doing that and working, some days I think I'll never finish writing my thesis."

"The fact that you're attempting higher education is commendable. You'll get it done," Mary said with an encouraging smile. "How's it going over at the office?"

Charlotte rolled her eyes. "Chaos. You wouldn't believe the stress. It was very irresponsible of Mrs. Blakely to just quit like that."

Quit? Mary hadn't gotten the impression Eleanor had quit her position. She had been dressed to go to the office when Mary saw her at breakfast this morning. "When did she quit?"

"Sometime between yesterday and today."

"There must be some confusion. Eleanor wasn't feeling well this morning, but I'm sure she would never intentionally let anyone down." At least Mary hoped not.

Charlotte shrugged. "All I know is that everyone over there is scrambling trying to do her job, and Virginia has been all over my case."

"I'm sorry things aren't going well. Do they need any help?"

"You can check with Virginia, but more bodies in the office won't solve anything. You can hardly breathe in there as it is." She sighed and gave Mary a small smile. "Oh, don't mind me. I'm just in a bad mood. I woke up late, and then that police chief questioned me this morning. I don't know why he has to act so mean."

"Mean?" Mary had known the chief to be gruff and impatient at times but never mean. "That doesn't sound like Chief McArthur."

"Well, he didn't seem very nice to me. He acts like he thinks I stole that necklace. He kept asking me where I was that night and who could verify that. It's none of his business."

"I think he asked everyone involved the same questions," Mary said gently. "He's trying to find out who had access to the safe and necklace. He asked Betty and me too. We were home all evening. He's just trying to cross all possible suspects off his list."

"I guess I can see that." She took a deep breath. "I suppose I just got huffy for no good reason. It doesn't matter. I was with Virginia. She wanted to start assembling some baskets we're going to raffle off to help offset the updating of the preservation equipment for the historical society. That's why I'm here. Virginia sent me over here to see if the shop owner would like to donate any items."

"If you need books, I'll donate some for the baskets."

"Your donation will be greatly appreciated, I'm sure. I'll tell Virginia."

"How is she doing?" Mary asked. "Was she upset about the article in the paper this morning?"

Charlotte nodded. "Personally, I think everyone is overreacting. That young reporter even asked me some questions, as if I had a clue to what really happened."

"Oh, you saw Penny Fuller?" Mary asked. Maybe Charlotte had been Penny's anonymous source. "Was this yesterday?"

"Early this morning. She was waiting at the building. She kept pestering me with questions, but I was running late and kind of rude."

"What kind of information did she want?" Mary asked.

"She asked if I had heard any news on the investigation and if anyone had taken photos of the necklace. Then her cell phone rang, and she left in a hurry, which saved me from having to tell her to go away since the police asked me not to discuss the theft with anyone."

"That was wise of you," Mary said, mentally scratching Charlotte off the list of Penny's possible sources for that morning's newspaper article.

"I guess I'd better get on with it," Charlotte said. "I hate asking people for handouts."

"Let me. I know Sophie," Mary said, taking pity on the young woman. She obviously wasn't having a very good day so far. "Hey, Sophie, did you know they are putting together raffle baskets for the shipwreck festival? They are raising funds for new historical-preservation equipment. Charlotte is taking donations over to the historical society."

"Sounds like a worthy cause to me. Go ahead and pick out some tea tins and a couple of teapots and bring them up to the register," Sophie said to Charlotte. "I'd like to put my business card in with them."

"Thanks!" Charlotte shot Mary a smile. "This will make Virginia happy, at least for a few minutes until the next crisis occurs."

Mary didn't think it would be that simple. Nothing these days seemed simple. She thought about the pill she'd given the chief. "Oh, Charlotte, do you have allergies?"

"Not a one," Charlotte said. "Why?"

"Just thought that maybe you lost something," Mary said as she gave the puzzled-looking girl a wave. "Catch you later. I have to get to the library."

Mary hurried up Main Street and turned left on Meeting House Road. She could see the town hall from the corner and wondered again what Tom was up to wanting to see the old contract. As she neared the end of the block, the redbrick, white-trimmed Ivy Bay Public Library came into view.

Mary opened the door, slipping inside to the serene atmosphere. The sunlight from the skylights in the high, vaulted ceilings bathed the blond oak bookcases and furniture, giving them a cozy glow. Four bronze sculptures lined one wall. Mary paused to send a silent hello to her grandfather Franklin. Her gaze lingered on his image, the stern face, spectacles, and wavy hair that tucked behind his ears. Grandfather Franklin had been an influential citizen of Ivy Bay. If it wasn't for him, this library wouldn't exist. He'd also helped get the historical society to landmark other important buildings. She wondered what he'd think about all the excitement this week over the shipwreck and treasure. He probably would've loved the idea of buried treasure and worked doggedly to make sure that the *Lady Beth's* memory was properly preserved.

Mary turned her attention back to the purpose of her visit. The library had free Internet access, an interlibrary loan system, and several online newspaper database subscriptions, but today, Mary was most interested in the microfiche machine, where one could read past issues of the *Ivy Bay Bugle*. She had used the microfilm readers before and opened a cabinet beside the machine where spools of the film were stored in shallow drawers.

She searched for the film dated 1986 and labeled *Ivy Bay Bugle*. After she loaded the film and scrolled through until she reached June 1986, she saw almost every issue carried a front-page story of the *Lady Beth's* discovery. Many of the articles contained photos of Richard and Horace with the university diving and excavation teams. In one article, there was a photo of Horace and Richard presenting the town with a $250,000 check as part of the contract they'd made with the town. She hoped Bea had been able to locate it. Her stack of articles grew as she printed copies of all she could find.

Mary skimmed ahead over the next year to see if there'd been any mention of the *Lady Beth*. There were a couple of articles featuring the exhibit at the Gosnold Museum. She printed out those, just in case they held useful information.

She wasn't sure what she was looking for, but somewhere there might be a clue to what was happening today.

Mary couldn't help but wonder if there was any truth to the rumors about treasure being stolen before the excavation or that the chest of gold was buried somewhere in Ivy Bay. Her grandma used to say "Where there's smoke, there's fire." Had Richard and Horace tried to cheat the town as some citizens thought? Was that contract, now missing, just a way to appease the people when they had already squirreled away riches? Or maybe Horace and Richard were as honest and forthright as Eleanor believed them to be. How could one be sure?

After she'd finished her search, she carefully returned the spools back to their proper place and then took her printed sheets with her to the library computers. The online catalog identified the books on shipwrecks or local Cape Cod treasure, but all were checked out.

Victoria Pickerton, the head librarian and Mary's friend, was at the circulation desk, checking out patrons. She looked up and smiled at Mary when her turn came to pay for her copies.

"You too, Mary? Everyone seems interested in shipwrecks and treasure these days. I've sent for more books on the interlibrary loan system, but we can't keep up with demand."

"That explains why all the books I want for research are checked out," Mary said. "I'll have to make do with these." She passed the stack of copies to Victoria.

"I'm glad you were able to find some information. You're the fourth person in the last week to use the microfiche to look up the *Lady Beth*."

"I'm not surprised," Mary said with a little laugh. "Everyone seems interested in shipwrecks these days, which will be great for the festival this weekend."

Victoria nodded. "It should be. In fact, a young couple from the historical society has been in a lot, trying to do research for the shipwreck exhibit. I wish I've been more help. In fact, he's the one I've ordered more books for."

Young couple? "Do you mean Tom and Charlotte?"

"Yes, that's them."

Once again, Mary wasn't entirely surprised Tom would be looking up information on the *Lady Beth,* being in the scuba business, but Horace was in charge of the exhibit and arranging for artifacts to be loaned for the day. Why would he have Charlotte and Tom doing so much research on it? After seeing how disappointed Tom had been at not finding the necklace, she suspected Tom's research had been more personal than for the festival. And Charlotte certainly could be working on this for her thesis, but after seeing the way she had smiled at Tom, Mary got the feeling that Charlotte's involvement was personal too. But in what way?

Mary paid for her copies as a thought struck her that she would like to know more about the coins and other kinds of jewelry that could have been on board the *Lady Beth.* "Do you have any books on antique jewelry? Or perhaps currency? Seventeen hundreds to eighteen hundreds?"

"Funny you should ask." Virginia's fingers clacked over the keyboard. "We have an excellent book on that. It was in high demand too, but after it was checked in last week, it apparently disappeared. There's a note here that it's still missing."

"Did it get shelved in the wrong place?" Mary asked, knowing how easy that could be from her experience in shelving books when she was a librarian.

"That would be my first assumption, but it's a rather large book and easy to spot. It has to be kept on the bottom shelf since it doesn't fit on the others. I'm assuming that someone took the book without checking it out." Which was a nice way of saying it could've been stolen.

"What did it look like?"

Mary leaned over the counter and looked at the computer screen to see the image of the book. The ornate cover looked familiar. She'd seen an identical book about an hour ago.

In Charlotte Rose's bag.

THIRTEEN

As Mary walked back to the bookstore, she couldn't stop thinking about the book she'd seen in Charlotte's bag. Maybe it wasn't the same one missing from the library. Or maybe Charlotte had just forgotten to check it out while she was doing research. Charlotte had seemed awed by the diamond necklace when she'd seen it in the historical society office, and being a historian, wanted to do research on antique jewelry. A more sinister thought crossed Mary's mind that Charlotte might be trying to find out the value of the necklace she'd stolen, but then Mary dismissed the idea. After all, Charlotte had said the chief had checked out her alibi for the time the necklace was taken.

Mary spied Virginia heading up the steps into the historical society office. She darted across the street before the light changed and followed her inside. The office seemed quiet. Too quiet after Charlotte's mention that it had been in chaos. Virginia sat at Eleanor's desk, her chin resting on her hand as she stared at the screen with a weary expression.

Mary knocked on the doorjamb, and Virginia jerked upright and looked over her shoulder. "Oh, hi, Mary."

"How's it going?"

"I'm having moments of panic that we're not going to get everything done in time."

"I saw Charlotte over at the Tea Shoppe. She was getting donations for the raffle baskets. Is she back yet?"

"She just left here to go to the dentist a few minutes ago. Poor girl was complaining of a toothache. I hope it's nothing serious."

"I hope not either," Mary said, thinking the toothache must've come on suddenly. Charlotte hadn't appeared to be in pain when she had talked to her.

"Did you need her for something?"

"It can wait." Mary wasn't sure how she was going to ask Charlotte about a book that might be stolen from the library. "I told Charlotte that if you want any mystery books for your raffle baskets, I'd be happy to donate some."

"That would be greatly appreciated. I'll send Charlotte over when she gets back from her dentist appointment. If she gets back before you close."

"I can drop them by your home if she's too busy. Charlotte mentioned that she's been working on the baskets there."

"*I've* been working on the baskets there," Virginia said with a huff. "Charlotte put in about a half hour on those baskets and took off. She disappears most evenings. I assume she's working on that thesis of hers. Except for working here, I've hardly seen her all week, and she's supposed to be helping me."

"If you need extra hands, I can volunteer to help with the baskets."

"Thank you. I'll let you know if I get desperate." Virginia let out a sigh. "Anyway, don't worry about the books. If Charlotte doesn't get back, I can pick them up on the way home."

"Okay, that sounds good."

Mary turned to leave, and Virginia asked quietly, "How's Eleanor doing?"

"She's been better. I think she wants to be here working on the festival."

"I know, but…" Virginia looked down at the desk. "Well, just tell her we're sorry and thinking about her."

"I'll do that," Mary said as she went out the door. Virginia was feeling guilty about whatever had transpired this morning between her and Eleanor. It also confirmed what Eleanor had feared. The historical society didn't want their reputation tarnished whether Eleanor had stolen the necklace or just had been careless to allow someone else to.

She crossed at the light and waited for a shiny red Jeep with the dealer sticker still on it to make a right turn onto Main. Tom Gordon was at the wheel, and his laughing companion, with her ebony hair blowing in the breeze, was Charlotte Rose. They roared past, heading toward the bay.

Hadn't Virginia just told Mary that Charlotte was going to the dentist? If so, she was headed in the wrong direction. She stared after them and suddenly realized that if Charlotte hadn't been with Virginia all evening putting together raffle baskets, Charlotte Rose didn't have a solid alibi for the night the necklace was stolen.

After a busy afternoon at the shop, Mary was eager to get home and discuss the discoveries she'd made this afternoon with Betty. Neither Charlotte nor Tom had solid alibis for the night the necklace was stolen. Charlotte could've gotten Virginia's key to get in the historical society's building undetected.

So maybe the intruder at Eleanor's house had nothing to do with the necklace. Or maybe it had been Tom after all, looking for the necklace before finding out later that it was in the safe.

She knew it was still too much guesswork, but maybe talking it out with Betty would provide some clarity and some ideas of what to do next.

She crossed the footbridge and hurried down the street to the house. She had Gus's carrier in one arm and her purse and a file of the *Lady Beth* articles she'd gleaned from the library in the other.

Mary opened the door and set Gus's carrying case down just as a loud thud reverberated through the house.

"Betty, are you okay?" Mary called, nearly tripping over the carrier in her haste to find the source of the sound.

She reached the kitchen and stopped short. All the kitchen cabinet doors and drawers were open. Dishes, pots, pans, towels, boxes, and cans were on the counters and table. On the floor was Mary's ice-cream maker, the one she used to indulge her love of creating sweet cold desserts.

Betty and Eleanor were standing over it. Betty looked up with a stricken look on her face. "Oh, Mary. I hope it's okay. If it's not, I'll get you one just like it."

Mary was speechless for a few moments. She knew the ice-cream maker was just an appliance, but it had been a gift from her dear, departed husband.

"What happened?" She looked around the room again. "What's going on?"

"We're organizing. Something that we've been putting off too long," Eleanor said with her hands on her hips. "When we're finished, the functionality of this kitchen will be vastly improved. In the meantime, we have to tear it down, so to speak, before we build it up."

"I see that. But why is the ice-cream maker on the floor?" Mary picked up the machine but failed to find a place to set it down.

"Well, we thought that since you only used it once or twice a month, it could be moved to a pantry shelf so we could have more space for the new set of casserole dishes," Eleanor said.

"I'm sorry, Mary," Betty said, still looking stricken. "It was my fault. It slipped out of my hands. Here, put it over here." She moved the mixing bowls from the counter into the sink.

Mary set the ice-cream maker down, trying not to let her fuming show. Betty with her rheumatoid arthritis shouldn't be carrying heavy objects around, especially when her symptoms were acting up. By the way Betty was rubbing the back of her hands, Mary knew that she must be hurting today.

Eleanor examined the hardwood floor. "Looks like it made a small scratch. Betty, have you considered refinishing the floor in a darker shade?"

"Uh, no. Not really. I like the lighter color. It makes the room brighter."

Mary could hear Gus meowing from the foyer where she'd left him. "I'll be back." She hurried to the front door and opened the carrier door. "Sorry, buddy."

The cat leaped out and darted halfway up the stairs and turned and stared at Mary. She sank down on the steps and rubbed her face with her hands. She knew she shouldn't be upset. It looked as though the ice-cream maker was fine, at least on the exterior. She noticed a small dent on one corner, but hopefully the machine would still churn her recipes into creamy ice cream. She'd have to test it later, when Eleanor finished her mission to organize them whether they needed it or not.

Poor Betty. Mary sure hoped that Betty wasn't just doing this to please Eleanor. From what Mary saw, they would be at it for hours yet.

Gus rubbed up against her back, and she pulled him into her lap. He tolerated a hug before squirming to get down again. Mary took a deep breath and closed her eyes.

"Lord, I know I've been praying for patience a lot, but please continue to help me and give me the knowledge to know how to help the situation. Please don't let my temper get the best of me. Thank You. Amen." She opened her eyes as she heard footsteps approach.

"There you are," Betty said, looking worried. "I'm sorry about the mess, and your machine."

Mary took another deep breath, determined to follow through on her prayer. "Betty, you don't have anything to be sorry about. The machine looks fine, and if it's broken, I will get it fixed. And if you want to reorganize the kitchen, that's fine too. Just tell me how I can help."

"Oh, I think Eleanor's got it all under control. I don't know what got into her. She lay in her room for most of the afternoon, and suddenly she came into the kitchen with all these ideas on how to reorganize. I didn't have the heart to tell her that we didn't need her help."

Mary's heart squeezed at her sister's compassion. "Of course not. Don't mind me. I was just taken by surprise, is all."

Betty smiled. "You're being a good sport, as always. If you're hungry, I made some sandwiches. They're in the refrigerator. I know it's not much, but the stove is covered with dishes."

"Sandwiches will be perfect. Henry invited us all out for a sunset cruise, if you want to come."

"That sounds fun, but I don't know if Eleanor will want to go right now. But we can ask. She's going to spend another night since her security system isn't upgraded yet."

Mary stood. "So she did go back to her house? I was just wondering if there has been any more damage."

"She met the security company over there for a little while. Everything seemed okay," Betty answered as they walked to the kitchen. Gus followed on Mary's heels, no doubt wanting his supper, but when he reached the kitchen threshold, he arched his back and hissed.

"Guess he doesn't like what we've done with the place," Betty said with a laugh.

Eleanor turned from where she was stacking dishes into a cupboard. "What? You don't like what we're doing?"

"I was talking about the cat," Betty said. "He ran away."

"Oh," Eleanor said in a dismissive tone. She picked up a gravy boat. "Do you use this, or should we donate it to Goodwill? This one has a small chip. I noticed you had another, and we should be mindful of excess."

Betty looked as though she did mind but wasn't going to say so. "Well—"

"Wasn't that a gift from Jean?" Mary asked, referring to their cousin.

"It could be," Betty said.

"Then you'd better hang on to it," Mary said. "What if she comes to Thanksgiving dinner and notices that you aren't using it?" She turned her head and gave Betty a subtle wink.

"Yes, Mary has a good point, Eleanor. I wouldn't want to hurt anyone's feelings."

Eleanor sighed. "Okay, but really, Betty, you shouldn't let sentimentality get in the way of common sense."

"I'm glad you're feeling better, Eleanor," Mary said.

"Thank you." Eleanor touched her fingers to her forehead. "I haven't had one that bad for a long time. I still have a touch of it, but hopefully with a good night's sleep, it will go away."

"I hope so," Mary said. "My mother used to get terrible headaches, especially during the spring because of the pollen. Maybe that's causing it. I know if I get congested, it can play havoc with my head."

"That could be it. I have pills for allergies, but I haven't taken any in over a month. Maybe I should try that." She lifted a casserole dish into the cupboard. "Could you please hand me that glass lid that goes with this?" She pointed to the table. "I'm thinking we could put a rack in here that would double your space if we could set the lids upright."

Mary picked up the lid and gave it to Eleanor. If what Eleanor was saying about taking allergy medication was the truth, then the red pill found at the historical society most likely wouldn't have been Eleanor's since she'd not taken any in several weeks. Mary thought she should feel relieved, but something just didn't feel right. Hadn't Mr. Ames said the recent storms had made the pollen worse? Either the pollen circulating now didn't bother Eleanor, or she hadn't told the truth about taking the medication. But why lie unless she didn't want the pill in the historical society office to be connected to her?

"Eleanor, Henry Woodrow invited all of us to go out on his boat this evening. Would you like to go?" Mary asked.

"Tell him thank you, but I am determined to finish up in here." Eleanor started to refold the dish towels before she placed each one in a drawer. "Who knows when we'll get another opportunity to work on the house?"

Betty looked at Mary with a wistful smile. "I'll stay here with Eleanor. Maybe next time. Have fun."

"I'm going to go change, then," Mary said, and headed upstairs. She was disappointed that Betty wouldn't go, but it wasn't like Betty could just leave Eleanor to finish on her own. As she reached the top of the stairs, Mary spied Gus's tail disappearing through the cracked open door into Eleanor's room. She hurried to the door. Gus had his claws on Eleanor's suitcase, ready to scratch.

"No, Gus!" Mary scolded. Gus sat on his haunches and licked his back leg.

"You don't fool me. You are up to no good." She picked up her pet, and as she turned to leave, something glinted at her from the dresser. It was a gold ring. Mary picked it up and gasped.

Richard's ring!

FOURTEEN

———◆◆◆———

Gus squirmed in Mary's arms, making her realize she'd been holding him too long while she stared at Richard Blakely's ring in her hand. What was it doing here? According to Eleanor, the ring had been in the pouch with the stolen necklace.

When had Eleanor gotten the ring out of the safe? She'd told the chief she hadn't reopened the safe until the next morning when she found the pouch missing. And she had told Horace how upset she was that the ring was missing.

Mary set the ring back down and carried Gus to her room. Her mind reeled, not liking where her thoughts were going, but if Eleanor lied about getting the ring out of the safe, what else was she lying about? Could it be that she had taken the necklace too?

She set Gus on the bed and stared blankly around the room and then remembered why she was there. She needed to change for the boat ride. She went to the closet and pulled out blue jeans and navy deck shoes. It could get chilly out on the water in early June, so she grabbed her wide-weave cable-knit beige sweater to wear over a yellow T-shirt.

She placed a hand on her stomach, which felt hollow. She so hoped she was wrong about Eleanor. After all, other people had stronger motives to steal the necklace. Tom Gordon had said his shop struggled. Charlotte Rose had massive student loans to repay. And the jury was still out on Horace Crenshaw, considering part of that necklace should belong to him if indeed he and Richard had an agreement. And the contract that specified it was missing.

She went to the bathroom and ran a brush through her hair and applied sunscreen to her face, neck, and arms. Even though it would be dark soon, the sun could still do damage, especially when reflecting off the water. By the time she was finished, she was feeling better. She'd just ask Eleanor about the ring. But when she returned to the kitchen, only Betty was on her knees putting pots into a cupboard.

"Where's Eleanor?" Mary asked.

"We ran out of liner paper, and she ran to the hardware store to get some more. She'll be back in a few minutes," Betty said.

"Here, let me help you with that." Mary reached for a pot.

"Thanks, but I'm almost done with this cupboard," Betty said. "You run along and don't keep Henry waiting."

Mary didn't want to leave, but finally, at Betty's repeated insistence, she got in her car and drove over to the marina. She hurried along on the broken pavement that ran along the docks and the shanties that lined the marina. The sounds of waves slapping on hulls and sail lines pinging against masts filled the air and helped soothe her troubled thoughts about Eleanor, and Richard's ring.

The canal that separated Cape Cod from the mainland provided a safe, well-kept harbor for commercial fishing boats and lobster trawlers, as well as the pleasure boats. She scanned the harbor for Henry's boat and remembered Henry mentioning the possibility of taking out a tour. Since it appeared he'd done just that, she settled onto a bench to enjoy one of Betty's sandwiches she'd been able to extract from the chaos of their kitchen.

Mary tossed the wrapper from her sandwich in the trash and spotted the *Misty Horizon* just coming into the marina. The clean white paint contrasted smartly with the navy trim, the matching lettering spelling its name on the side. She'd been right about the tour, as several people sat on the deck or leaned over the gleaming rails. He'd need some time to finish up with his customers.

Mary waved at Henry and pointed to one of the shanties with a sign that read the Dive Shop. He waved back, indicating he understood.

The wide, faded-blue shop door sagged and was propped open. The building could use a good coat of paint, and patches on the walls barely covered where it looked as if someone had kicked in the wood.

She passed a barrel filled with water that tinged the air with an antiseptic scent. Black diving masks and snorkels bobbed in the solution. Several brightly colored dive tanks leaned against the wall. Mary stepped into the dim coolness of the interior. A naked lightbulb hung over the scant selection of dive equipment. Judging by the condition of the shop, Tom wasn't kidding when he said his business was struggling.

"Can I help you?" A petite brunette with a sunburned nose and sapphire-blue eyes stood behind a cluttered counter. A name tag on her tie-dyed T-shirt indicated she was Bri.

"I was hoping to talk to Tom Gordon if he's around," Mary said.

Bri smacked her gum as she pointed to a blackboard with a schedule chalked on it. "Tom is out with a group, but due back any time. If you don't want to wait, I can give him a message, if you want."

"I can wait for a few minutes, thanks." Mary perused the offerings on the counter that included bottles of solution to keep masks from fogging up, a variety of gauges, an assortment of protein bars, and packets of decongestants.

Mary picked up a packet. The pills on the front of the package advertising the contents were small, round, and red. Similar, if not identical, to the pill she'd found in the historical society office.

"Do you need decongestants?" Bri asked.

"Oh no. Not right now." Mary set the package back. "I was just surprised to see them for sale in here."

"Yeah, we sell them all the time," Bri said. "Divers use them sometimes if they feel stuffy. Otherwise, they can get severe sinus pain while underwater. Right here." She touched the bridge of her nose and forehead. "It's rad bad if you ever get it."

"I can see why they would be important, then," Mary said. It was puzzling, though. Horace and Tom were divers, and Tom even sold the over-the-counter pills, but both denied knowing anything about the pill she'd found in the office. And why do that unless they were trying to maybe cover their tracks. This discovery did offer other possibilities besides Eleanor dropping the pill when she'd been alone in the office.

Mary cast another glance at the decongestants and then studied the dive times posted on the wall. Tom had a dive class scheduled Tuesday mornings, which fit with his alibi, but he still could have taken the necklace the night before. Horace Crenshaw was listed for a group the following afternoon.

"Excuse me," a man said rather loudly. He had a diving tank in each hand. Mary moved out of the way so he could get around to the end of the counter.

She walked to the door and glanced outside at the docks. Henry's boat was tied up, and the passengers were getting off. They looked like a family. The father was holding a string of fish, and a young boy still wearing his life jacket was jumping around him with excitement. The mother scuttled around him, holding out her arms so he wouldn't fall into the water.

No sign of Tom Gordon or his boat yet.

Mary noticed a shelf of diving and travel books on the far wall and picked up one on diving shipwrecks. She thumbed through it and noted that the *Lady Beth* was mentioned. She tucked it under her arm to purchase and selected a notebook labeled *Dive Journal*. Inside were lined pages with places to record dates, locations, water conditions, visibility, geography, aquatic life, depth of the dive, and blank lines to make notes.

"Come right over here." Bri came up the aisle, showing the man where they kept dive booties. After she got the man trying the booties on, she sidled over to Mary. "Do you dive?"

"I've been snorkeling but never scuba diving." It had been on John's wish list to try it one day, maybe on a Caribbean cruise, but they had never gone.

"You should go out sometime. We have people your age that really enjoy it."

"I'll keep that in mind." Mary held up the dive journal. "Do all divers keep records like this?"

"They're supposed to. Good divers do anyway. They need it when they first get certified and later when they're trying to get further advancement and classes like deepwater dives and rescue dives." She turned back to the man who couldn't seem to figure out his size.

Mary remembered that Eleanor had said Richard had kept records of artifacts he had recovered. Surely he must've kept a dive journal too. She hadn't seen one on his shelf with his collection, but he probably stored them somewhere. She'd have to ask Eleanor.

Mary moved over to a round wire display with postcards and picked out one of every kind that had the *Lady Beth* featured on it. She was reading the backs of them when two twentysomething men walked into the shop.

"You know, just once I'd like to find something spectacular on one of these dives, like the diamonds that woman found," one of them said.

"We may be looking in the wrong place. She found it on the beach, not out in the bay," his companion said. "And remember, she lost it. How stupid was that?"

"It was stolen, dude."

The other man laughed. "So they say. I bet she just doesn't want to pay taxes on it."

The words to set them straight on the facts rolled to the tip of Mary's tongue, but Henry was coming in the door.

His green eyes warmed at the sight of her. "Find something good?"

She managed a smile. "*Lady Beth* postcards and a book on shipwreck diving." She'd tell him about the decongestants later.

Mary turned to Henry. "Let me pay for these and I'll be ready to go. Eleanor and Betty couldn't make it."

"That's too bad. It's really nice out on the water this evening." He chose one of the dive magazines on the counter and thumbed through it as Mary moved to the cash register.

Mary glanced over her shoulder at the guys who'd been so critical. They were looking at racks of wet suits, still chatting, although Mary couldn't make out what they were saying. Horace could be correct. People were jealous of other people's success and invented all kinds of false scenarios. Eleanor had a right to be worried about her and Richard's reputation. She just wished that she knew Eleanor was truly innocent.

A rack with coral-and-shell necklaces and bracelets sat on the counter. She'd seen Tom and other young people wearing them.

Mary remembered how Ashley had wanted one like Penny's anklet. None of these were as pretty as Penny's, but they looked fun and beachy. Maybe she could get one for Ashley's birthday.

"Those are made locally, if you were wondering. Aren't they awesome?" Bri said. "If you want something special, though, you can order something like mine." She came around the end of the counter and showed Mary her green, blue, and black coral-and-shell anklet. Mary thought it was prettier than the ones offered for sale, but wasn't quite as stunning as Penny's anklet with its rich red-and-black tones.

"I like it. It's different from the ones on the counter," Mary said.

"This one was custom made. It has some Tahitian pearls in it."

"Who is the artist?"

"Horace Crenshaw. He collects the materials all over the world. You should see what else he has. If you want, I can tell him you're interested."

"I know Horace," Mary said, impressed and surprised by his craftsmanship. "I'll talk to him if I decide to get one. Thanks, Bri."

Bri went to help another customer, and Mary turned to see a stack of black-and-white brochures lying on the counter labeled *Ivy Bay Treasure Map*.

"Those maps are based on Tom's research," Bri said. "If you want one, they're only five dollars."

Mary picked up a map and noted that it was copyrighted by Tom Gordon for the current year. The map drawing of Ivy Bay and the surrounding area looked handcrafted and old-fashioned. The legend indicated that *X*s on the map showed possible sites of treasure in Ivy Bay. The site of the *Lady Beth* shipwreck was clearly marked with a large *X* and several smaller *X*s dotted along the shore and in town. She took a closer look and then gasped. An *X* was set centered squarely over a lot that was now occupied by Eleanor's house.

FIFTEEN

————◆◆◆————

"Can Tom just do that? Make up a map that targets people's property? There was an *X* right over Eleanor's house and another by mine. Is that legal?" Mary asked Henry who was steering his boat out across the smooth water. No wonder people had been snooping and digging around Eleanor's place.

Henry pushed on a lever and increased the boat's speed. "I suppose someone could sue him if they thought the map was causing people to harm private property. But if the maps are historically accurate, I don't think there'd be much of a case."

Mary sighed. She certainly didn't want Tom to be sued. If the maps were accurate, it showed he'd been doing a lot of research on the *Lady Beth* shipwreck. That explained the library visits, but she still wondered why he had wanted to see the contract between Richard and Horace and the town.

She looked over at Henry and felt guilty for not being better company. After all, Henry had been trying to provide her with a relaxing distraction by inviting her for a ride.

Henry Woodrow, like his father, was a fisherman by trade. He'd grown up in Ivy Bay and spent most of his life on or near the water. He was an excellent captain and knew the best waters. His company, Woodrow Fishery, kept up a brisk business, with Henry delivering fish to local merchants and restaurants. Sometimes he chartered fishing trips or tours of the shore like he had today.

Mary felt comfortable aboard Henry's forty-eight-foot commercial fishing vessel with aluminum poles, gurdies, and a trolling rack on the back. She leaned back in her seat in the pilothouse, watching Henry adjust the electronic navigating equipment. Seagulls swooped behind them, no doubt wanting to make sure that if any fish were thrown overboard, they'd have first pickings. There was no way to tell them this was a pleasure ride, not a fishing expedition.

A medium-size boat appeared in the distance. It was designed with a step-down back platform close to the water.

"Divers." Henry reversed the engines to slow them and then cut the engine down to a low idle. "We'd better not get any closer. See the flags?" He pointed to an orange flag bobbing on the surface. "There are still a few down there. This is where the *Lady Beth* sank."

Mary stood so she could see better, not that there was much to observe but a tall metal marker with a light on top. She'd been out here before, but the *Lady Beth* hadn't meant much to her other than being part of Ivy Bay history. Now it seemed to consume her life. Henry handed her binoculars.

A blond muscular man was helping a woman on board the small boat. Tom Gordon. That must be the group he'd taken out, and Bri had said he'd be back any minute. They were running really late according to the schedule that Mary had seen on the wall, but even from a distance, it looked as though everyone was having a great time. Faint laughter echoed over the water. No doubt being the last dive of the day allowed them to stay out longer.

Two more people climbed up on the boat and started shedding dive gear and then their wet suits. Tom grabbed a line in the water and pulled in the orange flag. A few minutes later, they took off back toward the marina.

"Do you want to go out farther, or is this okay to stop for a while?"

"This is fine. I like being close to the *Lady Beth* tonight."

Henry gave her an odd look but didn't ask questions. He had brought munchies. Tortilla and pita chips with homemade seven-layer dip, fresh red grapes, and cookies from Sweet Susan's Bakery. He offered her a glass bottle of root beer.

Mary helped herself to the food. She'd eaten the sandwich, but the salty air was making her feel hungry again.

"How are the boys doing?" Mary asked, referring to Henry's two grandsons who lived in Boston.

"Oh, they're keeping their mother hopping," Henry said. "They are thinking of coming down for the Fourth of July and spending the week. Brody e-mailed me that he can't wait to go fishing."

Mary smiled at the love in Henry's voice whenever he talked about his kids and grandchildren. His twin daughters, now grown and out on their own, were a testament to what a wonderful, caring father he was and now an amazing grandfather too. He'd also been a good friend and confidant of Mary's when they'd been children, and even though they hadn't seen each other most of their adult lives, that connection was still there. Consequently, Mary felt comfortable confiding in him now, so she didn't hesitate when he asked her how the investigation was going.

Mary updated Henry about the discoveries surrounding the missing necklace, her list of possible suspects, and finally about her dilemma concerning Eleanor. "So you see, I'm not even sure that Eleanor isn't involved, and I feel terrible about that. Betty would be so upset if she knew that Eleanor is one of my suspects."

"I don't think you're being unreasonable. From what you told me, Eleanor had motive and the means to take the necklace. If she has Richard's gold ring, she must've been back in that safe at some point before the pouch and necklace disappeared," Henry said.

Mary nodded, feeling miserable. "I need to talk to her. She is going to have to report the recovery of that ring to the police if she hasn't already." The fact that Eleanor hadn't shared that she had the ring now just made her appear guiltier.

"What is your gut feeling about her?"

Mary leaned back on the seat cushion. What *did* she feel, exactly? "I guess I really am having a hard time believing that Eleanor would risk her reputation and standing in this town for the necklace. I don't know if she needs money. She seems to have always been financially secure, but what if she's in trouble now?"

"Is there anyone you could discreetly ask about Richard and Eleanor's finances?"

"Betty's son Evan might know," Mary said, but she dreaded having to ask him. Nobody wanted to think their uncle and/or aunt might be a crook.

They were silent for a few moments, listening to the boat creak and water slap on the hull. Mary drank some root beer and changed the subject back to the grandchildren, a much happier topic.

A cloud drifted over the moon, reminding Mary of the fog they'd had that morning. She pulled on her sweater, and Henry stood and stretched. He checked his instruments.

"There aren't any storms forecast for the night, but the fog's expected to roll back in soon. We'd better head back in now."

Henry did a wide sweeping turn, and they skimmed the waves toward the lights on the shoreline. Mary could pick out Betty's and her house. Mary wondered how Betty and Eleanor were doing with the organization project. If it made Eleanor feel better to get more involved in Betty's life right now, then Mary decided she would support whatever Betty wanted to do. Eleanor would be going home tomorrow anyway. Maybe.

The wind picked up and stirred up more waves, causing the boat to rock some, but Mary enjoyed the ride back. Henry slowed the boat as they hit the No Wake zone and headed for his slip.

The marina was dark with just a few dock lights. Only a few people wandered about, dark shadows under the dim lighting.

"Is that Tom?" Mary asked, watching a man carry a knapsack on his back toward Tom's boat. The bag must've been heavy because the man was stooped over.

"Looks like it. That's the Dive Shop slip," Henry said as the *Misty Horizon* lined up with the dock. Mary knew the routine and went down to the deck and pushed bumpers over the side so they hung between the boat and the dock. Mary braced herself for a little bump, but Henry slid the boat along the dock as smooth as glass.

Tom had reached his boat, and as he swung the knapsack over the railing, an object fell to the deck. Tom jumped on board, and a few seconds later, the engine fired to life.

The *Misty Horizon* came to a stop, and Henry jumped onto the dock to tie her off. He helped Mary to the pier. Tom's boat was still there.

"Tom dropped something on the deck. I'll be right back." Mary hurried up the dock and crossed to the next section, but by the time she reached Tom's slip, the boat was pulling away.

"Tom!" she yelled, but the boat was headed into the bay.

Mary spied a metal tube lying on the dock. That must be what he dropped.

Henry came up behind her. "I tried to radio him, but he didn't answer." He looked at the object in her hand. "What's that?"

She picked up the object. "It looks like a mug, but the bottom is missing. Guess it wasn't important." She handed it to Henry, and he moved back so he could see it better under the overhead lamp.

"I think it's a tankard. It's been in the ocean for a while. See the encrustation on it?" Henry turned it over. "Hard to tell how old it is."

"Do you suppose Tom could've found it on the *Lady Beth*?"

"If he did, he's being really careless with it. The divers aren't supposed to excavate on the dive site without permission, but they can pick up things outside the protected radius. And they are supposed to register anything of significance that's taken out near the wreck site. It's a protected landmark now."

Mary watched Tom's boat head out into the ocean. Why was he going out at night alone? Could he be doing something illegal, such as excavating the *Lady Beth* in secret? She looked down at the tankard. Or had he found another wreck? She shook her head. It could be her imagination was going wild again and he was simply going for a ride.

She looked up at the Dive Shop. The door was shut, and the light was out. Henry stood, staring out at the water, obviously deep in thought. She waited until he turned his attention back to her.

"I'll take the tankard with me and bring it back to him tomorrow," Mary said. "I need to talk with Tom anyway."

"Just watch your back," Henry said as he walked her to her car. "If Tom is guilty of stealing the necklace and finds out you're suspicious of him, who knows how he will react?"

That advice applied to the rest of the people on her suspect list, Mary supposed. Right now, she didn't know which of them to trust or believe. Could any of them be dangerous?

SIXTEEN

————◆◆◆————

Mary yawned as she strolled up the walk to the house. The windows were dark, but Betty had left the front porch light on for her. She climbed the steps and stopped. Sandy adult-sized footprints crisscrossed the front porch.

She glanced quickly around the moonlit yard. None of the shadows stirred. The familiar sounds of crickets chirping and distant lapping waves glided softly through the night air.

She skirted around the footprints and let herself in the front door. A night-light lit the stairs where Gus sat. How he always seemed to know when she was coming home, she never could figure out.

Mary quickly moved through the house and checked out the back windows for any signs of who the footprints might belong to. Everything looked normal, and she turned back to the kitchen and tried to decide if she should go upstairs. She felt a little unnerved. A cup of tea sounded good. She set her purse and the tankard on the table, and some of the encrustation flaked off. She opened the drawer to get a plastic bag to store the tankard in, but the drawer was full of pot holders. She pulled another one open and discovered baking utensils. After hunting for a while, she finally located the plastic products and tucked the tankard in a ziplock bag.

The teakettle was on the stove, so she poured water into it and set it to boil. She opened an overhead cupboard and grabbed a cup for her tea. At least they were still in the same place, but the tea wasn't. She hunted through the cupboards and found many other things had been moved.

"What are you looking for?" Betty stood in the doorway to her bedroom.

"Oh! You startled me," Mary said with a little laugh. "I'm looking for tea."

"Over here." Betty reached down, pulled a basket full of tea boxes out from a lower cupboard, and set it on the counter. "Things are a little mixed up, but it got Eleanor's mind off her troubles."

"That's what I figured. It's fine." Mary went to get a spoon, which of course wasn't where it was supposed to be either.

"Okay . . ." She turned around as Betty pulled out a drawer that used to hold dish towels.

"Eleanor said the utensils should be closer to the table." Betty handed the spoon to Mary and then giggled. Mary giggled with her. What else could they do under the circumstances?

"Bets, were there visitors here earlier?" Mary asked.

"No. Why?"

"There are man-sized sandy footprints all over the front porch."

Betty raised her eyebrows. "How strange. We were in all evening, and I didn't see anyone or hear the bell."

"I guess we're going to have to watch for people on the property." Mary explained about the treasure maps at the

Dive Shop and how one possible treasure site was near their home.

"Oh, you're kidding?" Betty said.

"I wish I were." Mary shook her head. "And with the people coming for the festival, we may even have more treasure hunters roaming about."

Betty seemed to think about that for a moment. "Well, look on the bright side—someone might find us a chest of gold, right out there in our backyard."

Mary laughed. "Do you want some tea? I'm making the sleepy kind."

"Sure. I wasn't able to fall asleep anyway."

Mary got another teacup out as Betty sat at the table. "How was your boat ride?"

"Very nice," Mary said. "We went out to the *Lady Beth* site. Tom Gordon had a group of divers out there."

Gus jumped up on a chair and sniffed the plastic bag on the table.

"Where did this come from?" Betty asked, picking up the bag with the tankard inside.

"Tom Gordon dropped it on the deck, and I couldn't get it back to him before he took off on his boat," Mary said. "I'll take it back over to his shop tomorrow, but I am curious about it, though. I wonder how old it is."

"Jayne or Rich might be able to help you figure that out," Betty said.

"Good idea," Mary agreed. Maybe she could catch Rich or Jayne in the morning before she opened her shop.

The teakettle started to whistle, and Mary grabbed it before it got too loud. She poured the boiling water over the tea bags and set the cups and saucers and spoon on the table.

Betty added sugar to her tea and stirred. Her expression seemed troubled.

"Everything okay, Bets?" Mary asked.

Betty blinked and looked at Mary. "Oh, sorry. What did you say?"

"I was wondering if you were okay."

"Yes, I'm fine. Just tired."

"You should be after all the work you did in here. How is Eleanor doing? Did her headache go away?"

"She seemed better, but I don't think today's headache was her usual kind of migraine." Betty stirred her tea again but didn't take a drink. "You know that call she got this morning?"

Mary nodded.

"Well, you probably guessed it was from Virginia. I called her later when Eleanor was upstairs lying down, and apparently, the historical society board felt that for Eleanor's sake and the society's reputation, Eleanor should step down as chairman of the festival and from her other positions as well."

Mary nodded. She had guessed as much, and Betty's statement confirmed the impression she had gotten when she stopped by the historical society office.

"Eleanor may have acted like she didn't care, but I think it has hurt her feelings greatly." Betty picked up her tea and set it back down. "I know I've been around long enough to know that sometimes people lead with their emotions and not their brains, but how can Virginia and the others doubt her so quickly? Especially after all the good things she's done for them and the town. Oh, I realize that Eleanor can easily rub people the wrong way since she thinks her way is the only right way to do things, but her kind actions have spoken louder than her words. They owe a great deal to her."

"I agree," Mary said quietly, although there were times Eleanor had gotten under her skin by the way she treated Betty and Mary. Eleanor and Mary would never be close. They were too different. But still, it was wrong to condemn Eleanor before the facts came out. She was being tried in the court of public opinion and losing.

Betty looked at Mary. "Thanks for letting me get that out. I've been stewing all day over it. I almost called Virginia back and gave her a piece of my mind, but I said a prayer instead."

Mary smiled over her teacup. "Good choice."

Betty lifted a shoulder. "I probably would've only made things worse." She gave Mary a hopeful look. "Have you found out anything new?"

"Yes, but I'm still not sure how helpful it all is." She updated Betty on the events of the day. Betty laughed when Mary told her how she'd run through the fog after Chief McArthur, and when Mary mentioned her suspicion that Tom and Charlotte could be partners in stealing the necklace, Betty nodded.

"I felt like there was something between them too, but I was thinking more of them dating rather than being partners in crime."

"I hope it is just dating," Mary said. She debated whether to discuss the discovery of Richard's ring in Eleanor's bedroom. If Eleanor had told Betty she'd found it, Betty would've mentioned it by now. Mary should probably ask Eleanor about it first.

"Mar?" Betty's voice penetrated her musing. "I'm going to go to bed. Thanks for being so understanding about everything and being there for Eleanor. And me." Betty gave Mary's arm a squeeze as she passed.

"No problem. You were there for me too when I needed you most," Mary said, referring to the dark days after John's death. She finished her tea and rinsed out her cup.

She picked up the tankard and checked to make sure the security system was turned on before going upstairs. Gus followed at her heels and then darted ahead of her. He rubbed up against Eleanor's door.

"Silly. Why are you trying to get in trouble?" She opened her bedroom door and went inside. Gus slinked in a minute or so later.

Mary changed into a comfy pajama set and headed to the bathroom. She reached for her toothbrush and realized neither it or the mug she kept it in were on the sink. She opened the medicine cabinet and discovered it in a new little plastic holder.

She stepped back and took a good look at the room. The hunter-green towels and floor rug were brand-new too. A ceramic dish containing shell-shaped soap had replaced her usual soft-soap container. She found it under the sink and put it back near the faucet. The kitchen must not have been enough to keep Eleanor busy. She didn't mind having new things, but she really didn't need them. Betty had done an excellent job decorating the house before Mary had moved in, and she had been content to leave things as they were.

She washed up and went back to her bedroom. Gus was on the windowsill, gazing out at the night. Wisps of foggy mist floated past the window.

Mary took her laptop on the bed with her and did a quick search on old tankards. She scrolled through the information but didn't see anything like what Tom had dropped on the deck. Her eyelids drooped. Either the tea was kicking in, or the day had finally caught up with her.

She closed her computer and turned off the light. She was too sleepy to even read herself to sleep, her favorite time of the day.

After saying her prayers, she snuggled down under the quilt. She glanced over to the window to check on her cat.

Gus was still silhouetted against the window, his head bobbing, as if he was watching something in the dark. It was probably a moth, but she got up and peeked out the window. In the distance, she saw a lone figure on the edge of their property near the dunes. Was he digging? She opened a dresser drawer and got out a pair of her bird-watching binoculars. It was almost too dark to see, but it was definitely someone digging in the restricted, protected area.

She got the treasure map out of her purse and confirmed what she'd told Betty earlier. Shame on Tom for putting temptation in people's way.

She called the police station and reported a trespasser on the dunes and possibly on their property. No longer sleepy, she turned on the light by the bed and reached for the Sue Grafton novel. She'd concentrate on someone else's mystery for a while. Tomorrow, she'd see if she could solve her own.

SEVENTEEN

M ary overslept the next morning. Picking up the PI novel the previous night had been a mistake, since the plot so hooked her she'd read until almost two in the morning.

She padded over to the window and gazed down at the beach, wondering if the police had caught whoever had been vandalizing the dune. She'd never noticed any lights outside the window, and Gus had eventually jumped down from the sill and curled up at the foot of her bed. At one point, after she'd turned out the light, she'd heard creaking on the stairs and then Eleanor's bedroom door opening and shutting. What had Eleanor been doing up at two in the morning? All was quiet after that, so probably nothing was wrong. Maybe Eleanor had just gone down for a snack.

By the time Mary had dressed for work, Betty and Eleanor were already in the kitchen. Eleanor sat at the table, reading the paper, and Betty stood in front of a waffle iron on the counter. She smiled brightly at Mary. "We're making Belgian waffles. Would you like one?"

"Sounds good," Mary said, and went straight for the coffeepot. She poured herself a full cup and drank it while she fed Gus.

"Eleanor, I'm afraid that Gus got into your room again. I got him before he could do any damage to your suitcase. I shut your door so he couldn't get back in there," Mary said, and refrained from adding that the door needed to be kept shut.

"He must sure like you, Eleanor." Betty smiled.

Mary took a deep breath. "I didn't mean to snoop, but when I was getting Gus, I saw Richard's ring on the dresser."

Betty gasped. "You found it?"

"Oh yes. It ended up in my purse at some point," Eleanor said. "I should've mentioned it earlier, but I was a little embarrassed. I thought I'd put it in the safe, but I guess I didn't. I just don't remember. I've had a few upsetting days."

Mary studied Eleanor's expression. Her cheeks flushed just a little, as if she really was embarrassed, so maybe she wasn't lying.

"You need to tell Chief McArthur you have it," Mary said. "It's listed as being stolen."

Eleanor paused in her reading. "Oh yes, of course. I'll take care of it."

Mary certainly hoped so, although she was a bit worried about the chief's reaction. No doubt he would want to know exactly when Eleanor had gotten the ring from the safe and if she'd taken anything else.

Mary glanced at the newspaper Eleanor was holding up in front of her. The main headline of the day was the hospital scandal, and it consumed most of the front page.

"At least this one is more accurate," Eleanor said.

"What's more accurate?" Mary asked.

"The article on the *Lady Beth* this morning. That young woman reporter called me yesterday, and I met her at my house for an interview. She actually wrote really nice things about Richard." She pushed the newspaper across the table for Mary to read. The beginning of the article was tucked in the corner of the second page.

"I think Penny did a pretty good job, considering there is really nothing new to add to what happened to the necklace." Betty poured batter into the waffle iron and shut the lid.

Mary swallowed more coffee, hoping it would zip into her nervous system. Her eyes felt gritty as she focused on the newsprint. Modern-Day Treasure Hunters was the title, and the article covered a recent wreck found off of North Carolina and questioned how much was there to discover out in the ocean. The article discussed the discoveries around Cape Cod, including the pirate ship *Whydah* and then moved on to the *Lady Beth*.

Penny had quoted Horace Crenshaw. "Ocean explorers never know what they are going to find in the depths of the seas. They may go on for years and never have a significant find, if ever. Yes, I got discouraged, but if I had stopped, we never would've discovered the *Lady Beth*."

"Richard loved diving," Eleanor was quoted as saying. "He grew up here in Cape Cod, and when he wasn't working, he liked to be in the water. He wasn't obsessed about finding treasure, but he loved to dive wrecks. He did research on the *Lady Beth* shipwreck and joined with Horace Crenshaw in the quest to find it. The day they found the wreck was one of the most thrilling days in their lives. And while they did recover some beautiful objects, Richard was very concerned about preserving the historical value of the artifacts. That was the true value in the items he recovered."

Mary read through the rest of the article that recapped the recent storm stirring up more artifacts that had been buried in the sand, maybe for centuries, and the discovery of the diamond necklace.

Mary agreed that article seemed fair and accurate, although the article did bring up the question, yet again, whether there was more discovered on the wreck that had never been reported.

Penny had even asked the question of Horace, "Do you think any treasure, particularly the rumored gold on the *Lady Beth*, has been plundered over the last century and a half?"

Horace answered with, "Of course, the *Lady Beth* has been out there in the bay for over 190 years. Who knows who may have visited the wreck? We'd like to think it had gone undiscovered all those years, but in reality, like the great pyramids, people could have accessed the site and time covered their tracks."

The waffle maker buzzed, and Betty opened the lid. "Perfect. Nice and brown. Mary, do you want strawberries or syrup or both?"

"Strawberries, please," Mary said. The smell of the hot waffle caused her stomach to grumble, and hunger set in.

She looked over at Eleanor, who had shoved her plate forward with half a waffle still on it. "I agree this is a better article than the last one." Johanna being listed as coauthor of the article may explain that. "At least it painted Richard and Horace in a more positive light."

Eleanor nodded. "The reporter apologized to me for the earlier article, or I would have never allowed her in my door. She said she had to write it in a hurry and was under a lot of pressure since Johanna was covering the hospital scandal and they are short of staff."

"Did she mention who she got the information about the theft from?"

"I didn't ask."

Mary glanced at a quarter-page ad for the Cape Cod Shipwreck Festival that promised a display of items recovered from the *Lady Beth* and other shipwrecks, maritime artist exhibits, food booths, book signings, a drawing contest of the *Lady Beth*, and other events related to the shipwrecks.

It looked as though it was going to be an exciting weekend, but Mary couldn't help feeling as if the countdown to the festival was like a ticking time bomb. More treasure hunters in town eager to make a discovery of their own. More speculation on the legendary chest of gold and its whereabouts. And more rumors about the stolen necklace and the theft being partly due to the historical society's carelessness, namely Eleanor Blakely. Mary prayed they'd recover the necklace or discover the thief by then.

Betty placed a plate with a golden-brown waffle, topped with strawberries and whipped cream, in front of Mary.

"This is wonderful, Bets." Mary inhaled the sweet scent. "I didn't even know we had a waffle maker."

"It totally slipped my mind, like the pasta maker we found on a top shelf while we were cleaning out cupboards. I used to make waffles for Edward and the kids on Sunday mornings."

Eleanor glanced over at Mary's plate. "I prefer raspberries on waffles. My housekeeper used to put them right in the batter as well as on top."

"They must have been delicious," Mary said, and smiled at Betty. "But I think this one is the best I've ever had."

Eleanor picked up the newspaper. "This article should be good publicity for the shipwreck festival. Of course, I would have placed the festival ad right by the article, instead of on page three, but apparently, nobody wanted my advice."

"I wouldn't say that," Betty said. "They probably just want to let you rest. Things will get back to normal once the police catch the thief who stole the necklace. Everyone is just on edge."

"Betty, I'm not that naive," Eleanor said sharply. "I was in charge, and in their eyes, I made us look like a bunch of inept amateurs, if not fools." Eleanor's gaze shifted down to the tabletop. "Maybe I did leave the safe unlocked."

"But you didn't take the necklace," Betty pointed out. "Even if the safe was unlocked, it doesn't excuse the thief. Anyway, everyone will cheer up when you show up with Richard's artifacts for the shipwreck exhibit."

"That reminds me," Mary said. "I was in Tom Gordon's dive shop yesterday, and he had divers' journals for sale. Did Richard keep a dive journal?"

Eleanor leaned back in her chair. "Yes, he was meticulous about keeping records about his dives."

"Would it be possible for me to get a look at the one where he kept records about the dives on the *Lady Beth*, particularly the day he found the diamond necklace?"

Betty's eyes widened. "Do you think there might be a clue in there?"

"Anything is possible at this point," Mary said. "I'd like to get a sense of what Richard's impressions were during the recovery period and the people he worked with." And if there was any hint of Horace or he hoarding some of the treasure as some about town thought. If someone had a vendetta against Richard or Horace, they may have felt justified in taking the necklace. Of course, the thief still would've had to have been someone close enough to hear about the recovery of the necklace.

"I can't think of anyone who'd even still be around here, except for Horace. But I don't mind you looking at it," Eleanor said.

"You could put it out in the display for the festival," Betty suggested.

"I'm having second thoughts about putting Richard's artifacts out for display," Eleanor said. "What if they get damaged or stolen?"

Eleanor hadn't seemed resistant to the idea of lending Richard's shipwreck artifacts the week before, Mary thought. Was she really worried or just upset over her abrupt exclusion from running the event? Mary had a feeling it was a little of both.

Betty looked at Mary, and she could tell Betty had concluded the same thing.

"I understand how you feel. We'll make sure someone guards his things," Betty said gently. "It would be a shame not to share at least some of them as tribute to Richard for his amazing discovery and your generosity to the town for sharing the profit with them."

"I suppose you have a point," Eleanor said with a delicate sigh. "It wouldn't be fair to Richard not to honor his memory. I'll think about it."

"I can help you pack up the things whenever you're ready," Betty said. "Maybe, meanwhile, you could look for the journal for Mary."

"I'll get it when I move back home today," Eleanor said.

"Thanks." Mary glanced at the clock. It was almost nine thirty. She'd have to hurry if she was to catch Jayne or Rich before she opened the shop. Mary quickly finished her breakfast and collected Gus's carrier. Her pet seemed wide-eyed and alert this morning, despite his late window gazing last night. He jumped right in the carrier without any enticing from Mary.

Mary said good-bye to Eleanor and Betty and set out for downtown with Tom Gordon's tankard.

Gems and Antiques was already open. Mary entered the shop, which to her was always an adventure. As she navigated the maze of New England heritage and European treasures, it was hard not to drool over the antique quilts or Paul Revere silver. The exquisite china, brooches, and jewelry from Europe were also tempting purchases, and the case of glittering jewelry, chock-full of gemstones, always drew customers.

"Hello," Mary called as she made her way across the store to where Jayne Tucker sat on a stool behind the counter. A copy of the *Ivy Bay Bugle* was propped up in front of her. Jayne and her husband, Rich, had owned the quaint shop for over twenty years. They traveled frequently around the States and Europe, seeking out estate sales and auctions to keep their store well stocked with antique treasures.

"Good morning, Mary," Jayne said, appearing as vivacious and lovely as always.

"Morning," Rich echoed. His bald head was bent over something in his hand. He looked up at her with his intelligent blue eyes and spied the plastic bag Mary held. "My! What have you got there? Another diamond necklace?" he teased.

"I wish." Mary smiled.

"Rich!" Jayne said, and looked at Mary. "My condolences on the loss of the necklace."

"Yes, I'm sorry, Mary," Rich said.

"No offense taken, but thanks. The necklace wasn't really mine, but I feel bad for Eleanor." Mary handed the bag to Rich. "I'm hoping you might be able to tell me what this is. I found this down by the marina. I was wondering if it came from the *Lady Beth*."

Jayne scooted off her stool and hurried over to see. "Oh, how fun."

Rich set the bag on the counter and carefully removed the metal cylinder. "It's a pewter tankard and definitely has been out in the salt water awhile, but I wouldn't bet on it being from the *Lady Beth*. It isn't old enough."

"Looks like it must've had a glass bottom," Jayne added.

Rich looked at Mary with a twinkle in his eye. "You know the story behind glass-bottomed tankards, don't you?"

"No. I haven't heard that one."

"They think that the glass-bottom tankards date back to the eighteen hundreds, which means one could've even been on the *Lady Beth*," Rich said. "The story goes that one day a captain decided to cut a hole in the bottom of his beer tankard and fit it with glass. That way he could always keep an eye on any scalawag strangers and his greedy crew even when drinking ale and playing a hand of poker."

He held up the tankard and glared at Mary through it. "I see you two scalawags. Better behave."

Mary and Jayne laughed. Mary wondered if Tom knew this tidbit of history. She supposed she'd better get the tankard back to him or she'd be as guilty as the thief who stole the necklace.

"I can look into the origin of the mug, if you'd like to leave it," Rich said.

Mary hesitated. "Well, it isn't mine, but I suppose that I can leave it here until this evening." She probably wouldn't get a chance to get down to the marina before then anyway.

"Excellent. I'll take some photos of it if I'm not done." He carried the tankard to the back room.

"Thank you," Mary called after him. She picked up Gus's carrier.

"Any news on the missing necklace?" Jayne asked.

"Not yet," Mary said. "The more time that passes, the less certain I become that it will be recovered."

"That's such a shame. It would have been quite an attraction for the festival," Jayne said. "You know what? All this talk and reading about the *Lady Beth* has me yearning to see the jewelry and other artifacts that were originally found."

"Me too," Mary said. Especially now. Maybe there had been something recovered at the wreck site that could give some clarity about the necklace they'd found. "I've never been to the exhibit. Horace Crenshaw has been working on getting some of the items to be displayed for the shipwreck festival, but I'm guessing they won't send the jewelry." After the theft of the necklace, she wondered if the museum would even trust the historical society with anything valuable.

"The museum is an hour and a half away," Jayne said in a musing tone. "We could go and call it a girls' lunch out." She grinned at Mary. "Think you could be spared from your shop tomorrow?"

"I think it can be arranged," Mary said, delighted at the invitation. Going to the museum with an antiquer like Jayne would be an experience. But more important, it occurred to her that Dr. Carlson worked there. Not only was he the one who'd appraised the other pieces of the *Lady Beth* jewelry, but because of Horace's phone call to him, he also had known early on about the recovery of the necklace. Had he mentioned it to other people?

"Let's say we leave at ten?" Mary suggested.

"It's a date, then," Jayne said gaily.

Rich strode out of the back room. "What's a date?"

"Sorry, darling. It's for girls only," Jayne said with a laugh. "I'll explain later. Have a great day, Mary."

"You too, and thanks for the help with the tankard." Mary closed the door behind her and crossed the street to her shop.

She unlocked the door and let Gus out of the carrier and ran through her normal opening routine: turning on lights, checking for any e-mail or phone messages, and picking up any books that had wandered with customers from their normal spots.

She eyed the table at the front holding the new arrivals. She probably should start replacing them with the next batch of new summer releases.

She flipped the sign on the door to Open, and as she settled behind the counter with a book catalog, the door opened and a mother with three young children entered.

"Good morning," Mary said with a smile.

"Hello." The mother gave her a smile as the kids saw the bathtub in the children's section and headed for it.

"You have very cute children," Mary said as the youngest of the three, a girl with dark, curly ringlets climbed inside the tub.

"Thanks. They can be really energetic, but they do love books. Quiets them down."

One of the little boys spied Gus sitting by a bookshelf and made a grab.

"Thomas! Don't bother the cat," the mother said, but Gus leaped nimbly away.

"Sorry." The mother rushed over to the children's section.

"No problem. Gus is used to customers of all ages. If you need help finding something, please let me know," Mary said. She was about to get up and see if she could entertain the children and give the mom a break when the door opened again. Rebecca and Ashley strolled in. Ashley took one look at the children and hurried over to them.

"Hi!" Ashley said. "Do you want me to read you a story?"

"Yes!" The little girl scrambled out of the bathtub. Her brothers followed her, and they sat with Ashley on the rug. Gus jumped down off a shelf and rubbed up against Ashley's back as she started reading.

The mother looked at her quiet brood with a relieved expression on her face and started browsing shelves.

Mary and Rebecca exchanged smiles. As always, Ashley was taking her role as helper in the bookstore seriously.

Rebecca put her purse in its cubbyhole and looked down at the catalog in front of Mary on the counter. "Anything look like a must-buy?"

"They all do," Mary said, smiling, "as usual. I'm going to have a hard time choosing."

"I heard the reviews on this one were excellent." Rebecca pointed to a new Joanne Fluke mystery.

Mary made a check mark by it. "Any others you think would be good?"

Rebecca bent her head over the catalog as the door chime rang, and Eleanor swept into the shop with a "Good morning."

"Eleanor! Did something happen?" Mary asked, her thoughts going immediately to Betty.

"Everything is fine." Eleanor's assessing gaze swept the room. "I just thought I'd stop by and help you for a while."

EIGHTEEN

***

Words froze in Mary's throat, and Rebecca looked at her with slightly raised eyebrows. Eleanor rarely came by the bookstore unless there was a very special event, and now she wanted to help out?

Eleanor finished her study of the shop and turned to the counter. "Hello, Rebecca."

"Good morning, Mrs. Blakely," Rebecca said.

Eleanor's gaze shifted to the catalog lying flat on the counter. "What are we looking at?"

"Uh, upcoming releases," Mary said. "I'm making an order for next month."

"That sounds interesting." Eleanor leaned over the counter, and Mary turned the order catalog so Eleanor could see the titles.

"What type of mysteries do you like to read, Mrs. Blakely?" Rebecca asked politely.

"I prefer classic literature. Now, Richard loved a good thriller."

"So does my husband," Rebecca said.

Eleanor turned to Mary. "Do you have any tea?"

"Yes, we do." Mary hopped off the stool.

"Oh no, I can get it. Don't trouble yourself. It's in the back, right?" She walked to the room where Mary kept her beverage supplies.

Rebecca looked as though she wanted to ask questions but then thought better of it. Gus opened a sleepy eye from behind Ashley where she was seated cross-legged on the rug, still reading to the three children who had come in with their mother. He stretched, arched his back, and then padded across the room to where Eleanor had gone.

Mary intercepted him. "Hold it, bud. Why do I think you're up to no good?"

She tucked the cat under her arm and checked on Eleanor. "Are you finding everything okay?"

Eleanor stood in front of the closet, picking up one box of tea and then another. "Is this the only variety you have?"

"Were you looking for a specific type?" Mary set Gus down by his food bowl.

"Oh, I was in the mood for some ginseng green tea, but I should've just brought some myself. It's loose tea. I find that the loose-tea infusers really bring out the flavor. You might want to provide that for your customers. I could bring some by. The Tea Shoppe carries them."

"That's nice of you, Eleanor, but—"

"Oh, it's no problem at all." She stepped back, studying the closet. "Do you know what would work well in here? Those little shelf organizers. They can double your storage space. I'd be happy to help you organize." She smiled at Mary and then looked past her at the wall. "I have a lovely painting at home, too, that I just don't have space for. The colors would be perfect over the love seat."

Gus took that moment to stick his claws in the arm of the love seat.

"Gus, no," Mary said.

He jumped down and ran out into the shop. Again, Mary wondered just what had gotten into her pet the last couple of days. He generally left the furniture alone. Was he upset that Eleanor had been a guest at home, and did he feel his territory was being threatened here now too?

As Mary watched Eleanor wander around the room deciding what else could be improved, Mary could sort of understand how the cat felt. Why was Eleanor really here?

"Maybe he just needs a scratching post so he's not so bored," Eleanor said.

"I'll keep that in mind. Thanks, Eleanor," Mary said. Gus had plenty of things to keep him occupied, including a scratching pad in Mary's bedroom. "Did you still want tea?"

"I'll just have some mint." Eleanor reached for the box.

Mary selected a teacup from the little collection she kept in the cupboard, filled it with water, and put it in the microwave.

"Have you thought of getting an electric teapot?" Eleanor asked when the timer dinged, and Mary carefully handed the cup of hot water to Eleanor. "That way the cups don't get so hot." She tore a wrapper off a tea bag and set the tea into the mug to steep.

"When we have a book signing or other event, I use coffee urns that will hold hot water," Mary said, but Eleanor didn't appear to be listening. She wandered over to the door where Mary stood and looked out over the shop as Ashley finished one book and picked up another from a stack beside her. A customer had come in with a toddler, and the child joined the others on the floor around Ashley.

"You know, Mary, I was just wondering if it is such a wise idea having Ashley read all those books to the children? Does that cut into sales if they can hear it for free?"

"No, I don't think so," Mary said. "Children love to hear stories over and over." And as if to prove Mary's point, the mother grabbed several of the books Ashley had read and ushered her three children over to the counter where Rebecca rang up the sale.

"You are quite a good salesgirl," Eleanor said to Ashley after the customer left. "In the good old days, little girls were supposed to be seen but not heard. We were supposed to wear dresses and call adults 'Ma'am' or 'Sir.'"

Ashley stared at Eleanor with a quizzical expression and looked down at her overalls. Rebecca pressed her lips together. Ashley was just being her usual friendly self, and in Mary's opinion, she was quite mature for her age.

"Ashley is a great help at the store," Mary said quickly, realizing that Eleanor was bordering on upsetting Ashley and Rebecca.

"Oh yes, I can see that, but don't you miss playing outside with the other children?" Eleanor asked Ashley.

"Eleanor, you know what?" Mary said. "Now might be a good time to head over to your house, before it gets really busy in here, and see if we can find Richard's dive journal."

Mary looked at Rebecca. "Can you cover here for a while?"

"Sure thing," Rebecca said.

Mary grabbed her purse. "I won't be long."

Eleanor kept up a brisk pace to her house that had Mary slightly winded. When Eleanor set her mind on where she wanted to go or what she wanted or do, she single-mindedly carried it out.

A No Trespassing sign was posted in Eleanor's yard. She glanced at it and said, "The security company must've put that there. I don't think it will deter a determined thief."

Or one that was after something specific, Mary thought.

Another dead-bolt lock had been added to the front door, and it took Eleanor two keys to get the door open. She stared at the new alarm control panel.

"Oh dear, I forget how this worked."

Mary stepped up next to her and studied the electronic screen. "How long do you have before the alarm goes off?"

"Twenty seconds." Eleanor pushed a couple of buttons, but the system still flashed a red Armed. She closed her eyes, and the seconds ticked by. Mary braced herself for the alarm to go off. Then Eleanor stepped forward and tapped in a series of numbers and the screen flashed green.

She stepped back. "Not bad for a slightly older woman," Eleanor said with a triumphant smile.

Mary grinned. "Nope. Not bad at all."

The house was eerily quiet, and the only sounds were their footsteps on the hardwood floors as they made their way to the office. Everything looked the same as when Mary had visited before, except for the gold ring on the glass shelf. Richard's ring.

"Richard kept his journals in the safe." Eleanor walked over to a large painted seascape of Ivy Bay. She tugged on the bottom of the frame, and it swung open to reveal a large wall safe.

"Do you mind looking away? I was told not to let anyone watch when I opened this."

"No, not at all." Mary turned to the desk and heard Eleanor spin the dial. On the desk, Mary noticed a colorful photo of Richard and Horace that she hadn't seen before. The men wore bathing suits and dive equipment. They were holding conch shells and had long, colorful shell-and-coral necklaces hanging around their necks and a circle of flowers on their heads. Both had goofy grins.

"Where was this photo taken?"

Eleanor looked over her shoulder. "Oh, that was Tahiti, 1988. I found it in the armoire upstairs. Horace and Richard were acting like a bunch of nuts. That was the last trip they took together. And the last time they dived together."

"Did they have some sort of falling out?" Mary asked.

"I'm not sure what happened. Maybe they just drifted apart. I asked Richard once if something had happened between the two of them, and he shrugged and said I was imagining things."

Somehow, Mary doubted that. Eleanor wasn't always tactful, like back in the shop with Ashley, but Eleanor noticed details.

"Eleanor, while you're in the safe, could you look for a copy of the contract that Richard and Horace made with the town about splitting the profits from the *Lady Beth* excavation?"

"I don't think I ever saw that contract, but I'll look," Eleanor said.

"And do you mind if I take more photos of Richard's artifacts, just so we have a record in case something else happens?"

"Go ahead," Eleanor said, sounding exasperated with whatever she was doing in the safe. The phone rang on the desk, and she crossed the room to answer it.

"Oh, hello, Frances," Eleanor said, and glanced over at Mary. "You'll have to call Virginia about that. I'm not over at the office today."

While Eleanor carried on the conversation, Mary snapped some photos of the items from the *Lady Beth*. Again, she wondered why the thief hadn't at least grabbed something.

She opened the lid on the pistol case. The pistol wasn't fully settled in its spot. She picked it up. Was it just her imagination or did it not feel as heavy as she had thought it was before? But then she hadn't been holding it by the handle when Betty had given it to her. She examined the gun, thinking that a lot of work went into the silver tooling. No wonder Richard had wanted to keep it.

"Here are the dive journals." Eleanor had hung up the phone and returned to the safe. She handed Mary three small books wrapped in plastic. "I didn't see the contract. Richard would've had a copy, but he might've kept it at his business office, and those documents either have been shredded or put in storage." Eleanor shut the safe door and tested the handle, as if it were a habit. Surely she would've done the same with the historical society safe, Mary thought.

Mary sat on one of the easy chairs and had just started to unwrap the plastic from the journals when Eleanor gasped.

Eleanor had sat behind Richard's desk with a stack of mail in front of her. She held up a letter. "What is it?" Mary jumped up and took the letter and read a computer-printed message.

I know your secret. What did you do with the treasure?
Make it right, or you will pay for your crime.

NINETEEN

❖◆◆❖

Eleanor, is there someone in Richard's past who would think you or he had committed a crime?" Mary asked as she paced Richard's office, the anonymous letter in her hand.

"I'm trying to think," Eleanor said, looking suddenly small and frail in Richard's large desk chair.

"Did he upset anyone he dived with? Especially during the excavation of the *Lady Beth*?" Mary persisted.

"Not that I know of, but there were jealous people around. Still are," Eleanor said. "You heard some of the comments people are saying about Richard and Horace hoarding the treasure and cheating people."

Mary sighed. That list of disgruntled people could be endless. She stopped in front of the desk. "Richard was in business. Did he ever owe money to anyone? Maybe never paid them?"

Eleanor started to shake her head but then hesitated. "There was a time in the late eighties that Richard's business took a downturn. He had to fire people. Some were angry. For a while, it looked like he might have to declare bankruptcy. But then suddenly, everything was fine."

"What happened?"

"A silent partner bailed him out."

"Who was it? Horace?" Mary asked. Since this would've occurred after the discovery of the *Lady Beth*, Horace may have had the funds to bail Richard out.

"No, I think Richard would've told me if it was Horace. He never divulged who it was. Richard rarely talked business with me. He had his duties as the provider, and I had mine in the home."

Mary resumed her slow pacing. Did Richard really have a silent partner, or as rumors had suggested, had he stolen something from the *Lady Beth*? Like a chest of gold coins or maybe some other jewelry. And how would she find out? Obviously, Eleanor didn't know, or at least she wasn't going to tell Mary.

Mary remembered her conversation with Henry on the boat about someone who could find out about Eleanor's finances discreetly. She hadn't had a chance to call Betty's son Evan yet, but she would as soon as she could.

Mary picked up her purse. "We need to take the note to the police."

Eleanor shook her head. "I can't."

"What do you mean you can't?" Mary fought to keep the exasperation out of her voice. "Someone is trying to blackmail you. This could be dangerous."

"We don't know that. He could just be some nut."

"Exactly, and you don't know what he will do," Mary said. *Lord, grant me patience.*

"If I take the note to the police, and they think there is a spark of truth in there, it will look like Richard or I did something illegal. Some people already do, including the police chief. I know I'm on his list of possible suspects. I don't want Richard's reputation tarnished, not after all the good he'd done in his life. And I don't want to live here if people don't think they can trust me. The Emerson family name means something, and I don't want it dragged through the mud."

Mary sighed and sank down in one of the easy chairs. Eleanor had a stubborn set to her chin, and Mary doubted she could change her mind. She reread the note.

I know your secret. What did you do with the treasure?
Make it right, or you will pay for your crime.

"What treasure do you think they were referring to?"

"I assume the necklace," Eleanor said.

"Did Richard and Horace ever talk about a chest of gold coins?"

"Yes, they thought the *Lady Beth* was carrying at least one chest of gold, but it was never found," Eleanor said. "Some say it's just legend, but Richard said that after reading some of the documents related to the ship, they highly suspected there was more out there. Assuming, of course, someone else hadn't found it first."

"And Richard never took anything from the ship that wasn't recorded?"

"Of course not," Eleanor said as she twisted her wedding ring around on her finger. She glanced at the note in Mary's hand. "Wouldn't I know if he did?"

Mary hoped so. She had caught the brief flicker of doubt in Eleanor's eyes.

"Mary, let's just give it a few days before we take this to the police. At least until the festival is over and people stop paying so much attention to the *Lady Beth*," Eleanor said. "If I get any more threats before then, I'll take the ring and note in to the chief." Eleanor looked up. "For Richard's and my sake, let's not stir up any more suspicion."

"Okay. We'll see how it goes for the next day or so," Mary agreed reluctantly. Because if Eleanor didn't go forward soon and update the chief, Mary knew she'd have to.

TWENTY

M ary lingered just inside the doorway of Gems and Antiques while Rich Tucker discussed a Tiffany lamp with a customer. She glanced out the window to see a young family enter her bookshop. The shop had been buzzing with activity when she got back from Eleanor's, and she'd been immersed in running her business until Rich called and said she could pick up the tankard.

After agreeing to not go to the police just yet, Mary had walked with Eleanor back downtown where Eleanor was meeting Betty for lunch. Eleanor didn't want Mary worrying Betty by telling her about the note. Mary hadn't made any promises, but she did tell Eleanor she'd try her best to help find the thief who stole the necklace.

Mary had Eleanor make a copy of the note for her. Mary still wondered about what treasure the author was referring to. Was it a treasure in the present, such as the diamond necklace, or something in the past, like the allegedly lost chest of gold coins, or maybe both? Whatever the author wanted appeared to be linked to the mysteries swirling around the Blakely family and the *Lady Beth*.

Mary surmised that the most important two mysteries that needed to be solved were: What had happened to the rest of the treasure aboard the *Lady Beth*, assuming it existed, and who had stolen the diamond necklace?

Rich looked over at her and held up one finger indicating he'd be a few minutes. Mary nodded and wandered around the displays near the door. An old ship's bell on a table caught her attention. The stately piece might look nice displayed by the deck in Betty's garden. Her sister sometimes put large conch shells out there, similar to the ones that had been in the Tahiti photo of Horace and Richard. She turned the price tag on the bell: $350. Mary turned the tag back over. Too pricey for the garden.

"Hi, Mary. Let me get your tankard," Rich said as his customer left the shop. He went behind the counter and brought out the plastic-wrapped cylinder. "I found a product number stamped into the pewter and was able to trace this particular item to the 1990s. Who knows how long it has been in the water, though. There are tests you could do, but it really wouldn't make a difference on how much it's worth."

"How much do you think it's worth?"

"In this condition, possibly five to ten dollars."

"Is that all?" Mary asked.

"Well, if you found one from the eighteen hundreds, you could get more than a hundred, maybe two. It all depends on the history, time period, the country it's from, and who made it."

"Doesn't sound complicated at all," Mary said with a grin.

Rich smiled. "This one was made in the United States. Cleaned up and restored, it could bring in more like twenty dollars. 'Course repairing it and putting glass back on would eat up a lot of that."

"Well, I have to say I'm disappointed it wasn't from the *Lady Beth*, even though I knew it was highly improbable," Mary said. "I appreciate your help." She paid Rich his usual fee for doing research and then went back to the bookshop.

If Tom supplemented his income collecting items like this, no wonder he was so upset on missing out on the necklace. It would take a lot of tankards, buttons, forks, and whatever else they had been collecting to even come close to a tenth of what the diamond necklace was worth. If she put herself in Tom's place, struggling to stay afloat, she could see how taking the necklace would be very tempting. He could even sell the diamonds off one by one over the years, and possibly no one would even notice.

Mary got to work on a stack of invoices she wanted to enter in her account files. Even with the surges of customers that besieged the shop periodically, the rest of the afternoon seemed to drag by. When closing time finally arrived, Mary locked up and hurried home. Betty wasn't home yet, and Mary assumed she was still out with Eleanor somewhere. She fed Gus and then wrote a note to Betty that she was going to the marina.

Mary grabbed a light sweater and drove over. Lights shone out the Dive Shop door. A large truck was parked in front, and boxes covered with drawings of diving equipment were being unloaded.

Mary didn't know a lot about scuba equipment, but she did know it was expensive. She skirted around the crates in front of the door and walked in the shop. Bri was behind the counter, issuing orders to the two men unloading the truck.

She also had a cell phone stuck to her ear and was ringing up merchandise on the cash register at the same time.

Mary got in line behind the man buying a set of flippers and studied the wall of photos behind Bri's head. In some of the boat photos, customers held up items they'd found. None of them looked like the tankard. Actually, none of the items—forks, spoons, glass bottles, and others—looked extraordinary, although the divers appeared excited. Mary supposed she'd be excited too, if she discovered something buried in the bay's sandy floor.

The man in front of her picked up his purchase and left. Bri looked at her. "Weren't you in here yesterday?"

"Yes, I was. I was hoping to be able to talk to Mr. Gordon."

"Again? He's out with another dive group but will be back any minute."

Mary sighed. That's what Bri had said yesterday, and it could be at least another half hour if Tom was still out at the *Lady Beth* dive site.

She held up the bag with the tankard in it. "Do you recognize this?"

Bri shrugged. "Looks like a piece of sea junk."

"It's a tankard. I believe it belongs to Mr. Gordon. He dropped it last night, and I didn't get a chance to get it back to him until now."

"You can leave it on the counter. I'll put it on his desk with the others."

"Others?"

She smacked her gum. "You know, with Tom's other stuff."

"I'd prefer to give it back to him in person."

"Suit yourself." Bri sidled out from behind the counter and pointed at the man carrying another big box in. "Hey, don't put that down there. It goes by the back wall." She groaned and said to Mary, "I have to watch them every minute."

"I see you're getting a lot of new equipment in," Mary said. "Business must be doing well."

Bri shrugged and was about to say something when one of the men dropped a box in the doorway. "Hey, you guys be careful. I'm not signing for that until you show me it's not broken." She headed to the door.

Mary backed over to the wall with the books and picked up one on the Florida Keys to look through, as space between the aisles was filling up with boxes. A door opened off to the side of the room. Was that Tom's desk in there? She was curious as to what consisted of "Tom's other stuff" that Bri had been referring to. She slowly moved in that direction, trying not to call attention to herself.

When she'd reached the door, she realized it was a small walk-in storage room. Diving equipment littered the floor. A beat-up metal desk was jammed by the wall. Another battered tankard sat on the cluttered desk, along with some other encrusted items. Most likely, they were small artifacts, but it was the empty knapsack beside the desk that really caught her attention. It looked like the same one that Tom had been carrying last night to his boat, only empty now.

A commotion at the front door heralded Tom Gordon and at least six dive customers, including to Mary's surprise, Penny Fuller. She wore a black-and-pink wet suit. She set her tank and yellow mesh bag down by the counter. Her eyes widened when she saw Mary walking down the aisle.

"Look what I found." Penny reached into a yellow pouch that was hooked to her suit and brought out a round small metal disk.

"What is it?" Mary asked.

"A button! Look at the detail on it." She handed the disk over, and Mary could make out a faint design on the flat side.

"This is very nice. Is it silver?"

"Probably just silver plated," Penny said. "Tom thinks it might be from World War II, like off a uniform. I was so excited and breathing so hard I almost ran out of air before the dive was over. That would've been embarrassing."

Mary smiled and handed the button back. "I didn't know you dived."

"Oh yeah. I have for years. A relative taught me when I was twelve. Do you dive?"

"No, although I've always wanted to try it."

"You should sometime. It's a great experience." She looked over at Bri at the counter. "I'd better check out. I need to get my tank refilled." She fairly danced her way to the counter.

The sound of air brakes filled the store, and the truck rolled forward. Tom Gordon came in holding a sheet of paper and went down the aisle. He took a knife from a sheath on his waist and slit the tape on a large box.

Mary waited until he finished opening the flaps and said, "Hi, Tom. I was hoping I'd catch you."

He lifted a scuba mask out of the box. "Oh, hello, Mrs. Fisher. What brings you down here?"

Mary held up the plastic bag. "Henry Woodrow and I were coming in on his boat last night, and I saw you drop this tankard on the dock. But by the time I got to your slip, you'd already left. It was late, after nine, so I just took it home with me."

"Thanks." He took the bag from her and set it on the counter. "That was nice of you to bring it back. I can't believe I just dropped it like that. I was on my way to gas up the boat for the next morning and must not have been paying attention."

"Easy to do," Mary said. "I'm curious. Where did you find it?"

"I don't recall exactly. Stuff like that is scattered all over the bay. Those storms sure stirred things up."

"Hey, Tom!" one of the delivery men called.

"I'd better get this delivery checked in. Thanks again for returning it." He backed away and went outside before Mary could ask any more questions.

Mary headed outside to her car. Tom had climbed in the back of the truck. She found it interesting for him to offer an explanation as to why he was out late on his boat since she hadn't asked him what he'd been doing. She could plainly see the gas pumps from where Henry had docked his boat last night. Tom hadn't been going in that direction. He had been heading out to sea.

TWENTY-ONE

M ary opened the door to the house, and only Gus greeted her with a meow. Betty still wasn't back. She wondered if Eleanor would be staying the night again. After their discussion back at her house about the note, Mary had strongly suggested Eleanor not stay home by herself until things calmed down.

She went to the kitchen and fixed a blueberry bagel with cream cheese and poured a glass of milk. She got her notepad out of her purse and flipped to the page where she'd listed possible suspects who could've stolen the necklace. Tapping her pen on Tom's name, she thought about the large delivery of equipment. Apparently, his business wasn't struggling as it had been. Well, obviously something was helping it if he could afford to buy all that equipment.

And then there was his statement about going to refill his tank with gas. Who goes way out into the bay and then turns around to get gas? The marina was the closest gas filling station for miles.

Maybe he was night diving at the *Lady Beth* or another shipwreck site that required permission and didn't want the authorities to know. The empty knapsack bothered her, though. It had been full when she'd seen him on the dock. What had he done with all the stuff? Sold it? But, even then, unless he was finding gold or jewels, he couldn't be making that much money. Not so much as the sudden change in what he could afford to stock his shop with or buy a new Jeep.

Tom was looking more and more guilty. She circled his name. He was the number one suspect on her list for now. She put a star by Charlotte Rose.

Gus pawed at her leg. "Are you hungry, bud?" she asked. She got up and stretched, then walked to the pantry. She turned to the shelf Betty had designated as Gus's and discovered cans of soup stacked instead.

"Okay, Gus, where's your food?" The cat food had been right there this morning. She searched all the other shelves until she discovered the cat supplies tucked on a bottom shelf in a corner. She had to bend way over to reach the cat tuna. How inconvenient this was going to be.

Was this Eleanor's idea?

Please, Lord, grant me more patience.

She blew out a deep breath. When this was all over and Eleanor moved home, she'd just talk to Betty and see if it was all right to move Gus's supplies back to a more accessible shelf.

She opened the can of food and fed Gus. Betty was still not back, and Mary remembered she wanted to talk to Evan about Eleanor and Richard. She picked up the kitchen phone and sat down by her notepad at the table. Betty kept her son's number on speed dial so Mary pushed the button.

Betty's grown son, Evan, was a busy architect who lived nearby with his wife, Mindy, and two young daughters, Betsy and Allison.

Evan took care of a lot of Betty's business affairs, and Mary just hoped that he knew about his uncle's business too. Being family, Mary knew she could confide in him about her worry for his aunt, but she still felt awkward discussing Emerson affairs. She just hoped that Betty or Eleanor had informed Evan about what was going on.

After several rings, Evan's voice came on the line. "Hello?"

"Evan, this is Aunt Mary. I'm sorry to bother you this late, but it's important."

"Oh, that's fine. You couldn't have gotten me earlier anyway. I just got back from a business meeting in Boston. What's happening?"

Mary tapped her fingers on the counter. "Well, I know this may be a bit awkward, but I need to ask you some questions about your aunt Eleanor and uncle Richard."

"Mindy told me a little about what was going on around here," Evan said, "but I've been basically out of the loop since Sunday. Maybe you'd better update me."

Mary summarized the last four days, and Evan let out a low whistle.

"Incredible. I go away for a few days and Ivy Bay turns into a den of thieves." He muffled the phone, and Mary heard him say, "I'll tell you in a minute, honey."

"Whoever wrote the note thinks that either Eleanor or Richard, or both, committed a crime," Mary said. "I can't help but think that the publicity of the found necklace may have influenced this."

"I know that people speculated that my uncle Richard and Horace Crenshaw took more than they ever reported," Evan said. "But you hear those types of things whenever there's this newsworthy a find."

"I agree," Mary said. "I had another thought. Eleanor mentioned that your uncle's business had troubles in the late eighties and it almost went under. People could've thought that he used the treasure to bail him out."

"I can see how the circumstances might look suspicious."

"Eleanor says Richard obtained a silent partner. Could maybe this partner feel he's been cheated?"

"No clue," Evan said. "Uncle Richard didn't discuss much business with me."

"He apparently didn't discuss business with your aunt Eleanor either. He never told her who his silent partner was," Mary said. "You can say no, and I will totally understand, but—"

"You want me to look into it and find out what happened back then. No problem," Evan said.

"Thank you." Mary breathed a sigh of relief. "And just so you know, there's another aspect to this too. Eleanor was the last known person to handle the diamond necklace and to put it in the safe. She was also in the office alone during a possible time the necklace was stolen. The police may be wondering about her financial situation too, as motive. I know Eleanor's family and Richard left her well-off, but if her finances are dwindling, it may make her look even more suspicious."

"It's ridiculous that they even suspect her." Evan sounded agitated. "Aunt Eleanor has been a solid, supportive Ivy Bay citizen her entire life, and Uncle Richard was too. They didn't have to share part of the *Lady Beth* treasure with the town or the university, but they did."

"I know. And there are others the police suspect too," Mary said, not wanting to disclose to him that she, too, wondered about Eleanor's role in the missing necklace. She still doubted that Eleanor was telling everything she knew about Richard and the *Lady Beth*. Eleanor may have some other motives that Evan could uncover with his research. She prayed that Eleanor hadn't done anything illegal.

"This has been really hard on your aunt," Mary said. "She's concerned about Richard's memory, as well as their reputations. I'm afraid that with people swarming into town this weekend, it will make the situation even more difficult."

"Don't worry, Aunt Mary. I'll discreetly make some inquiries and see what I can find out."

"Thanks again, Evan. Please give Betsy and Allison a nighttime hug from me."

"Will do. Talk to you soon," Evan said.

Mary put the phone down and felt some of the burden she carried to find out the truth lift. She just hoped it wouldn't be too long before Evan got back to her.

The kitchen door opened, and Betty called out, "Hey, we're back."

Mary grabbed up her notes and stuffed them in her purse as Betty and Eleanor, laden with shopping bags, came into the kitchen. From the variety of bags they heaped on the table, it appeared they had visited at least half a dozen shops.

Eleanor beamed. "You should see all the wonderful things we got for the house. This place is going to look marvelous. Betty outdid herself."

"I'm sure she did." Mary smiled at her sister. "She has marvelous taste."

"We did find some cute things." Betty gave her a weary smile. "Eleanor knows the best places to find bargains."

"You'll have to come with us next time." Eleanor opened the refrigerator and selected a bottle of water.

"That would be fun," Mary said. Or not. Eleanor's bargains could still be gaspingly expensive. Mary preferred shopping with just Betty, but it was nice of Eleanor to make the gesture to include her.

Eleanor poured the water into a glass. "I'm going to go change into something more comfortable. Don't you dare show Mary what we bought until I get back."

Betty sank into a chair after Eleanor's footsteps could be heard going up the stairs. "I suggested shopping to distract her from worrying, and the next thing I knew, we were headed to Boston."

Mary grinned at Betty over the pile of shopping bags. "Looks like you succeeded in distracting her."

Betty nodded. "I think so too. She's going to stay here tonight again. She said she'd feel safer. Have the police found out anything yet?"

"I haven't heard," Mary said. Now if Eleanor had let Mary take her to the police station and turn over the note, she might have been able to find out something from Chief McArthur.

They spent the next half hour examining Eleanor's and Betty's purchases. They unpacked scented candles for the living room, cheerful kitchen towels, a new apple-shaped rug for in front of the kitchen sink, two royal-blue casserole dishes to replace Betty's older dishes Eleanor had insisted on donating to Goodwill, a stainless-steel stockpot, and coffee and tea from a Boston specialty shop.

"And this is for you." Eleanor lifted a box out of a bag and passed it Mary. It was a red electric teapot. A very nice one.

"I thought you could use it at the shop so you didn't have to heat up water in the microwave," Eleanor said.

Mary's first reaction was to say it was too expensive. There were simpler models that would work just as well. But Eleanor looked so pleased with herself that Mary just said, "Thank you, Eleanor."

Betty gave Mary a grateful smile from behind Eleanor's back.

Mary stood and covered a yawn with her hand. "Well, I need to head off to bed."

"But we're not finished." Eleanor walked over to some shopping bags by the back door. She bent to pick one out and let out a screech. "Eek!"

Gus's head popped up out of the bag.

"That cat!" Eleanor said as Mary hurried over to get her pet.

Betty laughed. "He's just having fun, Eleanor."

Eleanor shook herself slightly, like a hen settling her feathers. "Do you want to see what else we got, Mary?"

"I'll look tomorrow." Mary tightened her hold on Gus as he started to squirm. She knew he would go right back inside the bag if she put him down. "I have a big day ahead. I'm going to the Gosnold Museum with Jayne Tucker to see the *Lady Beth* artifacts."

"Why are you doing that? Don't you have things you have to do around town?" Eleanor's tone sharpened to the point that Betty glanced at her.

"I'm going for research," Mary said pointedly. "I want to find out as much as I can about the *Lady Beth* and the excavation. Maybe something in the past is linked to the disappearance of the necklace."

"Oh well, that could be fun. We could all make a day of it," Eleanor said. "That is, if Betty and I are invited, of course."

"You're welcome to go," Mary said almost too brightly to hide her reluctance to include Eleanor. She wanted to do research without Eleanor hovering around and directing their activities.

"We can't, Eleanor," Betty said coming to Mary's rescue. "We were going to choose which of Richard's *Lady Beth* artifacts we're going to display at the festival and then pack them in boxes."

Eleanor sighed. "You're right. I forgot. Maybe next time, Mary."

"Okay, good night, then. Pleasant dreams." Mary headed upstairs with Gus. She got ready for bed and looked longingly at the Sue Grafton novel on her nightstand, but first she was going to review Richard's dive journals. She unwrapped the plastic from the leather-bound books. Inside were pale, featherlight tabulated pages with Richard's bold handwriting filling in the details of each dive including dates, locations of the dives, the depths reached, and descriptions of what they found.

Mary fluffed up her pillow and leaned it back on the headboard as she skimmed through the pages, looking for mention of the *Lady Beth*. Predictably, most of the dives were in the summer, with occasional spring and winter dives. On several dives, the *Lady Beth* was mentioned, but only in the context they were in the wrong location.

Finally, she reached the entry for June 12, 1986. "*LADY BETH* FOUND!" Mary felt goose bumps just reading that. She could only imagine how excited Richard and Horace must've been. She read through the excavation dive notations. Richard had recorded lists of their findings, a lot of which Mary hoped to see the next day at the museum.

As Mary read through the pages, she noticed that there were symbols drawn on the sides of the pages. She tilted the book more to the light. There was a flower, an anchor, wavy lines that were filled in, and various shapes, like boxes and triangles.

Mary smiled. Richard Emerson was a doodler. So was Mary, although she'd curbed the habit somewhat when the habit became a nuisance. She'd find herself drawing things, without thinking, on the edges of order sheets or important papers.

Richard's doodling didn't fit the general impression she'd had of the dignified, slightly stuffy man she remembered. It just showed that you didn't really know a person. She liked this whimsical aspect of his personality.

She read on about the excavation, feeling Richard's excitement through his words on the journal pages. Richard had been very detailed. There was even a notation about losing his diver's pouch and the necklace, but no mention of the contract that was drawn up. She read over the list of items they'd chosen to keep, such as the dueling pistols.

She moved on through the journal, and the dives to the *Lady Beth* grew fewer. From her research, Mary knew the site had eventually been classified as a historic landmark and permits were needed to excavate any items within the underwater boundaries. Items found in the vicinity had to be recorded with the state historical register, which made her wonder again if that's why Tom was going out at night. Maybe he didn't want anyone to know what he found.

She came to the end of the journal and found two folded sheets of paper tucked inside the back cover.

She opened them up and discovered they were photocopies of what looked like tattered, old letters. The handwriting was small and a bit difficult to decipher.

She lifted Gus off her legs and went over to the closet and got John's magnifying glass out of one of the boxes. The magnifying glass made it easier to read the letter. Both of them were addressed to My Dearest Sarah and signed by Yours Truly and Forever. Whoever had sent these letters obviously wanted to remain anonymous to anyone but Sarah. She read the first one.

My dearest Sarah,

As the journey on the Lady Beth grows longer, so does my affection and longing for you. I pray that I continue to possess your heart. I keep your glove in my pocket, and my dream night take me back to the church picnic in the meadow when I first saw you, a beauty sitting among the spring flowers.

We have visited many interesting ports. Our cargo is growing with many wondrous items. As I promised you, I have worked hard to secure our future. The captain's demeanor grows colder toward me daily. I know not what I may have done, except that I have been more successful than others in acquiring and trading merchandise. The ship will dock in the Bahamas in a day to collect a family who is paying for transport. We will visit Florida and then head to Boston. Soon, my darling, we will be together.

Yours Truly and Forever

Excitement rippled through her. Whoever had written these letters had been on the *Lady Beth*, but who was *Yours Truly?*

My dearest Sarah,

I hope this letter finds you well and happy for my arrival that will occur within a fortnight. Boston is our next port. My enduring love belongs to you. Do not despair. I have kept my promise. Despite unscrupulous carryings-on, I have secured our future through ingenious means and can only hope that your hand will be mine.

Yours Truly and Forever

She read the second letter, which appeared to be later since it mentioned that Boston was the next port. If this was the final voyage, then the *Lady Beth* never made it to Boston, she realized with a pang. How sad.

Mary tucked the pages back in the journal, wondering about the "unscrupulous carryings-on" and how Yours Truly secured his fortune. And what would that fortune consist of? Gold? Silver? Gems? Or something else in the cargo. Spices were valuable back then.

Richard had kept these copies of the letters, so they had to be of significant historic meaning. Maybe Sarah and Yours Truly were just key figures in shipwreck lore, although Mary hadn't seen the letters before in her research. But were they more than that? Eleanor had mentioned that Richard had found documents referring to more treasure on board the *Lady Beth*. Were these letters a clue to where that treasure ended up? If so, did Richard ever find it, and more important, where was it now?

TWENTY-TWO

"O uch!" Mary rubbed her shin that she had just bruised by smacking it into the chair. A chair that shouldn't be there. What was it doing on this side of the living room?

She looked up and realized most of the living room furniture had been rearranged. When had that happened? Mary had come down to get a glass of milk after she'd finished reading the letters last night, and everything had been normal then. Had Eleanor been up in the middle of the night moving furniture? How she managed it by herself, Mary didn't know.

She limped into the kitchen. Eleanor sat at the table in her bathrobe, her chin propped up by her hand as she stared into her coffee mug. Mary gestured toward the living room. "When did—"

Betty's slight shake of her head signaled Mary not to say anything more. Mary gave her a nod and headed for the coffeepot. She poured herself a cup. The coffee had an exotic taste. "This is good."

"That's one of the coffees Eleanor picked up yesterday," Betty said. "It's called Tahitian Sunrise."

Eleanor looked over at Mary. "It was one of Richard's favorites."

"I can see why," Mary said. The hint of coconut reminded her of the photo of Richard and Horace in Tahiti. Maybe that's what had prompted Eleanor to pick this flavor.

"Thinking of Richard, have you ever seen these letters before?" Mary reached into her purse and pulled out Richard's dive diary. She passed the photocopies to Eleanor.

Eleanor skimmed them. "Yes, I remember them vaguely. Richard collected all kinds of things about the *Lady Beth.* Why?"

"I was just wondering why Richard would keep copies of these in his journal."

"I wouldn't know," Eleanor said. "Maybe he just liked them." She passed the letters to Betty who'd come over to see what they were talking about.

"Do you think the originals might be at the Gosnold Museum?" Betty asked.

"If not, Mary could ask the historian over there. Dr. Carlson worked with Horace and Richard on the wreck," Eleanor said.

Betty gave the letters to Mary. "These are so romantic and sad. I'm assuming whoever wrote these died in the wreck."

"Reports say there were no survivors," Mary said, feeling sad too. She knew what it felt like to lose the one you loved.

Betty sighed. "I wonder whatever happened to Sarah."

Good question. Maybe Mary would find out today. She fed Gus and quickly fixed herself a bagel to take with her. She wanted to get to the shop early to get some work done before she left for the museum.

"I'm going to leave Gus home today," she said to Betty. "I'm not sure how long I'll be gone."

"Gus can keep me company in the kitchen while I bake. I got recruited to make corn bread for the fire station's booth at the festival. They'll be selling chili."

Eleanor looked up. "I have a recipe for cheese and onion corn bread that really complements chili."

"I was planning on just plain ole corn bread," Betty said. "But I suppose I could do both."

Mary left them talking about recipes and finished getting ready for work. She headed for the shop an hour earlier than usual. It felt strange stepping out to go to work without Gus's cat carrier. She lifted her face to the clearing blue sky.

Thank You, Lord, for such a glorious New England day.

She hurried across the footbridge over the cranberry bog with light steps and headed up Main Street. She waved at Tess Bailey who was sweeping the sidewalk in front of the ice-cream parlor.

Two town workers were hanging a banner over Main Street that read Cape Cod Shipwreck Festival. Virginia stood on the sidewalk watching them, her hands on her hips, looking cross.

Mary went inside her shop and worked at balancing the accounts until it was time to open and Rebecca arrived with Ashley in tow. Mary stepped outside as Jayne rolled to a stop in a yellow vintage convertible. She laughed at Mary's expression.

"It's a 1969 Chevrolet Corvair convertible. Rich picked this up in Pittsburgh for a song since it didn't run before Rich worked on it. My dad used to drive one like this. I thought it would be more fun than the truck. Do you mind if we have the top down?"

"Not at all," Mary said with delight as she slid onto the passenger seat and put on her seat belt.

"There's an extra scarf in the glove compartment." She patted the sapphire-blue filmy scarf that captured her auburn curls. Mary took out the red one and put it on, feeling very like Grace Kelly in *To Catch a Thief.* Maybe Mary would find some clues today to catch a thief herself.

The drive up the coast took longer than expected, with early summer traffic clogging some of the little towns. But the route was worth it, especially today with the bay sparkling under the azure sky. They passed the time talking about the festival. Jayne and Rich had been recruited at the last minute to help with decor, which meant Jayne had to be back by three this afternoon to help set up.

Jayne pulled up to a white block building set on a bluff overlooking the water. From the brochure Jayne gave her, Mary learned that the museum architecture was 1970s postmodernism, which incorporated lots of glass block, deep-seated windows, and a dramatic shed roof. In an area where historic quaint houses and buildings were the norm, one would have thought the museum would've stuck out like a sore thumb. But, over time, the white concrete had weathered as the natural rock and dunes around it, and it blended into the landscape.

The museum was named after the famous explorer Bartholomew Gosnold, who had sailed from England with a small crew. During their journey, they'd stopped and fished in these Atlantic waters and caught so many cod that Gosnold named the area Cape Cod. Despite the efforts of later explorers and settlers to change the name, it stuck.

If the exterior of the museum seemed simplistic, the interior made up for it. The light that shone through the glass block near the ceilings bathed an interior full of the colors and rich textures of treasures and artifacts collected from the dangerous and exciting journeys of men and women who explored the seas.

Mary could've spent hours just in the outer room featuring the history of the early Cape explorers such as Gosnold, Champlain, Hudson, Smith and Hunt, Dermer, and Pring, but they'd come to see the *Lady Beth* exhibit housed in the heart of the museum.

Mary approached the receptionist behind a marble counter and inquired if Dr. Carlson was in and if she could get an appointment to see him. Luckily, he had an opening in a half hour. Mary told her she'd be back.

"I just love coming here," Jayne said after they'd paid for the tickets and began wandering through the exhibits on their way to the museum center. "So much history. There's a story behind each button or fork or flask. I think that's what really keeps me in the antique business. The human side. The stories of real people who have had these things in their lives."

Mary nodded, enjoying Jayne's passion. "That's what draws me to books. Granted, novels are fiction, but the characters are based on real human traits, and the plots, if they are done well, can mirror our lives or lives we wished we had. I love to escape into their worlds."

"I guess that makes us explorers of a sort," Jayne said. "I explore people's lives through antiques, and you explore the human experience through books."

"So true," Mary said with a smile.

Two cannons guarded the entrance into the *Lady Beth* exhibit. The cannons were the only ones recovered in the wreck, although according to the experts, the *Lady Beth* should've had four. But no one seemed to have a record of where they had disappeared. Another mystery, Mary thought.

On the wall of the entryway were photographs of the excavation, many with shots of Richard and Horace. One photo showed the two men receiving a reward for historical preservation. They were a study in contrasts. Richard wore a dignified dark suit. Horace, on the other hand, was clad in a tropical shirt and shorts with sandals. A colorful coral necklace, similar to the one he had adorned in Tahiti, hung around his neck.

The entire room was devoted to the *Lady Beth*. A ship model dominated the center. Glass cases lined three of the walls containing similar items to those Richard had in his office. Glass bottles, plates, silverware, cannonballs, and several pistols, but not as fancy as the ones Richard and Horace kept.

Surprisingly, the shelves contained a lot of ladies' personal items, such as hand mirrors, silver combs, and boxes beset with precious stones. Mary moved on to the jewelry display. Several glittering necklaces, bracelets, and a tiara were draped on black velvet. The pieces did resemble the necklace Mary had found in Richard's pouch.

"Beautiful," Jayne said softly. "Did the necklace you found look like these?"

"The pattern is similar. I have a photo of it." She found the photo on her phone and showed Jayne.

"The necklace is gorgeous, and it does look similar to the ones here. I wish I got to see it before it disappeared," Jayne said. "I hope you get it back. But I've been in the business too long to expect much. When people steal easily identifiable items like that, it's less risky to extract the diamonds to sell and melt down the gold."

"It's too bad. The necklace was still in pretty good shape, although some of the diamonds were missing." Mary leaned toward the glass to examine the jewelry in the display. The defects were barely noticeable. "Like these here. If you look close, some of the diamonds are gone too."

Jayne studied the jewelry for a few moments. "I didn't even notice, and I'm supposed to be able to evaluate these things for a living," she said, sounding disgusted with herself. "They look well crafted, though, except for the missing diamonds. The pattern of the missing stones is interesting too. Like they just randomly fell off. In pieces that have been bashed up against a rock or something, you see more concentrated damage. Of course, they were in the water for decades, so who knows what they've been through."

Jayne moved on to the next window case, and Mary spied a case of documents and maps. She hurried over, wondering if she'd find more letters like the ones she'd found in Richard's journal.

Several letters that had been written from sailors and passengers of the *Lady Beth* to family and friends were placed under a glass countertop so visitors could get up close to the letters. Mary would've loved to spend time reading the flowery language and the glimpses of their lives.

As she reached the end of the counter, Mary found what she was looking for. Two yellowed letters, penned in faded ink, addressed to Sarah. Eagerly she reread the last letter from Yours Truly and Forever.

According to the Lady Beth timeline on the wall, Yours Truly died about twenty days later, pursued by pirates and then caught in a storm that ran them into a sandbar.

Mary read the brass plaque under the two letters: Letters from James Paul Vanderstrom to Sarah Jane Whitmeyer.

How marvelous! She now knew the identity of Yours Truly and Forever, author of the letters, and Sarah's full name. And something else...

James Paul Vanderstrom's initials were JPV. She'd seen those same initials in Richard's office. She whipped out her phone and scrolled through the photos she'd taken of the pistol case. The initials on the cover of the case *were* JPV. She'd found the original owner of the pistols. Since Richard had copies of the letters in his journal, he must've been researching the owner too. But was that all Richard had been looking for?

According to his letters, James Paul Vanderstrom had gone out to seek his fortune so he could wed Sarah Whitmeyer. In the last letter to his love, he mentioned unscrupulous carryings-on and that he had secured his fortune in an ingenious way. Did he mean he'd taken his fortune someplace safe?

Maybe the rumors were true that after escaping the pirates and anchoring in the bay, the crew took some of the fortune they collected and hid it on land. Then when they returned to the ship, perhaps to ferry more across, the storm had hit full fury and all perished.

Mary looked over at the jewelry display. But why leave these beautiful and valuable diamonds behind on the ship? Why weren't they taken off with the coins if they thought the pirates might close in? Jayne sidled up to her. "A gold doubloon for your thoughts?"

Mary raised her eyebrows, and Jayne laughed.

"Okay, so it's a chocolate doubloon. There's a basket over there." Jayne handed her a gold foil-covered chocolate.

"I'm thinking about lunch," Jayne said. "There's this place on the way back that looks like a shack, but they make the best cod chowder on the coast."

"The best, huh? I'm looking forward to that." Mary glanced at her watch. "I can see Dr. Carlson in a few minutes, and after that, I'll be ready to go." She took one last look at the sparkling diamond jewelry and followed Jayne out of the exhibit.

"I'm going to check out the gift shop," Jayne said, heading for the small shop at the entrance.

The receptionist smiled as Mary approached. "You can see Dr. Carlson in a few minutes." She gestured to an open book lying flat on the counter. "Did you sign the guest book when you came in? If you put your e-mail address, we will keep you up-to-date on museum events."

"No, I didn't." She signed her name and added her e-mail address to the page. As she set the pen down, her gaze caught a name near the top of the opposite page.

Tom Gordon, and on the next line was Charlotte Rose. Dated two days ago. First the library and then the museum. One thing was abundantly clear—they were all doing research.

Was this where they'd come on the day Mary saw them drive away in Tom's Jeep? Charlotte had told Virginia she was going to the dentist. What was so important about a museum visit that made her lie?

"You may see Dr. Carlson now." The receptionist gestured for Mary to follow her to the far end of the counter to a door. She pushed open a steel door to a huge office that seemed to double as a restoration room, with tables and shelves full of objects in various stages of cleaning and repair.

A slightly stooped, silver-haired man with deep blue eyes rose from behind a desk. He wore brown pants and a black long-sleeved shirt, and his skin was deeply suntanned like Horace's from years of being in the sun. He came around the side and firmly shook Mary's hand. "Mrs. Fisher, how nice to meet you. The receptionist mentioned that you're from Ivy Bay and are related to Richard Blakely."

"That's right. Richard is my sister's brother-in-law."

"It was a sad day when the world lost Richard. Good man. I enjoyed very much working with him on the *Lady Beth* excavation. I assume, then, you were the one who found the diamond necklace?"

Mary nodded. "Yes, it was on the beach, still in Richard's pouch."

"It was tragic it was stolen. My condolences. Horace had mentioned that the necklace had been stored. That act of carelessness was inexcusable. As I told him, the necklace should've been transported immediately here where we have adequate protection, but then hindsight is twenty-twenty."

"I'm still hoping it will be recovered," Mary said, trying not to let her irritation show. Everyone just assumed Eleanor had been careless. And from a look around the room, even here, people left out plenty of artifacts for the taking of a clever thief.

"I'm hoping you may be able to help me with some research." She explained about the copies of the letters she'd found in Richard's dive journal. "I was wondering if the fortune James Paul Vanderstrom secured was ever accounted for?"

"Ah yes, Richard had mentioned to me he had an inkling on where more of the *Lady Beth* treasure could be, but apparently, he never actually found anything significant. As I recall, a couple of other researchers looked into it too. We were able to secure some of the ship's record of what may have been on board from the purchases it made at ports on its voyage, but, back to your question. If James was able to somehow smuggle something like a chest of gold coins off the *Lady Beth*, he did it so well it has remained hidden to this day."

"That's disappointing," Mary said. "Do you think it's in Ivy Bay someplace?"

"There's no reason not to think that, except that many have searched over the years. If you're interested—"

The phone rang. "I'm sorry. I need to take this," Dr. Carlson said. He picked up the receiver and turned his back to Mary.

Three gold coins and chips of what looked like broken glass lay in a shoe box lined with black velvet on the desk. A bottle of what appeared to be some kind of cleaning solution and cotton swabs lay beside it. The coins looked similar to the ones in Richard's office, but still partially covered with sediment.

Dr. Carlson hung up the phone. "I'm afraid I have been called away on some urgent business." He reached over and shut the lid on the box with the coins. "I'll walk you out." He ushered her to the door.

As they moved into the lobby area, Mary asked, "Do you know Tom Gordon? He runs a dive shop in Ivy Bay and takes groups out to the *Lady Beth* wreck site."

"Tom, oh yes. I met him the other day. A determined, ambitious young man. He's very interested in our research here and is helping finance one of our expeditions this summer. In fact, I was going to ask if you might be interested. Even if you don't want to go along on the trip like Tom does, you can help fund it. If we find anything valuable, you will get a percentage of any profits from the artifacts." He picked up a brochure from the counter. "You just never know when you might get lucky."

TWENTY-THREE

T hanks again, Jayne." Mary waved as Jayne pulled away from the curb. It had been a productive outing, and Mary felt as though her friendship with Jayne had grown. All the way back, she'd pondered about what she'd learned. The news that Tom Gordon had invested in one of the expeditions sponsored by the museum seemed incredulous considering he'd told Mary his shop had been close to bankruptcy. This only made her more convinced that Tom had come into some wealth. Perhaps from a stolen necklace.

Her thoughts had shifted to the other mystery surrounding the *Lady Beth*. She had been thrilled with the discovery of the names of Sarah and Yours Truly, although she wasn't sure of the significance of it yet. Dr. Carlson had confirmed that Richard was still researching the supposedly lost *Lady Beth* treasure. Whether the letters were a clue still remained to be seen. And if Richard had found the gold or other treasure, even just a part of it, he hadn't shared the discovery with anyone. Perhaps he had used it to save his business and created the story of having a silent partner. She hoped Evan had been able to find out something.

Jayne had dropped Mary by the historical society office. Mary wanted to talk to Charlotte. She hoped she was wrong and hated to think the young woman was caught up in something that could ruin her future. If Charlotte was involved in the theft of the necklace or knew something about its disappearance, maybe Mary could convince Charlotte to make a deal and try to save herself.

As Mary approached the office, Horace came out the door, his arms overburdened with a load of boxes. She grabbed a small box that tilted precariously from the top.

"Thanks," he said. "I guess I should've made another trip. Glad you came along when you did. There are breakables in there."

"I was just heading in to talk to Charlotte."

"Well, you missed her and everyone else. They all left in a huff."

"Oh dear. I hope everything is okay."

"She and Virginia had some sort of fight. Charlotte apparently wants to quit working at the office after the festival. Got a new job at the Dive Shop. I guess she and Tom are an item, if people use that word anymore."

"Is that right?" Mary said, although she'd already guessed as much since they had been spending so much time together.

Horace stopped in front of a Jeep, a much older model than what Tom had been driving.

"Looks like you're moving," Mary joked as he set the boxes on the sidewalk.

"Actually, I am sort of moving." Horace smiled. "I'm taking my stuff home because I just got funding for a new project near Belize. A colleague of mine is closing in on the site of *The Commander*, which went down in 1789." He opened the door and started loading his boxes.

"How exciting," Mary said. "When do you leave?"

"I should've left by now, but I didn't want to let the committee down since they are overloaded without Eleanor." He took the small box Mary was holding, set it inside, and shut the door. "You know, I don't think it was fair how they treated Eleanor. It came from some of the other board members. Whenever you rise to the top in an organization, there is someone waiting to knock you down. Eleanor had stepped on toes over the years."

"Is that what the problem is?" Mary wondered who on the society board he was referring to. "I assumed they were just trying to protect the society's reputation rather than it being personal."

"Could be. Maybe it was a little of both."

"Horace, can I get your opinion about something else?" Mary asked.

"Sure. My opinion is freely given whether people want it or not." He chuckled.

"I found some copies of letters written by James Paul Vanderstrom to Sarah Jane Whitmeyer in one of Richard's dive journals. Do you know why Richard would've kept them?"

"I don't recall those exactly, but there were a lot of documents we went through. I'm sure it was just historical curiosity." He jingled his keys.

"I assume that since James Paul Vanderstrom's initials were on the pistol case, he was the owner of the pistols that you and Richard kept from the excavation."

"Ah yes, that's right. I have one of the pistols. Did you know that Richard won the case with a toss of the coin? Tails, I believe. He always was lucky."

"Oh well, that probably explains it. I just thought that since the letters were tucked in his dive journal they were of special significance other than just finding the owner of the guns."

"Such as?"

"James mentioned in the letter that he'd made arrangements to secure his share of the fortune. Could Richard have thought that this was a clue related to the rumored lost chest of gold coins or other treasure?"

"Wouldn't that have been something?" Horace said with a small smile. "But we'd all concluded that the chest was just legend."

"Dr. Carlson seemed to think that the theory had merit. I talked to him today at the museum."

Horace grimaced. "Well, as much as Dr. Carlson is respected in some circles, be careful. He's a shark waiting to gobble up what he can. Now, I've used him in the past only because he is a leading expert on artifacts in the era of the *Lady Beth*, but he can be ruthless if he wants something. He'd love to make another discovery to add to his list of triumphs. He probably tried to soak Richard for more funding by agreeing with his crazy theory. Carlson didn't ask you to invest in his expeditions, did he?"

Mary felt a little disappointed. "He did, but without much pressure." She'd tucked the brochure he'd given her in her purse. She skimmed it on the way home, and the minimum investment suggested was a thousand dollars. To join an expedition, the cost started at 3,500 dollars. Again, she wondered about where Tom's suddenly improved income had come from that would allow him to invest in or even join an expedition.

"Dr. Carlson mentioned that Richard had been interested in doing more research before his death. I assume this may have been after you two parted ways."

Horace gave her a sharp look. "Parted ways?"

"I'm sorry, that was a thoughtless thing to bring up," Mary said hastily and went on to explain. "It's just that I saw a photo of you and Richard in Tahiti. Eleanor said that was the last trip and dive you two did together. She thought you may have had a falling out with Richard."

"Eleanor tends to overdramatize," Horace said with a shake of his head. "We just got on with our lives. Now, the way I see it, if Richard had found anything valuable after the excavation, he would've shared it with me and the town. That was our agreement. Unless, of course, he wasn't an honorable man."

A sense of forced lightness in his tone caused Mary to think maybe Horace did carry a grudge about something, after all.

"From what I've heard, he was," Mary said.

He lifted a shoulder. "Case closed, then." He gave her a kind smile. "And you be careful; treasure hunting can be really addicting and cause people to do things they normally wouldn't." He went around to the driver's door. "Have a good day."

"You too. Maybe I'll see you tomorrow at the festival," Mary said. "I hope you have a great trip, if I don't get a chance to say good-bye."

"Thanks, Mary, and don't worry too much over Eleanor or anything else. Things tend to work out in the end."

Mary watched him drive away. Horace didn't seem to think the letters were anything significant beyond identifying the owner of the pistols and case, but there had been a slight tension in his manner. Horace could be totally right about Dr. Carlson's motives, but what if there was some merit to the theory that it wasn't just a legend or rumor and there really was more treasure somewhere in Ivy Bay?

Maybe the key lay in finding out more about Sarah and James. It wouldn't hurt to look into them, even just for curiosity's sake. She might be able to trace Sarah's and James's lineages at the county clerk's office, since all local records of births, deaths, and real estate transactions were kept there.

She glanced at her watch. Jayne and she had made good time on the drive back, and she still had an hour before she'd told Rebecca she'd be back. She pulled out her cell phone and called Rebecca, who assured Mary that everything was running smoothly and to take her time.

Mary hurried down Meeting House Road to the clerk's office and found Bea sitting behind the counter in her usual place. Her reading glasses had slid to the end of her nose as she studied some sort of manual in front of her.

"This is somewhat of a shock." Mary closed the door behind her. "Usually there's a long line this time of day."

Bea looked up with a smile. "I hope you need me to do something. Anything would be preferable than reviewing new government regulations. I've nodded off twice already. Save me."

"Well, I think I can save you from boredom for a little while. I need to do some research."

"Oh, bless you!" Bea shoved the big binder to the side and grabbed a notepad and pen. "What do you have for me?"

"I need to see if I can locate someone, actually two people, who may have lived in Ivy Bay around 1824."

Bea paused in her writing and looked up at Mary. "Why do I get the feeling this has to do with the *Lady Beth* shipwreck?"

"Because it does." Mary smiled. "There was a man on the *Lady Beth* named James Paul Vanderstrom, who wrote letters to Sarah Jane Whitmeyer. I was hoping to find out a little more about them and if their descendants are still in the area."

"All right. We need to check the birth and death records, but the computer is broken today." Bea nodded toward the monitor in the corner. "I have a call in to Megan, but she won't be able to get over here until tomorrow." Megan was Bea's granddaughter and a whiz with computers. She was the one who had built the database for the county clerk's office so people could search for all kinds of pertinent information in one place.

Bea slid off her stool. "We'll have to do it the old-fashioned way and search through the files in the basement, unless you want to wait until tomorrow for Megan to get the database working again."

"I'm fine with checking the files." Mary actually enjoyed hunting through the old records. She followed Bea down the stairs into the basement, careful to hang on to the solid handrail. The basement contained the really old files from the sixteen, seventeen, and eighteen hundreds. Bea made her way through the rows of boxes stacked six feet high, stopping every few feet to read the labels in the dim overhead lighting.

"Ah, here we go, 1800–1950. Let's start with these." They spent the next half hour digging through the records. Much to Mary's disappointment, they didn't find anything under Vanderstrom. That meant James probably wasn't from Ivy Bay nor had family in the area. But with more searching, Mary found several records for the Whitmeyers, listed as owning or having owned property in Ivy Bay.

"Here's a marriage record of Sarah Jane Whitmeyer to a George Martin Jefferson in 1830," Bea said triumphantly, handing the document to Mary.

So, Sarah had married someone else six years after the shipwreck. Mary's gaze lingered on Sarah's signature and felt a kinship. Mary knew that heartbreak of losing a man she loved. At least Mary had many years with John. She hoped Sarah had found happiness with George.

"Now we can see if there are any Jeffersons still in the area." As Bea pulled pertinent birth and death certificates from the files, Mary made a chart of the lineage.

Sarah Whitmeyer Jefferson had three children: two sons and a daughter. One of the sons had died in childhood. The surviving son, George Junior, and daughter, Martha, had grown up and married. Bea was able to find records of their children, but information on the lineage got sketchy after that, meaning the family could've moved out of the area. Only two possible descendants were still listed as being born in the county. Rachel Jefferson and Jonathan Myers.

Bea looked up. "What do you think? Is this going to help you find whatever you are looking for?"

Mary smiled. "Well, we'll soon find out."

"Mary, do you have a moment?" Rich Tucker said over the phone. "I have something you'll want to see."

"That sounds intriguing. I'll be over as soon as I can." Mary hung up the phone and turned back to the customer who'd bought a set of Sherlock Holmes novels.

"I'm hoping my son will enjoy these as much as I did at his age," a fortysomething man said as Mary bagged up his purchase. "He liked Hercule Poirot."

She added a couple of her custom-made bookmarks to the bag. "Then I'm thinking he'll like Sherlock too," she said, glad to see a father promoting classic mysteries. "Enjoy."

She waited until the customer had departed and then told Rebecca she needed to run over to Gems and Antiques. "I'll be back to close up."

She hurried across the street, wondering what Rich had found so interesting that he needed her to see it.

The Closed sign was on the door, but she found it unlocked as she pushed it open. Gems and Antiques was empty of customers. Only Rich was behind the counter with an assortment of crusty-looking objects spread out on it.

"Hey, I heard you had a great time at the museum," Rich said. "Jayne couldn't stop talking about it before she went home."

"I enjoyed it too. It was worth the trip up there." In more ways than one. Mary stopped in front of the counter and looked at the metal pieces on the counter.

"Is this what you wanted to show me?"

"Yes. Two people came separately into the shop today with these two knives, bolts, nails, and what looks like pieces of a lantern, and this mug. They're coming back tomorrow to pick them up, but I wanted to show you something." He picked up one of the dull-looking knives that had encrustation on it.

"First of all, I was examining the two knives. At first glance, they look as if they'd been in the salt water a long time, but in reality, I think they were altered, maybe washed with acid and then soaked in a material that created the look of encrustation. But these couldn't have been in the ocean for as long as it appears. See where the manufacturer names would be on these pieces? It's scratched off, but I was able to pull a few numbers off this one. The knives were made in the last year."

Mary sucked in a breath. "And they look antique...."

Rich nodded. "Now, I've already identified this mug as probably from the 1940s. One of the nails could be nineteenth century, but the rest of these could've come from any hardware store." He held up a hand. "But wait, before you say anything else, I have one more thing to show you."

He lifted a cleaning rag that had been covering an object on the counter. "Recognize this?"

Mary nodded, at a loss for words. It was the same tankard she'd found on the dock and returned to Tom Gordon.

TWENTY-FOUR

❖◆❖

Normally, Mary would've enjoyed the walk home in the balmy June air, but today she was too distracted. She knew now what Tom was up to: planting fake antiques for his dive customers to find. If he was clever enough to fool his customers, then those treasure maps may have been created as a diversion. A break-in at Eleanor's could be attributed to one of the many treasure hunters swarming her property and could steer suspicion away from Tom. Pretty clever if one didn't know Tom had a motive.

After he'd discovered the necklace wasn't at Eleanor's house, he could've teamed up with Charlotte to steal it from the office. She knew where the combination was kept and could've gotten ahold of Virginia's key to the office. Even if Tom acted alone in the theft, Charlotte seemed to be involved in whatever he was doing now. If he'd been spending money like it appeared he had, chances were the necklace was no longer in Ivy Bay, or if it was, it wasn't in one piece.

Before she left the shop, Mary had put in a call to Henry, updating him on what she suspected might be going on. He offered to let her know if he spied any more suspicious activity. Mary planned to get down to the marina as soon as she could to speak to Tom.

As she entered Shore Drive, she noticed a cat sitting on the fence near her house. The Holmeses, who lived down the street, owned a cat, Tiger, with similar coloring as Gus. She wondered if they knew Tiger was outside. But as she got closer, she realized the cat on the fence wasn't Tiger. The cat looked like—

"Gus!" Mary called, breaking into a trot. Oh dear! Had Eleanor let him out again?

The cat flicked his tail and crouched as a butterfly fluttered by. He made a flying leap, missed the butterfly, and landed on the far side of the fence.

"Gus, come here." She rounded the fence.

No cat. Her heart rate slipped into a higher gear as she hurried to the back of the house. She forced herself to slow down. This was ridiculous. She knew she shouldn't be this worried. After all, Gus had survived as an outdoor stray before she'd taken him in. But he had been acting a little out of character with Eleanor in the house, and now with lots of strangers coming into town for the festival, she couldn't help but be a little concerned.

Gus wasn't on the deck. Had he gone into the marsh?

"Mrs. Fisher, what's wrong?" Tyler Walinski asked. Thirteen-year-old Tyler lived next door with his older brother and his mother.

"I'm looking for my cat, Gus."

"Oh, I just saw a cat run over that way." He pointed toward the garden. "Do you want me to help you catch him?"

"It may just make him run if you try to grab him out here," Mary said. "But if you could help me look for him and let me know when you see him, I'd appreciate it. We just have to be careful not to scare him." Or turn it into a game of hide-and-seek. Mary knew the cat would love that. "You circle around on the beach side, and I'll check the garden from this end."

"Okay." Tyler took off at a trot toward the dunes.

Mary checked around the bushes and plants in the garden. Where was her cat? She stopped and took a deep breath.

"Dear Lord, I know You see each sparrow that falls. You brought Gus into my life when I needed him the most. Please take care of him and bring him home soon."

"I see him," Tyler called softly and waved at her from the path leading to the beach. Gus was nosing around the dune not far from where she'd found Richard's diving pouch.

Footprints dotted the sand dune from treasure hunters, but she, too, paid no mind to the additional Stay Off the Dune signs that the beach patrol had been forced to put up. Right now, she was more concerned about getting her cat back before he wandered farther.

She approached the edge of the dune. "Gus. Come here."

Gus stared at her for a few seconds and then continued on with his sniffing. She wondered what he could smell that so captured his attention. Mary carefully maneuvered up the side of the dune.

"Ma'am!" someone called. Gus looked up, his eyes widening.

Mary looked over her shoulder to see a deputy she didn't know approaching. Deputy Wadell had said that they had to patrol the beach because of all the treasure seekers on it.

"I'm just getting my cat," Mary called and turned just as Gus launched into a flying leap. She caught him in her arms and hugged him tight.

"Great catch," Tyler said.

Mary gave the policeman a thumbs-up, and he waved before veering toward a group of teens digging a big hole in the wet sand.

She stepped carefully down the dune to where Tyler stood. "Thank you for helping me find Gus. Remind me to buy you an ice-cream cone this weekend."

"You don't have to, but cool!" He jogged back up the path toward his house.

Mary's stomach felt hollow after all the adrenaline expenditure as she marched with Gus to the back door. He put up little resistance, apparently tired after his adventure.

The smell of frying onions hung in the kitchen air as Mary entered. Betty stood at the counter, mixing hamburger into a meat loaf. She looked over her shoulder with a smile. "Dinner will be ready in an hour."

Mary set Gus down and realized her shoes were full of sand. She backed to the door and took them off on the stoop before entering again. "Where's Eleanor?"

Betty rubbed the remaining meat loaf from her fingers. "She's upstairs, napping. Why? Do you need her?" She turned and caught sight of Mary's face. "What's wrong?"

"Gus was outside. I specifically *told* Eleanor not to let him out, but she doesn't listen. I've tried to be patient, haven't I? We took Eleanor into our home, and I've been running around town trying to salvage Richard's and her reputations. She's careless with other people's things, and if you haven't noticed, she lacks empathy for anyone else. Can't she see that the week has been hard on all of us? Doesn't she ever listen to anyone?"

"Wait! What are you talking about? Gus was outside?"

"Yes! Eleanor told me how her cats have always been outside pets, but I asked her not to let him out. She had opened the door for him the other morning. I would have had no idea where he was." The words rushed out of Mary's mouth like a storm surge, and she had trouble catching her breath. "It was just one little request, but she didn't respect my wishes. You know how much Gus means to me; why can't she?"

"Mary, I'm so, so sorry."

"You have nothing to be sorry about. This wasn't your—" Mary stopped when she realized that Betty looked almost ill.

"This must be my fault," Betty said. "Eleanor has been upstairs for hours. Some children came by to sell candy bars for a fund-raiser. Gus must've snuck out when I went to fetch my purse. He was eating out of his dish, and I didn't even think to look for him later."

Mary sank down on a chair as waves of guilt and regret hit her. She had never wanted to make her precious sister feel bad. "You have nothing to feel sorry about. I apologize for my outburst. I overreacted and jumped to conclusions. Gus is fine. It's just been a challenging week," Mary said as she caught a flash of movement out of the corner of her eye. Was that Eleanor in the hall? There was the sound of someone on the stairs and then a door closing overhead.

"Oh dear. I think Eleanor overheard me," Mary said with a deep groan. "That was terrible of me to complain about her. I feel awful."

Betty laid a hand on Mary's shoulder. "Don't be so hard on yourself. You've been so nice about letting Eleanor stay here. And other than letting Gus out the second time, you didn't say anything that isn't true. Exaggerated a little, but still true."

Mary patted Betty's hand. "You're the best sister anyone could ever have."

Betty smiled. "Remember that the next time Eleanor needs to stay with us."

Mary stood. "And now I'd better go apologize to Eleanor."

Before she could make it to the top of the stairs, the phone rang. Betty called out to her, "Mary, it's Henry. He says it's urgent."

Mary hurried back to the kitchen and took the phone. "Hi, Henry. What's going on?"

"Tom is setting to go out on his boat, and he's carrying a bundle like he did the last time we saw him."

"I'll be right there, Henry." Mary hung up the phone. "Betty, I need to get down to the marina. Don't wait on dinner for me. And I'll apologize to Eleanor when I get back."

On Friday evenings, the small marina was usually busy with weekenders vying for the best guest-docking sites. Tonight, it was even more congested, and almost every slip was full, which Mary thought bode well for more attendees at the shipwreck festival in the morning.

The *Misty Horizon* was docked in her usual slip, and Henry was hosing off the decks. He jumped down onto the dock when he saw Mary and turned off the water.

"It looks like they're about ready to take off," Henry said, looking over at Tom's boat.

"Okay, I'd better go to talk to them now, then," Mary said, feeling a little nervous.

"Do you want me to come with you?" Henry asked as Mary hesitated.

Mary smiled. He was such a good friend. Always there when she needed him. "I do, but I think I'd better go alone. I might get more information out of them if it's just me."

"Okay, I understand. I'll be close by if you need me."

With a deep breath, she crossed over to a neighboring slip. "Hello, Tom!" Mary called. "Permission to come aboard?"

Tom looked up from untying the boat's rope from the dock. "I was just getting ready to cast off, but sure, come on board." He turned to secure the line.

Mary climbed up the steps. A knapsack lay on the deck along with scuba tanks and gear.

"Why aren't we leaving?" a female voice called from below.

"We have a visitor," Tom called back.

Charlotte Rose came up from the stairs below deck, carrying a clipboard. "Oh, hi, Mary. What are you doing here?"

"I need to talk to Tom and you—"

"Is this about the shipwreck exhibit?" Charlotte asked with a scowl. "I already told Virginia twice that Tom and I will supervise the exhibit from one to three tomorrow afternoon. I'm working for Tom part-time now, and she can't have me at her beck and call." A gust of wind blew her dark hair into her face, and as she brushed it out of the way, something flashed on her finger. A diamond ring.

"That's a pretty ring," Mary said.

"Oh, thanks!" Charlotte smiled at Tom. "It was a gift."

"Well, I haven't talked to Virginia about the schedule. This is something entirely different." Mary took a deep breath and turned to Tom. "I know you've been seeding the bay and probably the shoreline with things that look like shipwreck artifacts."

Charlotte bit her lower lip, her gaze on Tom as he let out a little laugh. "You have quite an imagination, Mrs. Fisher. Why would I do that?"

"To capitalize on the recent discovery of more artifacts from the *Lady Beth* and the gold coins. If people kept thinking they might stumble across something valuable, they'd want to use your services."

"Tom…," Charlotte began, and Tom silenced her with a look.

"I'm not the only one who knows," Mary continued. "One of your customers visited Rich Tucker asking the value of the items. Rich discovered that some of them were unnaturally altered."

"Tom, if Rich Tucker knows—"

"Charlotte." Tom took her hand. "No one can prove that those items came from me."

"But we can," Mary said. "Remember that tankard you'd dropped on the deck and I picked up? I took it by Gems and Antiques to find out more about it. That same tankard showed up there again today." Mary paused for a moment while Tom took in the news. "You know," she said finally, "you can fix this before it goes too far."

"I haven't done anything illegal," Tom said, his teeth gritted together. "I never said the things were from the *Lady*

Beth or any other shipwreck. I can't help it if people assume they were. Some of the items actually did fall off of ships. I bought some real artifacts cheap off eBay. Nobody's getting hurt. It's all in fun, right?"

"You're not going to tell people, are you?" Charlotte asked. "We already stopped doing it. In fact, last night was our final time, and we were going to ditch the rest of the stuff where it wouldn't easily be found." She glanced down at the knapsack on the deck near Mary's feet. "Anyway, yesterday Bri handed me the bag with the tankard. I thought it was something new. I'm sorry, Tom."

"Even if I don't say anything," Mary said, "eventually people will catch on, and that will affect Tom's reputation and business. If I've noticed that you've been spending a lot of money lately, others may too and think you exploited your customers."

"Tell her, Tom!" Charlotte tugged on his hand. "What can it hurt now? Besides, Mrs. Fisher can keep a secret. We can't have the police or people snooping around right now. It's very important."

"I don't understand," Mary said as she shifted her gaze from Charlotte to Tom. "If you're hiding something—"

"We found the *Lady Beth* treasure," Charlotte said.

TWENTY-FIVE

Y ou...what?" Mary asked, stunned. Of all the things she thought they might confess to, that wasn't one of them.

"Charlotte!" Tom almost shouted. "Enough. What are you doing?"

"Being smart about this." Charlotte turned to Tom. "If the police start investigating, the news of the discovery will come out too soon. If Mrs. Fisher understands what's at stake here, she won't tell. Right, Mrs. Fisher?"

"Wait." Mary held up her hand. "Are you talking about— Do you mean that the chest of gold actually exists?"

"I had been doing research for my thesis, and I stumbled across an old map of Ivy Bay in a book from a thrift store," Charlotte said. "And then Tom noticed an anomaly on an old handwritten map that wasn't found on other maps. He is so smart. Tom has a degree in geology, you know."

"What anomaly?" Mary asked.

"It's okay, Tom. Tell her." Charlotte tugged on his hand. "I once heard Eleanor Blakely tell Virginia when they were discussing who to get to help with the valuable artifacts for the festival that if you could trust anyone's integrity in the town, it was Mrs. Fisher's."

Eleanor said that? Mary was shocked. Eleanor had never seemed to have a high opinion of Mary. It suddenly made Mary feel all the more guilty about what she'd said about Eleanor earlier.

Tom sighed. "I got the idea the day you found the necklace. Everyone was looking along the shoreline. You searched the dunes, in a less obvious place. Maybe it was luck, but I started looking in places that people had already written off as possible sites of buried treasure."

"And then I showed Tom the map I'd found," Charlotte said.

"There was a small spit of land about three-quarters of a mile north of here that over time eroded and went completely under water about 170 years ago," Tom explained. "It took us a couple of trips, but we eventually found the remains of the chest under the sand. Unfortunately, most of the chest had disintegrated, but we did find the name Lady B on a portion of it. Only a handful of gold coins were easily accessible." He shrugged. "We just got lucky."

"It wasn't luck. Tom knows what he's doing," Charlotte said, pride shining in her eyes. "It's from being smart and doing the research."

Mary thought over what she'd just learned. "So you were out on the water that night the necklace was stolen?"

Tom nodded. "Yeah the GPS records our route with date and time."

"But you two told the police you were both home," Mary added. "Aren't you worried they will find out you lied?"

"Well, we didn't want to tell them where we went unless we absolutely had to. Besides, it was partially true. We were each home at some point that night," Charlotte pointed out. "We were hoping the thief would be caught by now."

So was Mary. "Now what?"

"Well, we're going to have to dig underwater," Tom said. "The gold coins are heavier than the sand, of course, so they could've sunk farther, and as the area eroded, they moved or maybe people found them. Remember the coin discovered last week by the tourist? That could've been from the same batch of coins we found, only it had settled on a higher layer, perhaps on rock. This is common when the surf becomes violent."

"Can I see the coins, Tom?" Mary asked. Their story rang with the sound of truth, but she still wanted to observe the evidence for herself.

"Not right now." Tom ran his hand over his head. "We sold a couple to help the business, but the others are hidden. We want to recover the rest before we tell everyone."

"And you consulted with Dr. Carlson at the museum?"

"Ah yes. How did you know?" Tom said, his forehead wrinkling. "It was supposed to be confidential."

"I happened to be there doing some research and saw a couple of coins on his desk. They looked similar to others found from the *Lady Beth*. There were also some chips that looked like glass or diamonds."

"There were a couple of pieces of jewelry among the gold. Earrings. A brooch," Tom said. "I'm assuming someone tossed some in the chest when they decided to transport the gold off the ship. Those small diamonds are what we gleaned from the sand."

"Is that why you have a library book on jewelry and currency?" Mary asked Charlotte. "I saw it when we were in the Tea Shoppe. It's listed as missing in the library catalog."

"What? Oh yeah." A rosy hue seeped into her cheeks. "I need to get that back."

"One other thing," Mary said, feeling like she was pushing her luck. "Do you realize the problems you've caused with the treasure map you're selling? With people tromping and digging on private property, someone might point the finger back at you and want to sue for damages."

"I told you people were going to get upset," Charlotte said to Tom, and then turned to Mary. "It was Penny's idea. She thought it would be fun and help Tom out. She had files of all kinds of documents about the *Lady Beth*. She said her great-uncle was big into shipwreck lore. She knew all the possible sites from her research. Tom and I figured that it would keep people busy looking in other places while we searched."

Tom cleared his throat. "What will it take for you to keep this find confidential for a while? Do you want a small percentage of what we find?"

"I don't want anything," Mary said, taken back a little. "I'm just trying to find out what happened to that necklace."

"We'll report the discovery of the chest soon. After we're sure there is more to excavate," Charlotte said. "Tom wants to give a portion of the profits to the town."

Another piece of the puzzle fell into place. "Tom, is that why you were interested in the contract between Mr. Crenshaw and Mr. Blakely with the town?" Mary asked.

His mouth dropped open, and he looked as if he was going to ask Mary how she knew about that too, but then shrugged. "I've always thought that Mr. Crenshaw and Mr. Blakely did the noble thing by sharing their good fortune with the town."

He glanced at Charlotte. "I—we thought maybe we could do the same."

After Mary assured them she wouldn't share their discovery with anyone who'd hurt their investigation, she returned to the dock, thinking that people could be so unpredictable. It hadn't bothered Tom to fool people by seeding the bay with artifacts or creating a treasure map that he knew would target residents' private property, yet he was considering sharing their newfound wealth with the town.

Henry gave her a questioning look as she approached him at the front of the dock. "How did it go? I could only hear snatches of the conversation, and none of it made sense."

"Well, my hunch about Tom seeding the bay and shore with objects for his customers to find was correct," Mary said. "But he's not the necklace thief."

"I see." Henry frowned. "Is he going to stop the seeding?"

"I'm sure of it. He now has a good motive to," Mary said with a slow smile. "Can you keep a secret?"

TWENTY-SIX

⬥

When Mary got home from the marina, she found Betty sitting on the living room couch working on a crossword puzzle. The lamps cast a cozy glow in the room. Classical music played softly in the background. It was a very relaxing scene, except Mary felt a little uncomfortable with the newly rearranged room. She liked the old arrangement so much better.

Betty looked up with a smile. "Did you find out whatever you needed?"

"Yes, but it wasn't quite what I expected. I told Henry because he heard part of the conversation and I'll tell you, but Tom wants this to stay confidential for a little while, and for good reason."

Betty leaned forward and lowered her voice. "What is it?"

Mary glanced over her shoulder.

"Eleanor is in her room," Betty said.

Mary sat down. "Tom and Charlotte may have found the legendary *Lady Beth* chest of gold."

Betty gasped, and Mary updated her on the day's discoveries. "You're amazing, Mar."

"I wouldn't say that. I was wrong about Tom and Charlotte taking the necklace. But at least the mystery of the lost gold may be solved." She sighed wearily. "Do you ever get that feeling that the answer to something is right in front of you and you just can't see it?"

"Frequently, especially when it comes to dealing with Eleanor. I think I finally know what she expects, and we can finally have a closer relationship, and then I do something that upsets her."

"I don't think it's you, Bets," Mary said as Gus trotted into the room and jumped into her lap. "How's she doing?"

"She ate dinner and said she wanted to go to bed early."

"Did she mention anything about overhearing what I said?" Mary endured more waves of guilt.

"No, but she was quieter than usual."

"I'm going to go up and apologize if she's still awake. And, Betty, I'm sorry for putting you in the middle."

"Mar, *nothing* you can do will ever make me not be grateful to have you for my sister."

"Is that a challenge?" Mary said with a smile. "Thanks, Bets."

Mary went upstairs and knocked softly on Eleanor's door. "Eleanor?"

When she didn't answer, Mary went quietly to her room and got ready for bed. She glanced at the novel, longing for the escape, but grabbed her Bible first. Despite her extremely productive day, she still felt out of sorts, most likely stemming from the guilt over what she said about Eleanor, and the fact she felt as though she was back to square one with the missing necklace.

She opened the Bible and skimmed the pages until she came to Matthew 7 and read where Jesus warned about not judging others and treating others as you wanted to be treated.

Thanks for the reminder, Lord. Please forgive me for my treatment of Eleanor. Help me to do better. And please help me figure out what happened to the necklace.

Mary closed the Bible. She had been quick to judge Eleanor and condemn her over Gus, without having the facts, and she'd been fairly quick to judge Tom's actions and assume he'd stolen the necklace. In both cases, she'd been wrong, and it was disconcerting, even if their actions had led to her conclusions.

She still didn't know what had happened to the necklace. Eleanor was still one of the prime suspects, especially now that Tom and Charlotte had proof of their whereabouts.

Mary lay back as determination to find the truth surged through her. She thought back to her trip to the museum and reviewed what she'd learned. It was easy to conclude after talking to Dr. Carlson that Richard had been seeking to find the lost chest of gold coins. He'd kept copies of James's letters to Sarah and not any of the others that sailors had sent home, so there had to be some significance, especially since James wrote Sarah he'd taken measures to secure his fortune.

But what if Richard had been looking for something else? Or...*someone* else? She again had a feeling the answer was right under her nose, but she just couldn't see it.

———

Mary sat up in bed, momentarily disoriented. She'd been dreaming she was in her bookshop, with the heavenly scents of Sweet Susan's Bakery drifting in from next door. But, she wasn't at the shop. The mouthwatering scent that filled her bedroom came from somewhere in the house.

Gus sat by her bedroom door, his nose in the air. He looked at her and meowed. Mary glanced at the clock. It was 6:00 AM. What was Betty doing up this early? And why was she baking?

She quickly dressed in slacks and a blouse and went downstairs. She stopped short in the living room. Everything had been moved back to the original way Betty had decorated the room. What was going on?

She walked into the kitchen. Eleanor stood at the stove, wearing an apron over her pantsuit. "Good morning, Mary. I hope you slept well."

Mary blinked. Was Eleanor actually smiling at her? "Good morning, Eleanor. It smells really good in here."

"That's the fresh cinnamon rolls in the oven. They'll be done in five minutes," Eleanor said. "Help yourself to some coffee. I made the Tahitian Sunrise blend again."

Mary cleared her throat. "Eleanor, about yesterday—"

"No need to say anything. I know your cat means a lot to you."

"But I shouldn't have overreacted like that and made the wrong assumption. I'm sorry."

Some emotion flickered over Eleanor's face. Was it guilt? It was gone before Mary could determine what it was.

"I have also been, perhaps, a little...overzealous while I've been here and offered advice not solicited," Eleanor said as she turned back to the stove. "Scrambled eggs and turkey bacon will be ready in a few minutes."

Betty opened the door to her bedroom and emerged in her bathrobe. She, too, appeared stunned to find Eleanor cooking.

Eleanor looked over her shoulder. "Good morning, Betty. Breakfast is almost ready."

"This is wonderful. What can I do to help?" Betty asked.

Eleanor turned the burner down. "Not a thing. Just sit and relax."

Betty gave Mary a questioning look. Mary just lifted a shoulder to indicate she wasn't sure what was going on.

Gus circled Mary's feet, and Mary went to the pantry to get Gus's food, only it wasn't on the shelf it had been on yesterday. She found the cans back in their usual spot. Eleanor must've been up all night returning everything to their original places.

Mary still felt guilty as she ate. Eleanor acted a little subdued but cheerful.

"So what are your plans for today?" Mary asked.

"We're going to take Richard's shipwreck artifacts and help finish setting up the shipwreck exhibit," Betty said. "And then we're meeting Evan and Mindy and the girls. Are you going to be there for lunch?"

"I should be," Mary said. She hoped she'd have some answers about the missing necklace by then.

Mary gazed at the papers and photos spread out on her bed. She was reviewing all the research she'd collected over the week, trying to find a common link between the *Lady Beth* excavation and the stolen necklace. Maybe there wasn't one.

Maybe the burglar had been someone who'd gotten lucky when he opened the safe at the historical society office.

Mary still found the coincidence too unlikely. More likely it'd been someone who'd seen or heard about Mary taking the necklace to the office, but why wouldn't they assume Mary had taken it home? Instead, someone searched Eleanor's house. Assuming the burglary wasn't a random crime or some treasure hunter looking for artifacts, perhaps encouraged by Tom's treasure maps, one might conclude that the burglar had to have known the history of the necklace and Eleanor's claim to it.

Lord, if the answer is here somewhere, please help me find it.

With the feeling that time was running out on ever recovering the necklace and salvaging Eleanor's reputation, she decided once again to focus on Richard's research and try to answer the questions plaguing her. What had Richard been looking for? Could the chest of coins be the fortune James had secured? Had he taken it off the boat? That just didn't seem accurate. The letter said he had been ingenious. Smuggling a chest of gold coins off a ship and rowing it to shore without anyone noticing was not impossible, but it would've been difficult.

Plus, the letter must've been mailed from the Bahamas before they sailed up the coast to Boston, so that would mean he'd already secured "his fortune" before the arrival in the bay. So what was it? Someone had to know the truth. Stories sometimes were passed through families.

She picked up the chart of Sarah Whitmeyer's possible descendants and looked up the phone numbers of the only two left in Ivy Bay. Rachel Jefferson and Jonathan Myers.

She tried calling Jonathan Myers first, and he flatly told her that he'd never heard of Sarah Whitmeyer Jefferson and not to bother him again.

The second call yielded a cautious hello from a female voice.

"Hello, this is Mary Fisher. I'm looking for Rachel Jefferson."

"That's me. You're not selling anything, are you?"

"No," Mary said hastily and explained briefly about the *Lady Beth* shipwreck and how she was trying to find the descendants of Sarah Whitmeyer Jefferson.

"I'm sorry. As I told the other reporter, I— You have the wrong person." The phone clicked off.

Mary stared at the phone. That didn't go well. There was something in the woman's voice, a nervousness that made Mary almost sure that Rachel Jefferson knew something about the wreck.

Mary glanced at the clock. She had a little more time before she should head into town. Mary read the key pages of Richard's journal again. Richard didn't mention anything about the gold, other than they had found a few coins at the shipwreck. She studied the photos of the diamond jewelry from Penny's article and the one she'd taken of Richard's artifacts. Her gaze lingered over the pistol, remembering her impression of how heavy it'd felt the first time she'd handled it.

Richard's doodles on the edges of the journal caught her attention again. The various shapes included a diamond and the numbers jotted next to them. 104W, 12E. Could they be...?

She consulted the list that she had compiled of the lineage of Sarah Jane Whitmeyer and noted the address of the land they'd owned. She then pulled up a map of the county on her computer.

Mary glanced back at the journal. The numbers on the journal page were map coordinates. She looked in the directory for Rachel Jefferson's address and located it also on the map. It was in the same vicinity as the coordinates.

Mary quickly printed off a copy of the map, grabbed Richard's journal, and stuffed all her research in a file. She hurried out to her car and headed out of town. She drove up the coast congested with summer traffic until she came to a small community consisting of several historic cottages on a hill overlooking the bay.

She slowed the car, hunting for Rachel's address. She finally found the cottage and parked. Her heart pounded as she walked to the door and knocked. She hoped she was right and not making a fool out of herself.

The door opened, and a petite middle-aged woman with curly dark hair and big brown eyes answered the door.

"Rachel Jefferson? I'm Mary Fisher. I called earlier."

The woman sighed and stepped back. "I was afraid this day would come. You might as well come inside."

TWENTY-SEVEN

◆◆◆

M ary raced back toward Ivy Bay. If her conclusions were correct, she might only have today to prove it. After she'd talked to Rachel, Mary had sat in the car going over her file of research again. She put in a call to Dr. Carlson and then Johanna, confirming her suspicions, and then took off for home. She just hoped her plan worked.

By the time Mary arrived at the elementary school ball field, the shipwreck festival was in full swing. She rushed by the booths displaying arts and crafts, fun games, and scrumptious-looking food, and headed for the large white tent that housed the shipwreck artifacts.

Everywhere, people appeared to be having a great time. This had been Eleanor's doing. Her baby. The other members had finished out the final details, but there wouldn't have even been a festival without Eleanor's passion and drive to make the event possible.

"Aunt Mary!" Evan Emerson waved and headed straight for her.

"Where's the family?" Mary asked, looking around.

"I'm not sure. I was supposed to meet them over by the chili stand at noon but had to run in to work for a while.

Anyway, I wanted to talk to you alone." He motioned for her to follow him out of the main stream of human traffic. "I did a little research and tracked down Uncle Richard's old bookkeeper. It took some wheedling, but he finally told me that it was Grandpa Emerson who'd bailed out Richard's business in the eighties. He gave him a loan."

"Well, that makes sense," Mary said. She should have thought about that as a possibility earlier. Eleanor's father had been quite wealthy. "But why didn't Eleanor know her father gave them money?"

"I guess because Uncle Richard's pride was at stake. You remember how he was."

Mary nodded. She also remembered how Eleanor had defended Richard as being a self-made man.

"Maybe we should just keep this between ourselves," Mary suggested. Eleanor didn't need to know about the loan. Let her continue to view her husband as the self-sufficient provider he was most of his life.

"I agree," Evan said. "There's no reason to tell her at this point." He looked out over the crowd. "I'd better see if I can find Mindy and the kids."

"Thanks, Evan," Mary called after him and then continued on to the tent.

Horace Crenshaw stood inside the door and greeted her. "I'm on security duty. Eleanor wouldn't leave any of Richard's things unless I stayed."

"She trusts you," Mary said, and took a quick look around. The interior resembled a museum. The committee had done an excellent job borrowing shipwreck artifacts to display. Old maps and paintings of Ivy Bay were hung from the walls. A jar set up for donations was already half full with green bills.

The *Lady Beth* artifacts were given the place of honor in the middle of the area. It appeared Eleanor had consented to provide all of Richard's collection. Horace had also contributed too, and Mary noted that both dueling pistols had been returned to their case.

On her way over to the festival, Mary had called Betty. She and Eleanor were going to meet her at the tent. While she waited, Mary lingered over the *Lady Beth* display and studied Richard's and Horace's dueling pistols. She picked up one and then the other.

"Mary, you're not supposed to touch," Virginia whispered to her. "You're setting a bad example for the others."

"You're right." Mary set the pistol down. She had confirmed her theory anyway.

"Mary, we're here," Betty called as she and Eleanor walked into the tent.

"What's this all about?" Eleanor asked, sounding irritated, and it was obvious she was pointedly ignoring Virginia. "I was just about to head home."

"I have some information to share with you. I think I know who stole the necklace."

"Who?" Eleanor said.

Mary looked over at Horace. "Could we clear the tent of visitors for a few minutes? I don't think we'll want other people to hear this."

Horace politely asked a couple of visitors to step outside for a few minutes, using the excuse they were having a security check.

"Hey, all!" Penny entered, wearing shorts and a T-shirt. "Johanna said you might have a story and asked me to get the details for her. She'll have to write it. I'm leaving tomorrow morning. It might just be better to call her."

"I think you'll be interested in this, and you may be able to fill in some of the details yourself. I just got back from visiting the great-great-granddaughter of Sarah Jane Whitmeyer."

"Who is Sarah Jane Whitmeyer?" Virginia asked.

"Sarah was the fiancée of James Paul Vanderstrom who had bought passage on the *Lady Beth*, along with some other explorers. He was going in search of his fortune so they could be married. Things must not have gone well toward the end of the journey. He'd written Sarah a couple of letters that ended up in the Gosnold Museum."

She pulled the copies of the letters from her bag and handed them to Penny. "Have you seen these before?"

"I might have with all the research I've done," Penny said with a shrug. She glanced at them and passed them to Virginia.

"James Paul Vanderstrom and his partners were supposed to split the fortune they had acquired on the journey, but James somehow discovered that the others were conniving to cheat him out of his share. So James decided to take matters into his own hands and scavenged through the valuables, taking a few items, including diamonds."

Mary passed out the photos she'd printed from her phone of the necklace Richard had discovered and an article on the museum that had some close-up photos of the jewelry collection. "If you examine the jewelry, you can see some of the diamonds are missing."

"I noticed the necklace was in poor condition," Virginia said to Betty. "So James pried the diamonds off the jewelry?"

"I assume by randomly selecting the diamonds to take off," Mary said, "he expected no one to notice until after the voyage, and he had smuggled the diamonds off the ship."

"What a cheat!" Penny said.

"To be fair, James could've tried to take them all, but being honorable, he only took what he thought was rightfully his," Mary said, noting Penny's reaction. It explained a lot.

Betty examined the photos. "But how did he get the diamonds to Sarah? He perished in the shipwreck, right?"

"The diamonds never made it to Sarah. They were hidden." Mary reached for the two dueling pistols, weighed them in her hands making sure she had the lighter one. She felt around the handle until she found the small indentation and flicked open the end.

Betty gasped. "The handle is hollow."

"Let me see," Virginia said. "Well, that's pretty incredible."

Penny pulled her camera out of her pocket and took a picture.

"If you noticed, the case has James Paul Vanderstrom's initials on it. James hid the diamonds in his pistol handle." Mary looked over at Horace. "The diamonds were never discovered until after the *Lady Beth*'s wreck was excavated."

"So you're saying that Richard or Horace had a pistol with a handle filled with diamonds?" Eleanor asked, and turned to Horace. "Did you know about this?"

Horace cleared his throat. "Not about the diamonds until recently, but I suspected."

Eleanor blinked. "But where are the diamonds now?"

"I'll get to that in a minute," Mary said. "Richard discovered the diamonds in the handle, but instead of telling anyone, he tracked down Sarah's descendant. He found out that she was in desperate need of funds for an operation for her daughter. The mother understood that she really didn't have a claim on whatever Richard had found on the *Lady Beth*. The last of the Vanderstrom line had died out, and besides, Sarah and James were never able to marry.

"The woman's story must've touched Richard, because later, he went back to see her and told her that his conscience was troubled. He had prayed about it, and he finally decided to give the diamonds to her."

Mary looked at Horace, trying to judge his reaction to the story, but his face remained stoic. "Richard also told the woman that his partner might make trouble, and she was never to tell anyone where the diamonds came from. The girl in need of the operation was Rachel Jefferson. Rachel still lives near Ivy Bay. If Richard hadn't helped them, Rachel might not be here today."

"I'm having trouble believing this." Eleanor gripped Betty's arm, as if for balance. "But I suppose, knowing Richard's character, I can see him doing it out of the goodness of his heart."

Mary turned to Horace. "Can you fill us in on the rest of the story?"

Horace didn't say anything for a long moment and then sighed. "I'm so sorry, Eleanor."

"What do you mean?" Eleanor asked. "What did you do, Horace?"

"Eleanor, I'd never do anything to intentionally hurt you, but you know that Richard and I had made a pact. If any treasure was found, we'd give part of the profits from the excavation to Ivy Bay and the university, and the rest we would split."

Eleanor nodded. "You all signed a contract."

"Everything went well during the excavation. We each got the pieces we wanted, even the dueling pistols. We flipped a coin, and Richard got to keep the case and one pistol, and I took the other. But about a year after the excavation was over, I noticed that Richard was starting to avoid me. I could tell something was up."

"Why didn't you just ask him?" Eleanor asked.

"I did, but he claimed nothing was wrong," Horace said. "Finally, one night I talked him into meeting me at a sports bar to watch a game. I purposely got him to drink a little bit too much."

Eleanor shook her head. "Horace, you know Richard wasn't supposed to drink because of his heart condition. What were you thinking?"

"Like I said, Eleanor, I'm sorry." Horace sighed. "Anyway, there was a commercial about the lottery on TV, and Richard made a joke about how I could've won the lottery by picking the right pistol. We were interrupted before I could pry more information out of him. Later, he denied saying any such thing."

Eleanor stared at Horace. "Why didn't you just tell me about this after Richard passed away?"

"I figured you had enough to deal with, and as time went by, it just seemed too awkward."

"Awkward? I thought we were friends." Eleanor's face flushed. "So instead of discussing this with me, you broke into my house?"

"I didn't break into your house, Eleanor."

"No, but your great-niece did," Mary said softly. "You switched the pistols, didn't you, Penny?"

"Me?" Penny let out a little laugh, her gaze shifting around the group. "Oh, come on, you don't think I'd—"

"Penny. Just tell them," Horace said, sounding weary.

"Horace! They can't prove anything," Penny said, and looked at Mary. "How did you find out that Horace and I are related? I've never been to Ivy Bay before, and I didn't tell *anyone*. We don't even look alike."

"There is a slight resemblance," Mary said. "Betty noticed it when you met her that day in the bookstore."

Betty nodded. "You can see it in the shape of your eyes and chin."

"There were other clues too," Mary said.

Penny's eyes narrowed. "Such as?"

"You both are in a brochure I got from the museum." She opened the brochure to an underwater expedition and revealed an underwater scene of divers hovering over a wreck site.

"How can you tell?" Virginia said. "They all look alike to me."

"This is Horace right here." She pointed to one of the divers. "I called Dr. Carlson, and he confirmed Horace had been on that dive."

"And that is Penny. You can't see her face, but you can see her ankle bracelet above her fin strap." Mary looked at Penny's ankle. "Your ankle bracelet has Tahitian pearls in it, and I heard you tell Ashley a relative made it. Bri at the dive shop had a slightly similar bracelet with Tahitian black pearls and mentioned Horace was the artist. You also mentioned how a relative taught you to dive."

"Who would've thought that my ankle bracelet would blow my cover?" Penny said to Horace. "So much for my undercover work."

Betty raised her eyebrows. "Young lady, I think you're missing a valuable point here. You'll have a breaking-and-entering charge to deal with."

"I admit nothing other than being Horace's great-niece," she said.

"You might fare better with a judge if you do tell your side of it," Mary suggested.

"I think she's right," Horace said.

Penny crossed her arms over her chest. "I'm not talking without a lawyer."

"Well, I think I can fill in some of the rest of the story. Correct me if I'm wrong," Mary said.

"Penny always had a strong bond with Horace because of his love for adventure. I checked and found out that he was also a professor at the University of Maine when you were a student. I'm thinking he told you about his suspicions about the *Lady Beth* pistols, about being cheated out of something, so you decided you wanted to help him. Or maybe you wanted whatever Richard was hiding for yourself."

"I wouldn't do that," Penny said, and looked at Horace. "If I did anything, it would've been for you."

"So being a reporter gave you an opportunity to investigate when the storms rolled in and news of *Lady Beth* artifacts surfaced. You already knew Johanna Montgomery through one of her nieces and got your professor to convince her to allow an internship. Then you slipped in hints of suspicion about Richard in the news articles you wrote and helped design a treasure map with Tom Gordon so there would be people swarming on Eleanor's property."

Eleanor gasped. "So that's why!"

"You got in through the window upstairs, didn't you?" Mary asked Penny. "And then switched Horace's pistol for Richard's, barely getting out when Eleanor came home. Sadly for you, the secret compartment in the hollow pistol handle was empty," Mary said. "You must've been so disappointed."

"This is some story, Mary. Maybe you've been reading too much of your own stock," Penny said, her laugh sounding forced, and her gaze shifted from face to face when no one else said a word.

"I'm assuming you switched the pistol back when you went to interview Eleanor. You did more investigation and were in the process of tracking down Rachel. She mentioned someone else had tried to talk to her about it. A reporter."

"I'm not admitting anything, but if there *were* diamonds in the pistol, then one-quarter of their value should be my uncle's, right?"

Horace sighed. "Penny—"

"The truth of how Richard cheated you and the town should be exposed," Penny said. "It's justice."

Eleanor shook her finger at Penny. "He did it for a good cause. You should be ashamed of yourself for judging Richard when you stole his necklace."

"I didn't steal the necklace," Penny said. "Do you think I'd still be here if I did?"

"You and Horace are both leaving town tomorrow. I assume you're going together," Mary said.

Horace sighed. "Yes, Penny is joining me on my next project, but she didn't steal the necklace. I did."

Eleanor and Betty gasped as Horace looked at Mary. "I realized moments after I'd lied to you about not knowing anything about that pill you found in the office that it was just a matter of time that you or someone else might eventually make a connection in their use for diving. It was a foolish mistake on my part both in accidentally dropping it and then pretending I didn't know what it was."

"I did get suspicious when I found out that divers sometimes use them," Mary said. Of course she had also suspected that the pill had belonged to Tom or Eleanor. "Why did you take the necklace?"

"I had a moment of weakness and felt justified, after Richard, who I trusted like a brother, obviously deliberately lied to me." Sadness filled Horace's eyes as he faced Eleanor. "I guess I always thought that maybe you knew about Richard cheating me, so I felt I had a right to the necklace. Or at least part of it. But Mary reminded me that you trusted me, and I'm having an attack of conscience."

"Oh, Horace, I didn't know." Eleanor placed her hand on his arm.

He took a deep breath. "Well, don't worry. The necklace is safe and sound. I sent it off to the Gosnold Museum to Dr. Greene, another historian on staff, *not* Carlson," he said to Mary. "He'll look it over and let us know what needs to be done to get it restored, and of course, evaluate the worth."

"Uncle Horace, what are you doing?" Penny said. "After what Richard did to you, that necklace should be yours. What you need is a good lawyer."

Horace draped his arm over Penny's shoulders. "You're so young. Things get complicated the older you get. I hate to admit this, but Richard actually did something noble by helping Rachel Jefferson's family, and he was right to assume I would've insisted on taking a cut of the diamonds. But you know what, Penny? I'm an old man now, and after the life I've lived, I hope I've learned more about compassion since then."

"But—"

He tightened his hold. "Someday you'll realize that the people you love are the real treasures. I didn't have any children of my own, and I realize how much I care about the times we spent together. Of all of our family, you and I are the most alike. Assuming that we don't end up in jail, I have a proposal for you."

Penny's eyes widened. "You really think we'll go to jail?"

Eleanor huffed. "What did you think would happen after you broke into my house?"

Horace looked around the group. "No matter how this turns out, I'm asking you, all of you, to keep Richard's secret about the diamonds he gave to Rachel's mother."

"I certainly will," Virginia said.

Mary's eyes met Betty's gaze. Her sister gave a slight nod.

"I don't know," Eleanor said. "This caused me a lot of trouble. I was afraid to be in my own house."

"But, Eleanor, do you really want to stir everything up?" Betty asked. "There will be people who will think that Richard cheated them by not splitting the diamonds with the town."

Eleanor frowned. "After this week, I'm not sure who my friends are anymore."

"I'm your friend, Eleanor," Virginia said. "Even though I haven't been a good one lately, I want to make it up to you."

"Couldn't there be some way that we can make this right for the town too?" Mary said. "Give them their share as agreed to in the contract, which is missing by the way."

"I have it," Horace said. "I wanted to use it as proof that Richard owed me. I agree with Mary. Even if the whole story about Richard and the diamonds comes out later, people should be mollified that the town got a donation."

He looked at his niece. "And you must never write about this."

Penny frowned and then blew out a sigh. "I was only doing this for you, Uncle Horace. I won't say or write a word. Okay?"

"Good, so we're all in agreement," Horace said. "We'll talk to the police, see if we can work out a deal, and then, Penny, after the trip to Belize, assuming we can still go, I'd like you to use those writing skills so we can write a book together on shipwrecks."

"I don't know," Penny said in a dull tone.

"I won't be able to afford that new sailboat I had in mind, but we can rent one and still travel around the world. And it might involve a lot of diving. Think you can handle that?"

"Maybe," Penny said. "I'll think about it. But if I do it, I want equal billing on the cover." She caught Mary's eye, and a smile twitched about her lips. Penny turned and gave Horace a hug.

Mary's bare feet left watery tracks beside her sister's footprints as they walked along the shoreline of Little Neck Beach. Gulls swooped over the lapping waves, calling to one another. Mary breathed in the briny air and lifted her face to the setting sun. It was a beautiful Sunday afternoon.

The shipwreck festival had ended with a spectacular fireworks show Saturday evening. Everyone had already declared the festival a phenomenal success and wanted to make it an annual event. The historical society board had begged Eleanor to come back and chair the event and others. Eleanor told them she'd think about it but privately told Betty she planned on going back.

Betty stopped to pick up a speckled brown-and-white clamshell. The beach wasn't as crowded as it had been over the last week. The treasure hunters weren't finding much, just the usual pieces of sea trash that washed ashore since Tom had stopped seeding the bay and shoreline with fake treasure.

Even the theme of the pastor's sermon that morning had been on the true treasures in life, such as God's words to live by and family and friends. It made Mary wonder if he'd talked to Horace when he chose the Bible text Psalm 19:10 to make his point.

They are more precious than gold, than much pure gold; they are sweeter than honey, than honey from the honeycomb.

"You just never know about people," Betty said with a small smile. "At least Horace seemed to really care about Eleanor. He could've taken Richard's ring too, when he stole the necklace. It was kind of him to put it in Eleanor's purse. He didn't have the heart to keep it from her."

"I'm just glad God nudged his conscience," Mary said.

Horace must have realized his rationale for stealing the necklace was flawed since he relinquished all claim to it in a quick plea deal with the police and local judge. Since the necklace was safe and sound at the museum and Eleanor didn't want to press charges against Penny for breaking into her house, it appeared that Penny and Horace would probably get off with a fine and community service. Penny got a lawyer and struck a plea deal. It had been suggested that they help in organizing teams to clean up the beaches over the summer, which was a passion of Horace's.

Ivy Bay would benefit from the situation in more ways than one since Eleanor had decided to donate the necklace to the town as long as Richard got credit for the find.

Mary looked at her sister. "Betty, I'm sorry that I wasn't more empathetic when Eleanor was staying with us. I realize now she just wants to feel needed and have family around her."

"Don't worry about it. My sister-in-law tends to reap what she sows. You were very kind, *and* you solved the mystery of the stolen necklace."

Mary looked out at the bay. She also knew the answer to another mystery that Tom would be revealing soon.

Betty's cell phone rang. "Why, yes, Eleanor, Mary is right here." She handed the phone to Mary.

"Mary, I wanted to invite you over tomorrow for tea with the book club. I hope you'll come. I want to thank you for all you've done," Eleanor said.

Mary was so surprised she couldn't answer for a few seconds. Eleanor rarely included Mary in her social functions, which had been fine with Mary since they'd never been close. The last week had been a strain on both of them. This invitation was a significant gesture on Eleanor's part. Mary's first reaction was to politely decline, but as she glanced over at her sister, she realized, as Horace and the pastor had pointed out, family was her real treasure in life, and that family included Eleanor.

"I'd be honored," Mary said, and realized she really was.

They are more precious than gold....

ABOUT THE AUTHOR

From her first introduction to the beginner readers with Dick and Jane, award-winning author Kelly Ann Riley has wanted to be a writer. She started penning tales at an early age and received special recognition for her short stories. Later, she became a reporter and the editor for her high school newspaper.

Now Kelly Ann enjoys writing inspirational romantic suspense novels and cozy mysteries. She lives in Alabama with her engineer husband, two grown-up children, and numerous pets. She loves visiting the East Coast and has wonderful memories of Cape Cod. She's an avid reader and, like Mary, she enjoys spending leisurely hours with a good mystery.

You can contact Kelly Ann through her Web site at KellyAnnRiley.com.

MARY'S MINT AND FIG DELIGHT ICE CREAM

1 14-ounce can sweetened condensed milk
1 5-ounce can evaporated milk
2 tablespoons sugar
2 teaspoons vanilla
2 cups whole milk
*2 cups peeled and coarsely chopped fresh figs**
*1–2 lemons to make ¼ cup juice***
2 tablespoons sugar
2 teaspoons chopped fresh mint

Whisk condensed milk, evaporated milk, two tablespoons of sugar, vanilla, and whole milk together in a large bowl. Cover and chill blended milk mixture for at least thirty minutes.

Process milk mixture in an ice-cream maker according to manufacturer's instructions. Remove ice-cream container from ice-cream maker and place in freezer for fifteen minutes.

Cut stems off of figs, peel, and coarsely chop to make two cups. Mix in lemon juice,** 2 tablespoons of sugar, and chopped fresh mint. Stir combination into prepared ice-cream mixture. Transfer ice cream to an airtight container and freeze until firm (approximately one to one-and-one-half hours).

*If fresh figs aren't available, you can try using dried figs. Cover dried figs with boiling water and set aside for two hours until soft.
**For more lemon flavor, try adding the zest of one lemon or to taste.

FROM THE GUIDEPOSTS ARCHIVES

For where your treasure is, there will your heart be also.

—Luke 12:34 (KJV)

The dew-streaked sign on the lifeguard station had been turned to read Off Duty. A fat child, out by herself, was dropping last night's shells into her pail. A bent, bronzed woman wandered barefoot into the edge of the ebbing waves. Except for these companions—and the strange solitary figure up ahead—I was alone on the beach that fresh Florida morning.

As I drew closer to the solitary figure, I began to be intrigued. He was walking the beach in a fixed pattern—a few paces one way, turn, come back almost in his own footsteps. His eyes were fixed on a metal loop at the end of a wand, which he carried in his right hand. The wand seemed to be wired to a set of earphones, clamped heavily over the man's head. Occasionally he would stop, dig at the sand with his boot, then move on.

He was a modern-day beachcomber. The apparatus indicated the presence of buried coins or metal jewelry through a series of clicking sounds in the earphones.

An interesting gadget. But in a way I pitied the man. Because in looking for treasure that might be buried in the sand, he was missing the treasures of the beach that were all around him: the sanderlings chasing the tide, the wave-foam blowing, the pelicans sailing in awkward beauty.

Lord, teach me to remove from my ears my own treasure-hunting devices that keep me from hearing You. Teach me to lift my eyes so that I can see the treasures You have planned for me to enjoy each day, free for the asking. —John Sherrill

A NOTE FROM THE EDITORS